PENGUIN BOOKS

LAND OF SAND AND SONG

Joyce graduated from the National University of Singapore with a degree in English and her contemporary YA novel, *Lambs for Dinner*, was published by the Straits Times Press in 2013 as part of a nationwide competition. She lives in the perennially sunny island-city of Singapore, where she publishes her short stories at *Muse in Pocket, Pen in Hand* and blogs at *The Writes of Passage* in between writing her next novel and dreaming about mythical worlds.

PRAISE FOR *LAND OF SAND AND SONG*

'Joyce spins an enchanting tale of magic, vengeance and romance in this new Asian fantasy world. *Land of Sand and Song* is brilliantly written with compelling characters, and you'll find it hard to put down this book once you pick it up.'

—Leslie W, author of *The Night of Legends*

Land of Sand And Song

Joyce Chua

PENGUIN BOOKS
An imprint of Penguin Random House

PENGUIN BOOKS

USA | Canada | UK | Ireland | Australia
New Zealand | India | South Africa | China | Southeast Asia

Penguin Books is part of the Penguin Random House group of companies
whose addresses can be found at global.penguinrandomhouse.com

Published by Penguin Random House SEA Pte Ltd
9, Changi South Street 3, Level 08-01,
Singapore 486361

First published in Penguin Books by Penguin Random House SEA 2021

10 9 8 7 6 5 4 3 2 1

ISBN 9789814954150

Typeset in Adobe Garamond Pro by Manipal Technologies Limited, Manipal

www.penguin.sg

To my father, for everything.

Contents

One

Desert Rose

It happened on a frigid, pitch-black night. The darkest night of the year, in fact.

Desert Rose heard the shuffling of feet and rumble of voices as shadows flitted past her tent. Her instincts told her to get out of bed and investigate, but the festivities of the previous evening had wiped her out and she didn't want to disentangle herself from sleep just yet. She could still feel Bataar's hand, warm around hers, as he danced with her around the bonfire. Next to her, Qara was belting out a folk song with the clanswomen—

The sound of a blade unsheathed made her jolt upright. Dread crawled under her skin. Desert Rose rubbed her eyes, collecting on her fingers the vestiges of kohl the older clanswomen had drawn on her eyes the night before.

She tiptoed over to her father, asleep in his bed across the tent, and shook him by the shoulders. 'Papa, wake up,' she whispered in his ear.

He stirred. 'What is it, Rose?'

'There are people outside. Armed.'

He was up in an instant, racing around the tent and throwing essentials into a calfskin bag as though he had prepared for this moment. 'You need to run . . . now,' he said, shoving the bag into her hand. 'Head east. Stay off open roads and lie low.'

'But why?'

He threw an ermine coat around her. 'No time for questions, *jig sarnai*.'

Despite him calling her by her pet name, *little rose*, the ripple of fear under his voice unsettled her to the core. His hands shook as he hurried her along towards the back exit. Scarbrow's hands never shook, not even when they were under attack by desert ghouls or raiders or when the clans battled among themselves. The chieftain of the Dugur tribe was unshakeable as a citadel.

Yet, tonight, he wasn't.

Something rustled outside the tent. A bated silence followed.

'Get your knives,' he said.

Clutching the bag her father had handed her, Desert Rose ran back to her bed and pulled out her double knives from under her pillow. 'What's going on? Who are we fighting?'

'*You* are not fighting, but keep your knives close. Go, *now*.' He gave her a firm push towards the back exit.

'What about you?'

'I'll catch up with you at the Oasis Capital in a few days. Wait for me there.'

The Oasis Capital. Her father had told her plenty of stories about that city and promised to take her there someday, but she had never imagined this was how they would make their first trip.

'No,' she said, dropping the bag. 'I'm not leaving you here alone. We go together.'

'Rose, please.'

But she only took a step closer to her father, gripping her knives tighter and hiding them behind her as she faced the entrance of the tent. By then, she could tell for certain that it was all the five clan leaders lurking outside—Blackstone's hulking form leading the way, Huol's diminutive one next to Bekir's slouched silhouette, with Erden and Gaan bringing up the rear. But why should they be running from the clan leaders? Her father was the chieftain.

They burst in without ceremony, Blackstone shoving the flap aside and waving in a soldier. The lamp in the soldier's hand threw their solemn faces into stark contrast.

The clan leaders were in full Council regalia—ermine coats and riding boots, not their nightclothes or the celebratory robes they had worn a few hours ago. How long had they planned to ambush them like this?

'Oh, good. You're both awake,' said Blackstone, his voice like the distant growl of thunder.

Her father drew himself to his full height and levelled Blackstone's gaze, but he spread his hands in greeting, as though this were nothing more than a friendly visit. 'To what do I owe the pleasure of this visit, my brothers?'

'The clansmen and I have come to a consensus, Scarbrow,' said Blackstone. 'We believe that in light of the recent events, where your decisions had not been for the interests of the Dugur tribe, you are no longer fit to be our leader.'

Desert Rose started forward, but a look from her father made her pause.

'Stay where you are, Scarbrow, and we won't hurt you,' Erden said, although he kept a wary eye on Desert Rose. Hadn't it just been a few hours ago that he called her father 'Chief' while pouring him another bowl of mulled wine, that he had called her the future of the tribe?

Her father raised his brows. 'You intend to hurt me?'

'Not if we don't have to. You are a reasonable man. Surely you understand that we are only doing what must be done.'

Desert Rose clutched her knives tighter, willing herself to remain where she was.

Blackstone's attention flicked to her. 'You're a strong fighter, Desert Rose. But surely you don't wish to fight against something that concerns the future of the tribe?'

'I'll fight anyone who hurts my father,' she snarled.

Gaan and Erden traded a glance, but Blackstone only looked amused. 'You may be skilled with your knives, but how confident are you against all of us?'

'Leave her out of this,' said her father. He looked each of the clan leaders in the eye. 'Must we come to this?'

Their faces were blank, remorseless. Only Huol's gaze fell to the ground.

'You gave us no choice, Scarbrow,' Blackstone said with a shrug. 'This concerns all our lives and you've been too weak for far too long. It's time for someone to make a change.'

'And I suppose you are the best person to.'

'The people need a strong leader,' Blackstone said without missing a beat. 'Someone to make the right decisions for them.'

'I always knew your ambition will get the best of you one day, *chono*.'

Her father had given her several veiled warnings to watch out for Blackstone. *There are those who seek glory over peace. Never leave your back facing them.* And even she could tell Blackstone had long been eyeing the chieftain's seat. He was always the first to question her father's decisions, and sometimes used the current unrest along the borders to stir up the people's discontent.

Had her father known all along that Blackstone would turn against him?

'You would rather take orders from that corrupt Oasis Emperor than defend your people?' her father said.

'No,' said Blackstone. 'I would rather take action and save the tribe.'

'And the rest of you.' Her father shifted his gaze to the other clan leaders. 'Do you also believe you're helping to save the tribe? By helping that greedy, lily-livered fool find the sacred spring?'

And there, Desert Rose realized, lay the heart of the matter.

It came down to the spring. It always did. Desert Rose had sat in on enough Council sessions and eavesdropped on enough private Council meetings to gather that, unlike Blackstone, her father never wanted to seek out the mythical spring, even if the stories about it were true, that it could enhance mortal life and bless it with worldly riches. 'A spring like that is not for us mortals to possess, much less exploit for worldly gains,' he once roared during a particularly heated discussion. 'Anyone who thinks otherwise is a fool.'

Blackstone always argued that it was their right to harness the power of the spring for the good of the tribe—'With a spring like that on our side, we could rule this desert'. Never mind that the quest would kill any traveller, or that it was sacrilegious to even go near it, and exploiting it would be to court divine punishment.

'It's a better option than going to war with Oasis Kingdom,' said Erden. 'We cannot survive any longer with forces invading from every corner. The Lijsal tribe has already agreed to ally with . . .'

'I don't care what the other tribes do,' her father roared. 'I will not sell out mine to the Oasis Kingdom.'

'Too bad, Scarbrow,' Blackstone said. 'You're overruled.'

Rage coursed through Desert Rose. Blackstone had always resented the fact that her father was elected as chieftain instead of him. How long had he been waiting for this moment, when he could finally snatch her father's place?

'Consider this a peaceful uprising,' Gaan said, stoic as usual. 'We all have the best interests of the tribe at heart.'

Blackstone's voice dripped with danger. 'Now, come with us quietly or we will take you.'

'*No,*' Desert Rose breathed.

Blackstone cocked his head at Desert Rose. 'And your daughter too.'

'Leave my daughter out of this,' her father growled, stepping closer to her.

'We need to cover our bases, Scarbrow. Surely you understand.'

'She's only seventeen. What threat can she possibly pose to any of you?'

'She's also your daughter. We wouldn't want her seeking vengeance on your behalf, after all.' Blackstone turned and nodded once behind him. Six soldiers immediately appeared and lined up in an imposing row. 'Seize him. And the girl too.'

'*Yavakh,* Rose!' her father cried. 'And don't look back!' He seized his sabre hidden behind a woven tapestry by his bed and lunged towards the soldiers.

But Desert Rose wasn't going to flee without her father. She whirled her knives and sprung at the soldiers. Her father was already wrestling with two of them. Even if she managed to take down the remaining four, she couldn't fight the clan leaders too. Quick as she was, Blackstone alone could pick her up and toss her over his shoulder like a rug.

The odds didn't matter now; she just needed to distract them long enough to help her father escape. She dodged an incoming sabre and kicked a soldier in the chest, sending him crashing backwards against the cupboard. The porcelain bird her father had bought her from a travelling market toppled off and smashed to the ground.

Meanwhile, her father had knocked out a soldier and was fending off another three at once. Blackstone unsheathed his sword from his belt. The other clan leaders followed suit and closed in on her father. At another signal from Blackstone, more soldiers burst into the tent with their weapons drawn.

'Papa!' Desert Rose cried. She dodged three soldiers to reach him, but Bekir and Huol cornered her against the other side of the tent.

She couldn't strike them. She couldn't. They had watched her grow up; they were almost like her uncles.

But what family member would betray them like that?

By the time she raised her knife, Blackstone and the others already had her father at sword-point. The remaining soldiers formed a defensive row, their blades ready for her.

'Enough of this, Scarbrow,' Blackstone said. 'Resist further and this blade goes deeper.'

With his sword firmly trained on the father, Erden now turned to the daughter. 'For your father's sake, I suggest you drop your weapons and come quietly with us.'

She exchanged a look with her father, caught the subtle shake of his head, and laid her knives before her.

'Seize her,' Blackstone ordered.

'Run, Rose!' her father cried, throwing off Erden and Gan and seizing his sabre again.

Perhaps it was the plea in her father's voice. But this time, she did as she was told, even though every part of her fought to stay with her father. She ducked through the back exit and out into the night. Her last glimpse of her father was of him swinging his blade as the clan leaders rounded in on him.

Outside, a desert storm was brewing. *A storm in winter?* Desert Rose glanced up at the sky. She had only ever witnessed a desert storm twice in her entire life, once when she was eight, before her father found her wandering in the desert alone, and when she was fourteen and got lost for two weeks in the Darklands.

She flinched as lightning slashed across the sky and thunder growled like a creature ready to pounce. The wind snapped at her feet. Was the crackle on her skin due to adrenaline or her being within striking distance?

Footsteps pounded behind her. Soldiers, close on her heels. They yelled at her to stop, but she only ran faster, skirting past the tents and towards the public square.

The dregs of last evening's revelry were still strewn about the campsite—silk caps and gowns, empty bowls of mare's milk and the charred remains of the bonfire that had seemed to blaze all the way up to the heavens. She wondered if the gods could hear her call now to keep her father safe.

How ironic that they should stage this coup right before the White Moon Festival, the one night of the year where all conflicts and grievances were to be resolved, apologies made, and debts repaid. Had the rest of them known their leaders would do this? Had they supported them even last evening when they had braided her hair, danced and laughed and toasted to the gods together?

She shook the thoughts out of her head and focused on putting more distance between her and the soldiers.

It was impossible to tell where she was heading in this darkness, even though she knew the camp by heart and could navigate her way to shelter and safety with her eyes closed.

She had grown up on these shifting sands. Papa used to tell her that the desert was magical. *It can take you anywhere your heart desires. But if you have no direction in mind, Fate can easily sweep you away.*

Papa. She allowed herself a moment to think about him. Had he managed to get away? Should she go back and find him now? Her footsteps faltered.

No, she would be of no help if she got captured too. If her father couldn't protect the tribe from Blackstone and the rest, then *she* would.

If only she were in her riding gear—she hadn't thought to change out of her dress from that evening, after all the dancing and merrymaking. Her dress, a delicate sapphire-blue gown that had glittered under the moonlight now seemed frivolous and impractical. It made her stumble several times until she gathered it up and hot-footed across the snow-dusted sand in her boots.

She left the campsite behind, racing through the dark with only the brilliant streaks of lightning as her guide, until all she heard was her own shallow, ragged breaths.

The sound of hooves made her slow down. Out of the gloom, a shadowy figure appeared about ten feet before her. She gripped her knives tighter as the rider dismounted and loomed towards her.

Broad, slightly sloping shoulders and messy wild curls. Desert Rose exhaled in relief. Some help, at last. She could always count on her childhood friend to take her out of this madness.

'Bataar,' she breathed, running towards the older boy.

But when she got close enough to him, the look in his eyes stopped her cold. There was none of that warmth he normally reserved for her, no hint of that indulgent smile he would flash her when she sometimes beat him and all the other clan boys at archery or horse-riding, no gentleness in his gaze he used to have when they lay beneath the stars on the darkest night of the year—one of the few times they were allowed to stay up past nightfall.

Bataar narrowed his eyes at her before raising a blowpipe to his lips. A sharp sting in her right thigh made her crumple to the ground.

He shot me, she realized. Bataar *shot me.* The shock paralyzed her as the dart wedged in her leg. She glared up at him, caught him wincing for the briefest moment before approaching her with the slow, wary steps of a hunter.

Night spun around her. She started to tremble. This was the drug the clansmen used on the animals they hunted. Now, she was just another prey to Bataar. Somewhere in the distance, lightning flashed across the sky, trailed by the rumble of thunder.

Desert Rose stared at Bataar's stony face as he pulled out his sabre and held it to her throat. 'Why?'

A hint of gentleness crept into the familiar timbre of his voice. 'It's what I have to do, Rose. Trust me, this is for the greater good.'

'You just shot me with a poisoned dart and you're holding a blade to my throat. Forgive me if I think you're full of shit, Bataar,' she spat.

He tightened his jaw. 'Scarbrow is no longer fit to lead us. You'll understand one day.'

Scarbrow. Not Uncle-Chief, like he used to call him. Had Bataar forgotten all the times her father had taken them both on excursions to desert towns and trained them in horse-riding when they were younger? 'He's my father,' she said.

'Well,' Bataar replied darkly. 'Blackstone is *my* father.'

So this was it for him. If Blackstone succeeded in his takeover, Bataar would be next in line for the chieftain position. She had always believed it was his father who wanted that destiny for him, but clearly she was wrong—it was more than that.

'It's nothing personal, Rose. The people just need a new leader, someone who will make the right decisions for them,' he said, echoing his father's words.

'The people voted for my father,' she snapped, 'who would never do something as low as ambush someone in the middle of the night and take him by force.'

Bataar's eyes flashed. 'What needs to be done must be done.' His gaze softened. 'We are not the enemies here. Believe me, Rose.'

The growing fog in her mind began to cloud her thoughts. Desert Rose was dimly aware of Bataar scooping her up in his arms and throwing her over his shoulder as he returned to his horse. She kicked and clawed at him with every ounce of strength left in her, but the poison was starting to turn her body numb.

Another deafening crack of thunder made Bataar pick up his pace. Desert Rose slid her shaking hand towards the darts on his belt. She only had one chance and no time to lose.

Bataar's horse let out a loud whinny as it reared. Bataar staggered backwards, his grip on Desert Rose loosening. 'Steady, Taban.'

With her last shred of fighting strength, Desert Rose yanked out two darts from Bataar's belt and plunged them into his back. He let out a cry, dropping her as his knees buckled. She went rolling and came to a stop just next to Taban's hooves.

Taban was a spirited horse. It had taken Bataar months to train him back when he was just a colt, and he listened to Bataar alone. Desert Rose flinched as Taban raised its front hooves again—but it only pivoted away, revealing the girl perched atop it.

'Qara!' Desert Rose cried.

Qara was gripping onto the reins for her life, her face white and tense. She looked tiny on top of Bataar's horse but leapt off with trained dexterity. Desert Rose yanked the dart out of her leg, gritting her teeth against the pain, then gathered the hem of her dress and pressed it against the wound.

'Can you walk?' Qara asked, helping Desert Rose to her feet.

Desert Rose shifted her weight to her right leg. 'I think so—'

Qara cried out and sank to the ground, clutching her calf and the dart wedged in it. Behind them, Bataar had his blowpipe at his lips, his eyes dark and grim.

Desert Rose removed the dart from Qara's calf. Qara whimpered, starting to shake as cold sweat broke out on her forehead.

Great, Desert Rose thought. *Now we're all going to die out here together.* Now when her father was counting on her to save them all. She fought through her dizziness and pain, taking deep laboured breaths as she helped Qara up the horse with trembling arms. Mounting Taban was a struggle, but Bataar was too busy tending to his own wound to stop them.

They could flee, find a quiet place to purge the drug and sleep it off. But Bataar was hurt too. He was hurt by *her*. Despite what he had done, she couldn't just leave him behind.

'Rose, let's go,' Qara rasped. 'They'll come looking for him, he'll be fine.' Desert Rose remained rooted to the ground, staring at Bataar. 'Rose, come on!'

She climbed up the horse behind Qara, scrambling to secure her footing in the stirrups. It took both her and Qara several attempts to tame the beast, but as soon as Taban complied, she secured the reins around her wrists and charged eastward.

It was all she could do to keep herself upright as the drug began to claim her. Qara, slumped against her, was already losing consciousness.

'There's a camp some distance from here,' she said. 'We can hide there at least until morning.'

'No,' Qara murmured. 'I have to go back before my father realizes I'm gone.'

'You're going back to them?'

'You and Scarbrow are the ones they're hunting. I'm not in danger.' Something unspoken passed between them—the understanding that Qara had known this might happen.

Blackstone would not give up so easily. Desert Rose had followed the older men on their hunts and games before, witnessed their dogged pursuit of their prey until they held the carcasses in their hands. And this time, she was the one being hunted.

'You're in no state to travel back on your own,' she said. 'Come with me—at least until we get the poison out.' Qara nodded feebly.

The ride to the next camp felt interminable. She and Qara were close to blacking out by the time they arrived, although Qara, untrained in metabolizing poison, seemed closer to the brink than her.

The camp was a small, nondescript one with only four tents, as far as Desert Rose could see. *Nomads?* she wondered. But their steeds (horses, not camels) suggested that they were not desert dwellers.

It was risky breaking into this camp without knowing whom it belonged to. The last thing she needed was to end up with desert bandits in her current state. But it beat staying out in the open for Bataar or some other desert nightmare to find them.

Thunder receded to a low faraway rumble. The oppressive air was releasing its hold as the last dregs of the storm faded away. How could it have passed so quickly? Rare as they were, especially at this time of the year, desert storms were violent, the downpour heavy enough to cause flash floods.

In the middle of the ring of tents were the remnants of an extinguished campfire. All the tents were dark, save for one illuminated by a lone lamp.

Desert Rose kept to the shadows, steering Taban out of sight from a couple of men on guard before dismounting with Qara. 'Go,' she whispered to Taban, giving the rein a light tug. She watched the horse trot off into the night, then limped across the sand with Qara in tow.

They stole into the smallest tent at the furthest corner of the campsite, which turned out to be filled with rations—clothing and medical supplies. Not nomads, then. Merchants? Desert Rose groped around in the dark and made a bed of sorts by stacking the bundles together. It was wide enough for Qara to lie on, at least. She tore open one of the bundles and pulled out a plain inner tunic to staunch the blood flow from Qara's calf.

'How are you feeling?' she asked as she bandaged Qara's wound with quivering hands, blinking to refocus her vision.

Qara bit her lower lip and shook her head. 'He injured you too.'

'I'll be fine,' she said. At the rate she usually healed, she might be able to recover by the next morning. Hopefully.

'He let you off easy, you know,' Qara said. 'Bataar never means to hurt you.'

Desert Rose ignored that. She tucked Qara's coat tighter around her, hiding her among the bundles as much as she could. 'I'll come for you in the morning,' she said.

A wave of giddiness hit her as soon as she rose to her feet, trembling like dust in the wind. She gritted her teeth and leaned against the bed post. Where could she go in this state? She could barely hold a knife, much less fight with it. But what if she never saw her father again?

Everything caught up with her in a rush. From the betrayal to the way the clan leaders cornered her father, how she had to run like a hunted animal, and now Qara putting her neck on the line by turning against Bataar and helping her escape. All for some magical spring that they had no claim to. All for power.

In that moment, her hatred burned bright and clear. If Blackstone was afraid that she would seek vengeance on behalf of her father, then vengeance was what she would give them. If the spring was what they wanted, then she would make sure that they never found it. She would thwart them in whatever way she could; she would make them pay for what they did to her father and her tribe.

That was her last thought before darkness closed in on her and she crumpled to the cold, hard ground.

The story of the Immortal Spring begins, as the name suggests, with two immortals in love.

Their love was a forbidden one. The Sky Princess was betrothed to the Lunar Prince to maintain the peace across the celestial realm, but she had already given her heart to the youngest Earth Prince, whom she had met on one of her clandestine trips down to the mortal realm.

The lovers met fortnightly (fourteen years, in mortal time) at the Celestial Pool in her backyard, the only place where they could sneak past the borders of heaven and earth.

When her father, the Celestial King, learned about their secret rendezvous, he waged a war against the Earth King and had the Celestial Pool boarded up so that the young lovers could never meet again.

The princess, doomed to an eternity of heartache, remains by the now dry Celestial Pool, waiting for the day she can reunite with her beloved. Her tears are said to flow from the heavens down to the Flaming Mountains, the highest mountain range in the world where the sky meets the earth.

And right behind the mountains is the Khuzar Desert, where a magical spring is said to fill up every fourteen years. It is where moonlight lovers like the Sky Princess and Earth Prince dream of visiting one day, where desolate souls go in search of a cure to their mortal woes, where the Elixir of Life itself is said to be hidden.

What irony it is, then, that men have lost their souls just to find that fabled spring!

—Excerpt from *Travels of the Lost Poet*, by Zhang He

Two

Wei

Wei sat at his makeshift desk, listening to the storm. He was no stranger to desert weather, having stayed out here for almost a full year now, but this storm was something else.

Never mind that it appeared out of nowhere in the middle of winter. It had also subsided as quickly as it had swelled, leaving the desert in an unearthly calm before a drop of rain even fell.

He had been worried that they would have to pack up and seek shelter at the nearest desert town in the middle of the night. It seemed like they were in the clear for now, but he knew better than to let his guard down out in the desert.

He shifted the table lamp closer and tried to focus on his map. They needed to figure out an alternative route, one that would help them evade the Imperial Army and lead them to the heart of the desert.

But the search was proving to be more futile by the day. Each night, before the men retired into their tents, Wei could hear the weariness in their voices as they spoke of the possibility of finally ending this quest. It was more brutal than the training they had received up in the Palamir Mountains as disciples of the Snow Wolf Sect. Bandits they could handle, but not supernatural creatures that burned with unearthly heat, creatures as old as the desert itself and twice as merciless; not the toll of constant vigilance and fear under the mercy of the elements. Out here, every day they managed to stay alive was a miracle.

Maybe it *was* a fool's mission to try and beat the emperor in finding the fabled spring. His father's obsession had dragged on for years and led countless soldiers to their deaths. Was he about to do the same with his crew?

But he couldn't give up now, not when his mother's life was at stake. Every day he spent here in the desert was another day his mother withered away behind bars, framed by Queen Wangyi (now the empress) for attempted regicide. If only he could find the spring, he would have the biggest possible leverage over his father to request for his mother's pardon.

But Wei knew he was running up dead alleys. He had spent the past year out in the desert with nothing but blind faith and folk tales to guide him. How could he possibly find a magical spring that was said to appear only in time of desperate need? All the books and the ancient texts he had managed to get his hands on couldn't point him in the right direction.

It didn't help that his father had declared that his rogue son had gone behind his back to learn magic and was now plotting a rebellion to steal the throne. If he didn't know better, Wei might think that his father was afraid of him.

Maybe he thought I'd be dead by now. That would probably give him something to rejoice over.

On days like this, Wei felt like he was fighting a losing battle, still chained to his father after all these years. All he could do was flee and hide.

A shadow looming outside the tent pulled him out of his thoughts. He reached for his sword on the table. 'Who's there?'

'It's me, Zeyan,' said the voice behind the flap.

Wei relaxed his grip. 'What is it?'

'We found an intruder. She's . . . well, you'll have to see for yourself.'

'She?' They had run into desert bandits several times, and rarely had those been female. Besides, why would she operate alone, especially in this weather?

They found her in the supplies tent at the furthest corner of the camp, sprawled on the floor near the entrance as though she had collapsed on the spot.

Underneath her thick ermine coat, she wore a flimsy but elaborately woven beaded dress that indicated she was from a desert tribe. Both garments were soaked with blood around her right thigh. She appeared no older than Wei—eighteen at most—and had probably seen better days, from the looks of her kohl-smudged eyes, her dress ripped at the hem, and dark, tangled hair framing her face.

A layer of sweat glistened on her forehead. Her brows pulled together as she muttered something indistinguishable in a fitful sleep. Even when Zeyan raised his lamp to her face, she showed no signs of waking.

'When did you find her?' Wei asked.

'Just,' Zeyan replied, setting down the lamp next to her. 'But she could already have been here for a while. She might be from the Dugur tribe. Their camp is not far from here.'

The woven hemp bracelet around her left wrist confirmed it, calling forth a memory of the Dugur tribe Wei thought he had long forgotten.

*

He had been no older than twelve when his father took him out to the desert. By then, Wei had heard enough stories about the wild to begin longing for it. Stories from the old generals about their expeditions out in the desert. How they had reached the brink of death with only the stars to guide them home. How they had faced terrors at night and broken down in despair before finally seeing daylight again.

As he and his father rode side-by-side under the merciless sun that day, flanked by an envoy of guards, Wei wondered how he would fare.

They came to a stop at the boundary marker where tribal land began.

His father spoke to him for the first time since they set out. 'You've always wanted to know what life is like outside the kingdom, beyond the Wall. Now you shall experience it. Spend the night out here and find your way back home in the morning.' He turned to leave without a backward glance.

Wei didn't think it was a tall order. This was his chance to prove his worth to his father, to show that he was deserving of a place in the palace. He would make it out of this desert alive.

But when night fell and the chill set in and he was still going in circles with only a compass as a guide, the first prickle of panic crept under his skin. Night in the desert was different from that in the Capital. Darkness grew as thick as the silence, the kind that stoked fears and bred monsters. Armed with only his dagger and barely any rations left, he didn't have a fighting chance.

Cold seeped into his bones, made its home in him. A shrill rattle came from the distance, followed by an unearthly shriek. Beneath him, the sands rippled like a stirring beast. A cry echoed through the night, lone and shrill.

Wei gripped his dagger tight. It seemed awfully possible to die out here.

The low bray of a camel made him whirl around. Out of the gloom, a girl about his age appeared with a lamp in hand. Behind her was a heavyset middle-aged man.

The sand stilled and the rattling ceased.

As they approached him, the girl exclaimed in a desert tongue, and Wei gathered enough to surmise that the older man was her father. She dismounted, came up to him and asked him for his name in the Oasis language thickened by her desert accent. He offered an alias, but his words came out slurred, thanks to his already frozen tongue.

'Follow us, child,' the man said in a smoother accent. The girl held out her hand without saying a word. He should have questioned their motives, considering what his father had said about desert folk, but he took her hand and followed them back to their tent, choosing, for the first time in his life, to lay his trust in a stranger over his own father.

*

Wei sometimes still wondered if he would have survived that day, had the desert girl and her father not appeared and taken him up for the night. He never learned the girl's name but could still remember how she and her father had spoken with a friendly ease that never existed between him and *his* father.

That memory had offered some comfort as he traversed the desert. Despite what he had been taught about desert people, his first experience with them was now one of the few warm ones he had.

He watched the desert girl struggle in her sleep now, her hair windswept and face grimy. 'I'll take it from here,' he told Zeyan.

If Zeyan was surprised, he did not reveal it, only nodding and retreating from the tent.

Wei didn't like to think of himself as a sentimental person. His time at the Snow Wolf Sect had taught him that the moment you allowed your emotions to sway your weapon was the moment your enemy had the upper hand. And the desert was the last place to let his guard down.

But the girl, in her current state, seemed far from a threat.

Wei pressed the back of his hand against her slick forehead. Heat rolled off her skin and she let out a moan. Had her wound gotten infected or had she been drugged? Either way, he gathered her in his arms and carried her back to his tent. After laying her down on his bed, he filled a basin of cool water and soaked a fresh towel in it.

The girl wrestled with the sheets, tossing and turning. 'I won't leave you, Papa . . .'

Wei returned to her side and wiped away her perspiration. She startled when he placed the damp cloth on her forehead, but did not wake.

'Shh,' he said, dabbing her forehead with the cloth.

Apart from the wound on her thigh, which appeared to have healed despite the blood on her dress, there weren't any other visibly major ones to tend to. But she continued fidgeting until he rested a hesitant hand on her head and hummed a broken tune from his memory. It was the one that the desert girl had sung all those years ago when she and her father took him to their tent. Somehow, it had stayed with him.

This girl seemed to recognize it too. Her fists unclenched and she sank into the pillow with a sigh at last.

There was little else he could do but let the night lull her to sleep. His scrolls and maps lay strewn on his desk, abandoned from earlier, but Wei sat by the desert girl, chasing away her fever until sleep eventually claimed him too.

At dawn, the visitor came.

Three

Desert Rose

Sleep caught hold of her at last, and so did the nightmares.

When she had nightmares as a child, her father would hum a lullaby about the girl from the mountains. But instead of the comforting timbre of her father's voice, she now heard a stranger's voice, deep and low, although it melted away before she could make out the words.

Desert Rose couldn't be sure if the young man she had glimpsed as she drifted in and out of sleep was part of her dreams, but the gentle tune he hummed recalled a half-forgotten memory about a lost boy she had once found.

When she was ten, she and her father had been on their way home with supplies from a nearby desert town when they found the boy and his horse before a sand devil could attack them.

A horse. In the middle of the desert. He had to be from the Capital. No nomad in his right mind would dare to brave the desert with nothing but a dagger, a horse, and far too little clothing for the night.

He was half frozen by the time they found him, curled up against his horse's side. To have eluded the ghouls and creatures under the sand up till that point was sheer dumb luck on his part. He hesitated before telling them his name, but thanked them multiple times in the Oasis language until they brought him to a desert town near the Capital the next morning.

Desert Rose sometimes still thought about that boy, what his life was like in the Oasis Kingdom. She still wondered what he had been doing out in the desert alone, and what he had grown up to be. She had told no one about the boy, but for that one night, she had a secret friend from the Capital that only she and her father knew about.

For some reason, amidst nightmares of lightning-streaked skies and stone-cold eyes, it was the memory of the Capital boy that cooled her fevered dreams.

*

She sprung awake at first light.

A damp cloth slipped off her forehead and landed in her lap. Her thigh throbbed when she moved but it no longer hurt, and the wound was halfway healed. As the crisp morning air chased away the remnants of a headache, events of the previous night rushed back.

The row of clan leaders standing before her and her father, backed by a row of soldiers. Bataar aiming a poisoned dart at her. She and Qara limping into a tent, both close to passing out. Her father telling her to run, his voice tight with panic.

Her father. Was he okay? Had he managed to escape? And Qara—where was she?

The distant rumble of voices pulled her back to the present. Something was wrong.

She eyed her surroundings, every muscle tensed. This tent was different from the one she and Qara had snuck into the night before. It was larger, sparser, with a makeshift table in the centre, strewn with maps and scrolls held in place by a sheathed sword. And instead of bundles of clothing, she was on a proper bed.

Where was she? How did she get here?

She threw off the covers and headed over to the messy table. This camp certainly did not belong to common travellers or merchants, judging by the contents on the table.

First, there were the maps. Maps of the desert carved up according to tribal territory. Maps of countries with exotic names—Lettoria, Bhagia, Chinnai, Kourtislavia, N'yong, Sorenstein, Mayweather, and more. Beneath those was a weathered-looking map of the Old World, detailed with the types of magic practiced in each region.

And then there were the scrolls. One of them, unfurled and pinned down by a chipped stamp, was filled with columns of characters written in a languid script. Desert Rose tried to piece the content together with what little she could read. *Celestial Pool . . . Magic spring . . . Flaming Mountains . . . Khuzar Desert . . . Men have lost their souls just to find that fabled spring . . .*

Indeed, she thought. She had heard too many accounts of hopeful travellers dying out in the desert in their search for the spring. When would they ever learn?

If the owner of this tent was doing research like this, he must be looking for the spring too. If so, everyone had an agenda for the spring—what was his?

She was about to unfurl another scroll when the voices outside grew louder.

'I already told you, I haven't seen anyone who fits your description,' a male voice said in an Oasis-accented desert tongue. 'You'd best be on your way.'

'You seem to be in a hurry to get rid of me,' the second man remarked.

Desert Rose recognized the tell-tale snarl beneath its human voice. That, and the smell of baked earth and rotting flesh. A chill slid down her back. *Sand hound.* The clansmen had sent a demon across the desert to track her down.

She was thirteen when she first encountered a sand hound. She had been separated from Bataar and Qara on one of their visits to the nearby desert towns, and it had come close to dismembering her when her father arrived and struck it down with an iron-tipped arrow. The demon had retaliated before dissipating, almost taking her father's arm with it.

'I happen to know that you're lying, traveller,' said the sand hound.

Of course it did. It could smell her. There was no fooling these sly shape-shifters, especially if they had already caught her scent.

She scoured the tent for her double knives, but they were nowhere in sight. Had she lost them last night, or had they been confiscated by the owner of this tent?

Either way, there was no time to look for them now. She would have to make do with the pair of silver daggers she found hung by the entrance, well-polished and engraved with the name 'Huwei'.

'I suggest you step aside, traveller,' said the demon. 'That's the tribe leader's daughter, and the tribe wants her back.'

The man barely missed a beat. 'I don't care who she is. I haven't seen her.'

She had to hand it to him for not flinching in the face of danger—then again, he probably had no idea he was talking to a demon.

'Do you know what happens to liars?' The sand hound's voice dipped to a growl. 'They are damned for eternity.'

Desert Rose stepped out from the tent, daggers behind her back. 'That's rich, coming from you. We all know you're damned for eternity yourself, demon.'

The sand hound was disguised as a slim man with a hooked nose and deep-set gaze. His white robe, impossibly spotless, flowed in the gentle breeze, and his eyes gleamed too brightly under the frail dawn light.

Despite all the training with Bataar and her father, Desert Rose had never faced off with a supernatural creature on her own. Her father had never let her, even though she had demanded on many occasions to follow the rest of her peers out into the wild. It was too dangerous, Scarbrow had insisted. But what good was being the tribe leader's daughter when she couldn't even protect herself against a sand hound?

It was thus with no little amount of recklessness that she now charged at the creature.

The hilts of the daggers were smoother than what she was used to, but the blades were keen and unforgiving. The demon dodged them with an almost leisurely ease before lunging at her with a hiss. She ducked and swung the daggers at it, just barely nicking its neck.

'Are those my daggers?'

Desert Rose caught a glimpse of the young man who spoke. He had the lean physique of a trained fighter and the steady gaze of a general, even though he appeared to be about her age.

Before she could reply him, the sand hound disappeared into a vortex of sand that flung him ten feet away, where he landed sprawled on the ground. It materialized again and sprang at her with a supernatural fury, blinding her with a blast of sand before grabbing her by the throat.

'You should know,' it rasped, 'that your father is dead.'

She froze. *Demons lie,* she told herself. The sand hound was especially known for its cunning—but it could also tell the truth sometimes. What if it was now?

'The clan leaders did the right thing, you know,' the demon said. 'It's time for a revolt. Your father would have failed to protect the tribe.'

'Shut your mouth,' she snarled.

'Look around you. This desert is dying day by day. Foreign armies are taking over the land and folks like us are forced to go deeper underground. What has your father done so far?'

'And you think the clan leaders helping the Oasis Emperor find the spring is going to save us all?'

The demon shrugged. 'If you can't fight them, join them. There's nothing left here to fight for.'

'You're wrong. There is still much to fight for, and we can still take our desert back.'

'If you insist,' it said, then clamped down on her arm with its row of jagged teeth.

Desert Rose cried out as the pain burned through her. The daggers slipped from her grip, but she managed to grab it by the neck. She dragged it towards the tent, intent on putting enough distance between the demon and its element. As long as it was in contact with sand, she would not be able to shake free of its bite.

It fought back with a force that almost tore her arm off, but her scream was soon drowned out by an unearthly shriek. She opened her eyes to find a sword piercing right through the demon's chest. The blade twisted, and there was the sickening crunch of bones. With a final strangled grunt, the creature's grip on her went slack.

Desert Rose stared at the sword-tip jutting out from the demon's chest, stained with blood black as ink and mere inches away from her face. Behind it, the young man's eyes blazed like twin fires in the night. A trail of sand hound blood crept down his face.

The demon crumpled to the ground and dissipated into the sand, leaving no trace behind, apart from its tarnished white robe.

All was silent again. Desert Rose let out a shaky breath. The pounding in her ears almost drowned out the soft wind that swept by.

Another man arrived—too late—to their aid. 'Wei,' he said. 'Is . . . everything okay?'

'Run-in with a sand hound,' Wei said. 'Zeyan, go wake the rest.'

Their voices sounded distant and muffled through the roaring in her ears. Her body grew heavy, but her head felt like it could float away if someone cut it off her shoulders. The world started to spin around her. She needed to find a quiet corner and purge the venom. Now.

Zeyan took a step towards her. 'Miss, are you okay?' His eyes widened when he noticed her arm. 'You're bleeding.'

Desert Rose glanced down. Her coat was soaked through at the arm, blood blooming from the puncture wounds. She gritted her teeth. 'I'll live.' A wave of dizziness struck her as she started to back away.

'Miss,' Zeyan said. 'I think you need medical atten—'

'I said I'll live.' But her legs buckled as soon as she started walking.

Wei dropped his sword and caught her by the arm, propping her up. 'You won't last a day in this desert with your injuries untreated,' he said with no little amount of exasperation.

She could try to prove him wrong and limp away, but even at the rate she usually healed, there was no way she could purge the venom faster than it was setting in. She would likely be dead before she reached the next desert town.

If Wei were planning to kill her, now would be a good time. But he only steered her back into his tent and sat her back down on the bed.

She focused on drawing deep, steady breaths. The Dugurians believed in channelling the elements for healing and strength. She had watched the *matisha*, the female shamans who healed and blessed the sick and injured, during their rituals. The first thing they always did was clear their minds.

She closed her eyes and focused on the desert's dry winds, the fire of summer and the frost of winter. She tried to draw the skeins of energy from the air and slow her shallow heartbeats to match the earth's pulse. But nature's power remained out of her feeble grasp. She had never excelled at the natural arts, having spent more time on horseback and archery.

A damp, warm towel touched her face. She jumped and opened her eyes to find Wei a mere foot away from her, dabbing away her cold sweat.

'How quickly does the venom spread?' he asked, frowning at her wound.

'What?' she murmured.

Wei tried again, this time in a desert tongue. His Capital accent, more refined than a desert dweller, smoothed out the edges of his words, making them sound almost melodic.

'It's okay. I understand the Oasis language,' she said.

The sand hound had left two deceptively innocuous puncture holes on her arm, but Desert Rose had heard tales of men driven mad from a sand hound's bite before killing themselves. 'It can be lethal, but the venom spreads slowly.'

She pinched the wounds the way her father had when he was injured by the sand hound. The sting made her hiss and grit her teeth, but she ignored the folded dry cloth Wei gave her to bite on. She tried not to cry out as the venom—black as night—burned as it oozed out into the dish Wei prepared. He cleaned her wound with a swipe of alcohol each time, and they developed a painstaking process of alternating between bleeding out the venom and cleaning the wound.

But as her blood cleared to a fresh shade of red, the chill began to slip away from her body and her vision sharpened again.

'Looks clean now,' Wei said at last, leaning closer to examine the injury.

It was hard to tell his exact age. There was a sobriety in his eyes that she saw in the older clan leaders and warriors who had returned from the border wars, but beneath that was the steely focus of a general's gaze. Despite his sun-bronzed skin, his features were chiselled but exquisite, recognisably Capital-bred. His garb—a plain black robe belted at the waist—was modest but sleek, rugged enough for the desert but sophisticated enough for the Capital.

Wei gave her wound one last swipe of alcohol for good measure before glancing up at her. Desert Rose turned away quickly.

The camp had roused by now. Voices outside grew louder as morning light reached further into the tent.

'How are you feeling?' he asked, reaching for a roll of bandages.

'Decidedly further away from the brink of death,' she said, her shoulders relaxing just a fraction. 'Thank you.'

His brows slid up. 'You attacked a sand hound knowing it could kill you?'

She shrugged. 'There are worse ways to die in the desert.'

'Indeed, getting shot in the leg with a poisoned dart would be a less heroic way than fighting off a demon.'

She ignored his remark. 'Did you see another girl when you found me?'

'What other girl?' he said, eyes narrowing.

Had Qara left the tent? Or was she still hidden there among the clothing bundles? Maybe, hopefully, she had managed to escape.

She shook her head. 'Nothing, there's no one else.' She nodded at the documents on the table. 'You mean to find the spring too?'

Wei made no reply.

Nations had gone to war over this land itself, torn the desert apart just to mine its treasures. Every day, she and her tribe lived under the threat of being invaded by these foreign treasure-seekers. She had watched her people die, caught in the crossfire, starved or parched to death as the tainted desert magic poisoned the very air, the water they collected, and the food they stored. They were corrupting the very thing they sought, and good men from various tribes had sacrificed their lives trying to protect the desert.

'The desert's magic is not for men to exploit,' she said.

'That depends on the cause for it,' he retorted. 'Anyway, I assume you are not going back to where you escaped from. Where to next?'

If he were headed to Oasis Kingdom, perhaps she could hitch a ride to the Capital. There was no way she could make it across this desert on her own without any rations.

'I have business in the Capital.' Her heart wrenched at the thought of her father's hurried parting instruction. *Please be there, Papa. Please be okay.*

'The Oasis Capital?' he echoed. 'That place will eat you alive.'

'I've lived my entire life in the desert and I just fought a sand hound. I think I can make it in a walled city with no magic.'

He nodded at her arm. 'You almost just died from fighting a sand hound.'

The tent flap flew open and Zeyan barged in, cutting her off mid-retort. 'They found us,' he said. 'The Imperial Army.'

Wei's demeanour darkened like a brewing storm. 'Gather everyone. We leave immediately.'

She could leave them now. The Imperial Army wasn't after her. But where could she go on her own? She was stuck with this ragtag crew for now.

'I know a faster way to the next desert town,' she said.

The desert was a living beast, merciless and wild. Its magic ran rampant, led by a mind of its own. Wanderers spoke of winds that whispered to them in the quiet hours before dawn and local tribes passed down tales of unspeakable creatures concealed by night.

And there in the heart of it lay a spring.

Buried so deep in the desert and hidden from sight, the magic spring had almost become a myth. A fabled oasis. A beacon of hope for lost travellers desperate for tomorrow.

But those who had lived during the reign of the Damohai, Children of the Desert, would remember how the spring had saved King Khotai's life when the Hesui Empire was under siege and he was exiled to the far corners of the desert. It had brought a man back from the verge of death.

As stories began to spread, so did the greed of men grow. They raced one another to get their hands on the spring water, the cure to all mortal woes and the answer to immortality.

But no mortal could lay rightful claim to it. All who tried never lived to tell the tale. Only fools believed they might possibly unearth the secret of the spring and mine its treasures.

*Legend has it that the spring will only awaken when the Damohai once again find their leader, who will rebuild the lost tribe and the fallen empire of Hesui. But until that happens—*if *it ever does—the spring remains as one of the most elusive mysteries of the Khuzar Desert.*

—Excerpt from *Land of Sand and Song: Tales from the Khuzar Desert,* by Lu Ji Fang

Four

Wei

They'd had close brushes with the Imperial Army before, but never *this* close, where the scouts were less than a day away from them.

As Wei joined the men outside his tent, a voice nagged at the back of his mind.

Aren't you playing right into his hand? That's what he wanted you to do when he imprisoned your mother, when he cornered you at every turn, forcing you closer and closer back home where he can kill you at last.

But he was tired of running. Of putting his friends in danger. Of being unable to protect his mother from palace politics. Of leaving everything to the chance of him finding some fabled spring.

Perhaps it was time to abandon his quest and face his father head-on at last.

The crew gathered before him in front of his tent, where he stood side by side with Desert Rose. She sized them up the same way they eyed her, but there was no time for introductions.

'Where are we headed?' Beihe asked.

'The Capital,' said Wei.

The men traded uncertain looks among themselves—and for good reason. It had been years since Wei had set foot near the Capital. As far as anyone was concerned, the rogue prince had died out in the desert and it was best to keep it that way.

Zeyan was the first to speak up. 'Wei, you know we can't return to the Capital. The emperor . . .'

'Yes, I am aware of what he plans to do.'

'We've spent all these years dodging the Imperial Army. Now you want to go to the Capital?'

Wei beat down the frustration rising in him and surveyed the men. There were only five of them, including Zeyan—a compact motley crew of vagabonds, deserters, and Snow Wolf Sect disciples seeking their purpose just like him. They had stayed by him even after learning that he was the disgraced Third Prince of Oasis Kingdom, even though all he had was a flimsy plan to find a fabled spring.

'It's been a year since we embarked on this quest, and our attempts have been futile,' he said. 'My mother is now a prisoner, and my brother's position becomes more precarious by the day. I will no longer run.'

He understood why the men shifted with unease. The emperor had decreed that anyone found with the rogue prince was punishable for being complicit.

'I don't expect you to join me,' he added. 'I only ask that you claim no alliance with me, should you choose to part ways.'

Silence fell. No one moved or uttered a word.

Wei nodded. 'Then let's get moving.'

Zeyan trailed after him as he went to ready his horse, speaking only when they were out of earshot. 'Wei, are you sure about this? Remember you were ready to charge home too, after learning about your mother's imprisonment.'

And he would have, had Zeyan not stopped his impulsive hide. He would have tried to break his mother free from the palace and likely gotten himself locked up too. But it had been almost a year since his mother's fall from grace, a year of him hearing reports from Zeyan's scouts about her suffering in the palace and not being able to do anything.

'Do you *want* to go home?' Zeyan asked.

'No. The palace has never been home for me. I just want to stop hiding.'

Over the years, he had just about convinced himself that he had chosen this life. That he enjoyed the freedom of being out in the desert, free of the inane politics and careful decorum of the palace, the whispers behind his back and barbed remarks from courtiers. Unpredictable and unknowable as it might be, the desert was something he could make sense of. It didn't have rules, but it also didn't have an opinion of him. Plus, he had learned more outside that walled kingdom than he ever had within it.

Lately, though, the questions were starting to creep in. Why should he be a stranger in his own kingdom and persecuted for returning?

Why should he have to leave his mother at the mercy of ambitious imperial consorts?

'And the girl is coming with us?' Zeyan went on. 'I heard she's the tribe leader's daughter. We've got enough problems on our hands without getting involved in tribe business, especially now that the emperor is working with the desert clans to find the spring.'

'So it's true, the emperor is behind all this,' said a voice behind them.

Wei and Zeyan turned to find said tribe leader's daughter stepping out from behind the horses, dressed in a fresh tunic, her hair tied up in a sleek ponytail. Now that she looked like a regular desert girl, it was easy to dismiss that supernatural flare he had seen in her eyes earlier as a mere trick of the light.

'Eavesdropping is rude, miss,' Zeyan said.

She ignored him, staring straight at Wei. 'If the clan leaders who captured my father are working with the emperor, does that mean the emperor is the one after my father?'

'If your father's been taken to the emperor, then he is most likely . . .'

Dead—or about to be.

'No, he's not,' she snapped. 'He told me to meet him at the Oasis Capital. He'll be there.' She repeated the last part to herself for good measure.

Wei said nothing else. He saw in her the same fire that had fuelled him as he rode out of the Oasis Capital when he turned sixteen. It was the look of someone who had nothing left to lose.

'Your funeral,' he said, repeating the exact words his older brother had said to him before he left the Capital all those years ago.

*

They set off that very morning. It felt good to be on the move again, to have a destination, even if it wasn't the one Wei had originally planned.

The desert girl—whose name, he learned, was Desert Rose—didn't question the urgency at which they travelled or the need for heavier disguise, nor did she flinch at the speed they rode. Although she didn't protest at sharing Wei's mount, she tried to keep as much distance from him as possible, and her hands would occasionally pat the knives at her belt like she was seeking reassurance from their presence.

In the years that he spent out of the palace, Wei had heard countless tales about desert beings, some of them as far-fetched as the dragon that lived beneath the shifting sands, and some that even the most sceptical travellers secretly paid heed to.

The story about the Damohai, Children of the Desert, was one that travelled far and wide—across the desert to the sweeping plains of Zzang in the north, the hidden valleys of Baldur in the west, and the bustling streets of Oasis Capital, where it was sometimes whispered as a bedtime story.

Descended from the Earth Prince and the Sky Princess's illegitimate and only son, the Damohai was a group of half-human, half-immortal beings. Legend had it that they were the original guardians of the desert, keepers of the Immortal Spring itself. Back then, King Khotai had ruled the ancient empire of Hesui, until a group of scientists commissioned by Zhaoshun—Wei's ancestor and the first emperor of the would-be Oasis Kingdom, who later declared himself the first Oasis Emperor—discovered a special type of herb that could temporarily disable their magic. It had wiped out half the Damohai, making it easy for Zhaoshun to lead the war against magical folk and drive them out of the desert. What remained was now, centuries later, a weakened group of castaways who practised their magic in the hidden corners of the Khuzar Desert.

Wei's own knowledge of the Damohai was gleaned from his teachers at the Snow Wolf Sect and further embellished by merchants with whom he had crossed paths in the desert. They had all agreed on the easiest way to spot one: it was all in the eyes, especially when their fight or flight instinct kicked in.

Desert Rose certainly wasn't an ordinary desert girl. He had caught that tell-tale flash of pale silver in her eyes, like a steel blade catching the moonlight, when she battled the sand hound. As the stories went, the Damohai's magic revealed itself in the face of danger as an unearthly light. Could she be one of them?

He gave voice to none of the questions in his mind as they rode. 'It's a half day's ride to the first desert town; we should reach the Capital in about five. Are you up for it?'

'Go as fast as you will,' she replied.

So they raced against the wind, chasing daylight.

Five

Desert Rose

Desert Rose was used to long journeys. She had travelled as far north as Vladov with her father many moons ago, and no desert girl trained in horseback was fazed by riding till nightfall.

But it was a different matter travelling in winter with a foreign crew and riding with a stranger against her back. She constantly reached for her knives tucked at her waist, the ones her father had given her when she was fifteen. With them in her hands, she could almost feel he was right there with her.

In the evenings, the crew would gather around a fire and trade stories while they filled their stomachs with meagre rations. As she ate alongside them, Desert Rose listened to the stories they narrated, mostly folktales and myths that she had heard as a child.

One told of Ji'an the One-Legged Wanderer, who had bested the crafty Wind Spirit to cross the desert. Another marvelled over the paradise of Utamila, Valley of the Gods, where good men, few and far between, were said to find their resting place among deities who welcomed them with open arms. Yet another, in a hushed voice, told of desert ghouls that now haunted the abandoned fortress of Ghost City, which had been consumed by a sandstorm brought about by an enraged djinn from the west.

But the story that made Desert Rose pay closer attention was that of the five Elementals who were prophesied to appear when the Damohai was on the brink of a revival.

It was said that the Elementals were scattered across the desert, and the sole survivor would lead the Damohai back into power so that they would, once again, reclaim the desert and protect the Immortal Spring, restoring the balance of magic between heaven and earth.

The narrator's account was flawed, though—the Elementals were prophesied to kill each other on their way to find the Damohai, and not, as he declared, be destroyed by their own powers. At least, according to the version Desert Rose knew.

Still, it was comforting to hear the stories that the men traded among themselves. It reminded her of the times she sat around with her tribe during Tsagen Sol and the desert felt as endless and deep as the night.

Wei would sit a distance away, just within sight but not close enough to join in on the conversation. Often, he would be lost in thought, brows creased and staring into space. Everyone left him well alone, as though his peripheral presence was the norm. Even with a travelling crew, he seemed to Desert Rose the loneliest person she had ever met.

Zeyan, the mild-mannered man whom she had seen conversing with Wei most often, approached her with grub and water at times. He had a kind demeanour that made her let down her guard a little, although she kept her answers brief. She still hadn't sussed out who these men were and what business they had in the desert other than what Wei's maps suggested. She didn't know why they were on the run, why they were avoiding open routes and convenient pit stops where most travellers camped for the night. And she would no longer trust another person until she had learned his true intentions.

Sometimes, she would glean a clue or two when the men spoke about the Capital. An offhand comment here, a curse at the emperor there, and Desert Rose gathered enough to understand that there was no love lost between them and Oasis Kingdom. Wei's expression would darken at the mention of the emperor, although he remained silent.

On the fourth evening, she went over and sat next to Wei, uninvited.

Surprise flickered past his face, but he didn't reject her company. 'If you're here to ask me about my research, I'm not taking questions.'

She nodded at the men around the campfire. 'Do you believe any of the stories they're telling?'

'I believe the world is much bigger than we think.'

'So you believe that the spring can serve you in some way or other.'

He sent her a sidelong glance. 'People won't risk their lives looking for it if they're not desperate enough.'

She hadn't thought of it that way before. She had always assumed that all who searched for the spring were driven by greed, not desperation. 'Why are you desperate for it then?'

He was silent for a long while. At last, in a voice so quiet it was almost drowned out by the crackle of the campfire, he said, 'I'm just trying to save the people I love.' He turned away, signalling the end of the conversation, before she could find a response to that.

They left the desert behind on the fifth day and crossed into greener pastures dusted with snow, which reminded Desert Rose of the powdered sugar rose cakes her father used to bring back from the Capital on his visits. As they neared the Capital, the snow grew into a thick blanket streaked by footpaths and roads.

They stopped in the most nondescript inn they could find, with a crumbling sign and no more than five people in sight, including an elderly innkeeper at the counter by the door. The furnishings were almost spartan, and faded lanterns swung in the four corners of the common area, casting a faint crimson glow on the walls.

Wei left his alias at the counter and asked for two rooms. With a brief glance at them, the innkeeper recorded his details and led them up a flight of rickety wooden stairs. Desert Rose kept her grip firmly on her knife hilts as she scanned the inn, half-expecting something to shatter the uncanny stillness any moment.

The doors to their rooms burst open as soon they reached the landing, revealing a swarm of soldiers in red and black livery, their swords drawn.

Wei and his crew barely missed a beat. They unsheathed their weapons and charged right back. Next to Desert Rose, the innkeeper ducked out of the fray, scurrying back down the stairs and leaving them to clash swords.

This is a trap, she realized. And they had walked right into it. The scouts had been staking out this inn, knowing they would pick the most remote and inconspicuous one in the vicinity.

She whipped out her knives and swerved just in time to avoid an incoming blade.

The handful of men in civilian clothing at the ground floor joined in, each one bearing arms embossed with the imperial crest. Wei and his crew backed against one another, forming a tight circle as they deflected blow after blow. One of the plainclothes soldiers dove for Zeyan, scraping his shoulder with his sword. Wei lunged at him, tackling him before throwing him over the banister.

The whoosh of a sword next to her ear made Desert Rose snap to attention. She spun around to find a soldier brandishing his sword at her and kicked him square in the chest, sending him tumbling down the stairs.

The remaining soldiers regrouped, forming an impenetrable wall that attacked relentlessly, cornering Wei and the crew into the room.

'We haven't touched Oasis soil. You have no right to take us,' Zeyan said. But the soldiers only inched closer, their weapons keen and ready.

'Don't waste your breath,' Wei said, meeting one of the soldiers' blades with his own. The shriek of steel against steel ripped through the still night—and then there was a cry of agony.

The soldier dropped his weapon with a loud clatter, sinking to his knees in front of Wei as blood sprayed from his gut where Wei had slashed him. Desert Rose flinched, gripping her knives tighter.

The soldier crumpled face-down on the ground, blood pooling fast beneath him. Silence grew as thick as the falling snow outside. Wei stood with his back against the window, flanked by his crew and braced for the next attack.

'You can tell the emperor that there are far less underhanded ways to capture a wanted man,' he snarled.

Desert Rose stared at him. What was he wanted for? How little she knew about this stranger, yet how she had trusted him, even travelling for days with him against her back.

Upon the silent order given by their leader, a man in a common blue tunic, the soldiers gathered their injured comrades and retreated.

Wei dropped his sword as they thundered down the stairs, then sank against the window ledge as blood dripped down his face, gleaming under the dim candlelight in the room.

The sound of muffled hoofbeats receded as the soldiers raced away on their horses. When the quiet of the night crept back in, Zeyan cleared his throat, eyeing Wei, who turned his back against them to stare out the window. Desert Rose peered at him, but his expression was unreadable.

Zeyan cleared his throat. 'They won't be back for now. Let's . . . stay here for the night as planned. I'll have a word with the innkeeper.' He brushed out of the room, sidestepping the wreckage and blood stains on the floor.

The others shuffled around with their belongings, leaving Desert Rose alone with Wei. She couldn't decide if she wanted to ask if he was okay or put as much distance between them as she could.

'Take another room,' he said without turning to look at her. 'You don't want to be in this one.'

She ducked out, glad for a reason to leave. Whatever he was running from seemed to have caught up with him, and she had no interest in getting involved.

*

She had stayed long enough. The already-growing unease she had felt as they neared the Capital now rattled hard inside her, urging her to leave.

She had to choose the right time to escape. Too early and she would be stranded in the freezing cold until the Capital gates opened; too late and the crew might have roused, and she knew from the past few nights that Wei was a light sleeper. They probably wouldn't even try to stop her from leaving, but she had never known how to say goodbye, even to strangers.

As soon as the sky turned deep purple, she crept out of bed and gathered her belongings. There was little to pack apart from her knives and some rations. With one last look over her shoulder, she stole out of her room.

The frail lantern light was all she had to go on as she inched down the hallway and the stairs, careful not to upset the creaky floorboards. Her outstretched hands reached the wooden door. A frigid gust of wind hit her in the face the moment she slipped outside, but it didn't matter. She was free. And she was on her way to the Oasis Capital.

*

The Oasis Capital.

Desert Rose had heard her father talk about it many times before. Winding labyrinths of houses and shops aglow with coloured lanterns.

Bustling streets lined with stalls and food carts filled with racks of candied fruit, sweet meats, and melons larger than her head. Buskers who danced with death and sold their art for pennies and cheers. Merchants from countries as far west as Sorenstein, and aristocrats dressed in furs and silks. Her father would describe everything to the last detail, and she would close her eyes and imagine herself standing in the heart of the city, taking in every sight and smell.

Her father was secretly fascinated with the Oasis Capital, even though he often referred to it as a 'depraved nation where magic goes to die'. It was a world apart from the desert, and although Desert Rose knew that he found his home in the shifting sands, she could tell from his wistful gaze that he had once loved and lost in that city.

She now stood before the towering double doors of the Capital, each wider than her tent and thrice as tall. Four guards in red and black livery stood before a pair of stone lions, stoic against the winter chill. Atop the walls that stretched beyond her sight, more guards kept watch at their posts. Even without the magic-resistant Wall, the Capital seemed impenetrable.

This was the furthest she had ever come alone. No amount of archery practice, horse riding or sparring could prepare her for this. She was going in with nothing more than what she had heard from her father and the handful of encounters she'd had with Oasis people.

At this hour, where late morning light scattered itself across the mist-covered mountains in the distance, a line of people was already forming before the gates. Some wore refined Capital-woven threads, others in roughly spun clothing. Some came trailing with servants, others with camels, carts and horses loaded with goods and wares. And then there were the desert-dwellers, the ones with hardly anything but the clothes on their backs.

Desert Rose watched as the guards let the locals in but stop a caravan of travellers dressed in desert garb—padded robes, sheepskin coats and leather boots, not unlike what she would have worn in regular circumstances. She glanced down at the men's attire that Wei had loaned her. It hung on her like an ill-fitting skin, but at least it looked more respectable than a torn, bloodstained dress and robe.

Part of her wanted to turn back to the desert, to everything she was familiar with. But she had come this far to find her father. To turn back now was out of the question.

She sucked in a bracing breath and hitched her bag tighter before joining the ever-growing line into the Capital.

The wait was interminable. The sun was well past its zenith by the time she reached the front of the line, where Capital folks and the rabble of frayed-looking travellers split into two separate queues. The guards combed through each carriage, scrutinizing every nook and cranny after getting the riders to dismount.

On the massive red brass door was a huge sign that read: *All who enter the Capital are to undergo mandatory cleansing. Failure to comply will result in immediate prosecution.*

A guard in front of her announced, 'Anyone without a Capital license or citizenship is to be denied entry. Citizens, please hold up your identity pass for smooth entry.' The guard took one look at her and drawled, 'Forbidden.'

It felt like a slap to the face. 'Why?' she demanded.

The guard shot her a glare. 'Did I not make myself clear just now? Foreigners are barred from entering unless they run a business here or have received permission from the imperial family, in which case I will need to see some documentation.' He leaned down to peer closer at her face. She forced herself to remain where she was. 'You reek of the desert. I'm sure you have no business being in the Capital, and we don't accept refugees. Now head on back.'

'I am not a refugee.'

'Fine. Then state your purpose.'

'I'm here to look for someone.'

'*Someone*,' the guard sneered. 'I'm going to need something more specific than that.'

Desert Rose bit her lip. What if he asked to know who her father was? Would she be putting him in greater danger if he were found? She didn't know what this new law decreed, but going by the guard's attitude towards her, she would be lucky if he didn't throw her back to the desert.

She tried to keep the irritation out of her voice. 'A family member. It's private.'

'Well, then I guess you're not entering the Capital, are you?' He looked over her shoulder. 'Next!'

The guard declared the next few foreign-looking folks inadmissible too. Unlike Desert Rose, they looked more resigned than irate, and a couple of them turned back with their camels, possibly to seek their fortunes at the nearest desert town or bazaar instead.

But Desert Rose wasn't done yet; she hadn't come all the way here to get turned away at the gates.

The ache in her heart swelled. If only she hadn't fled. If only she had stayed with her father. If only she had disobeyed him this time. They might have been in danger, but at least they would be together.

She lurked around the periphery, observing the people who were granted entry and those who were turned away, until the line finally dissipated. Daylight was dimming when she gave in to the notion of seeking shelter for the night at the nearest inn. But she couldn't go to the Travelling Horse, not without any currency on her, and she couldn't stay out here either, not unless she wanted to freeze to death.

When she spotted the well in the distance, she thought she was hallucinating. She was parched, she was weary. Surely her mind was playing tricks on her.

But no, it *was* a lone, crumbling—almost abandoned—edifice sitting by the corner of the wall, rimmed with snow.

It was foolish to hope to find water in the well in the middle of winter, but she approached it anyway. She reached for the rope and lowered the bucket down the well until a tiny splash echoed up. Hardly daring to believe her ears, she drew up the bucket and found it half-full.

Water never tasted as sweet as it did then.

The distant sound of hooves made her freeze. She squinted into the darkness, pressing close to the shadows.

Two pairs of guards on horses broke through the twilight gloom, their boots crunching on snow. Behind them was an ornately carved carriage with the drapes half-open. A young man peered out from within.

It was too late to hide.

The man emerged from his carriage in a smooth, practised motion and held up a small lamp, careful to avoid blinding her. His pristine ivory robe seemed to blend in with the snow-covered ground. Something about him—perhaps his steady gaze or his long, slender fingers around the lamp handle—that made her feel boorish in comparison. She was all too aware of the water dripping down her chin, but didn't want to draw attention to it by wiping it off.

The man, however, did not seem to notice. 'It's too late in the evening for anyone to be out in the cold like that.' His accent was smooth and polished as the gilded lion-headed brass-knockers on the Capital gates.

Hers sounded like rough desert rocks. 'It is by no choice of mine.'

'Were you trying to enter the Capital?'

She nodded once but offered nothing more.

'The entry regulations are stricter these days,' he said. 'If you're not from the Capital and don't have pre-existing business here, you will need a guarantor to help you enter.'

An involuntary sigh escaped her. But his next words sent a thrill of hope racing down to her freezing feet.

'I can help you enter the Capital.'

In the Capital, hands are full, but hearts are empty.

—A Dugurian saying

Six

Meng

It was nightfall by the time Meng reached the Capital gates. His journey back home had been delayed by a bunch of bandits who had scrambled away as soon as they realized whom they were trying to rob. There would thus be no fanfare to welcome him home, just a quiet reception at the gates—just the way Meng preferred.

It had been a long ride and an even longer trip; one week in Lettoria had taken more out of him than he had expected. Meng could feel his eyelids starting to droop—

But what he spotted in the distance made him do a double take.

It was dark and chilly enough at this hour for travellers to start seeking shelter and warmth. But the figure crouched by the well outside the Capital seemed impervious to the cold as she gulped down the water she had collected from the old well.

A well that had been dry since the start of the year, ever since the drought and famine hit the Capital hard.

The girl seemed to be around his age, but she looked as hardy as the next desert dweller. Her cheekbones were high, though without the haughty slant of Capital girls', and her gaze was keen, unlike the doe-like one that most girls around here cultivated. She tensed when she noticed them. As far as he could tell, she was alone and had no belongings, save for a leather pouch. Her eyes lit up when he offered to help her enter the Capital, but flicked to his entourage with the caution typical of desert dwellers.

'What's your name?' he asked. She hesitated. 'It's okay. You don't have to tell me if you don't want to.'

'You want to help me?' she asked instead. 'Why?'

Her speech contained no social formalities or courtesy markers. Coupled with her rough accent, her blunt question sounded rude enough for one of his guards to take a threatening step forward. Meng dismissed him with a wave and gave the girl a wry smile. She didn't seem to understand the feat she had pulled, or maybe she had no idea how long the well had been dry until she came about. But he knew, and he was certain of what he saw. And a girl like her should not be turned away at the gates.

'It might seem hard to believe,' he replied, 'but not all Capital people function without a heart.'

Her façade cracked, just a little, at his joke. The decision was obvious—it didn't matter how she entered the Capital as long as she did. 'Thank you,' she said, as he helped her to her feet.

'You may ride with me,' Meng said. 'How did you manage to arrive at the Capital on your own?'

'I had help,' she admitted. 'It's a long story, but I hitched a ride with a group of travellers.'

'And they left you at the gates?'

'I parted ways with them earlier.'

'And what is it that you seek in the Capital?' She chewed her lip. 'I can't be your guarantor if I don't know your purpose here.'

'I wish to see the emperor.'

He wanted to ask her why, of course. What business would a desert girl have with the emperor? Perhaps his father's alliance with the desert tribes had upset the peace. But he wasn't about to push her—not right now.

'Very well,' he said.

'You're not going to ask why?'

'This is between you and the emperor,' he said. 'You understand that you will have to be stripped of all magical abilities before entering the Capital? It's the law.'

Ever since relations soured with the southern colonies and western forces pressed ever closer, many visitors were now banned from entering the Capital altogether, and those who were granted entry were now subject to three rounds of cleansing, a measure that the emperor declared was necessary to keep everyone protected within the Wall. A measure that Meng knew was meant to convince the people that the emperor was safeguarding the kingdom—whatever helped to restore the people's belief in the emperor that the famine had undermined.

'I don't possess any magical abilities.' She seemed genuinely certain of that, even though a strange light in her eyes, almost otherworldly, shone through the winter fog.

Never mind the new decree. Meng knew his father would want him to bring her into the palace.

'Then let's get you into the Capital,' he said.

Seven

Desert Rose

Desert Rose had dreamt of visiting the Oasis Capital many times in her life, but never had she expected to enter in this manner—in a fancy carriage with a handsome Capital stranger instead of her father.

She sat less than a foot away from her guarantor, taking in the lavish interior of the carriage, the folds of his silk robe, and the faint whiff of a foreign spice on him. Hazelwood, from the south. The more affluent merchants from desert towns often wore it.

But this man didn't seem like a mere merchant, if the reception at the gates was any indication.

She shrank back from the window when the veil was drawn by the carriage-bearers. Four more guards came forth to receive them.

They sank to one knee before the carriage and greeted in unison, 'Welcome home, Your Highness Prince Meng.'

Prince? He was a *prince*? No wonder he seemed so certain he was able to help her.

Desert Rose tried not to let her surprise show, especially when he glanced at her. She was aware of the guards' attention shifting to her. One of them raised his brows upon recognizing the girl he had turned away at the gates.

'You desert rat—'

'She's with me,' Meng said, pulling out from his travelling bag a red wooden plaque inscribed with gilded characters. *Access.* 'You will speak to my guest as you would speak to me.'

The guard dipped his head, chastened. 'My apologies, Prince Meng. Please proceed to the cleansing pavilion with your guest.'

Prince Meng gave a nod and let the curtain fall back down.

'Helping desert girls enter the Capital doesn't seem to be the norm here,' Desert Rose remarked as they went on their way.

'Only if you're needlessly paranoid, like my father,' he replied.

They rode through the Capital gates with no other delay, and headed down a short, pebbled path that split from the main road. At the end of the path was a small garden where the cleansing pavilion sat, a simple circular shelter with a jade-green roof. Two officials sat before a stone table, tending to two steaming teapots, while a scribe perched next to them with his brush and scroll.

The cleansing process involved drinking a cup of pale, bitter-smelling tea with *ticha* leaves, emerald green and diamond-shaped, floating in it. *Ticha*, when consumed raw, was lethal. Desert Rose remembered someone had once tried to poison her father with it, years ago, and they had later found the culprit with *ticha* leaves stuck under his boots.

Prince Meng drained both his cup and hers. 'Best not to take on an empty stomach,' he told her. The guards exchanged a glance but did not dare to protest.

The scribe looked up from his scroll and shot her a pointed look. 'Your name, miss,' he said. 'For record purposes.'

Desert Rose hid a grimace. She couldn't get out of this one. 'Sarenai Mul.'

'Mul,' Prince Meng echoed as the scribe made record of it. 'You're from the Dugur tribe?'

Of course, her second name would give her away in a heartbeat. But Prince Meng understood her pursed-lip nod and did not press any further.

They travelled through the city unimpeded. It was just a little after dinner time, but the Capital remained abuzz with lantern-lit inns along the canal, shopkeepers packing up their wares or folding up their booths, and stray groups of boisterous nobles loitering around, reeking of rice wine. The commoners, Desert Rose supposed, had retreated into their homes for the evening, away from the cold. A faint whiff of canal rot hung in the air and the wizened trees lining the near-empty streets gave off an air of desolation, but the city's sights and sounds took Desert Rose's mind off her problems, if only for a while.

'Sarenai,' Prince Meng said, interrupting her thoughts.

'You may call me Desert Rose. That's what my name means, anyway.'

'If you wish.' He tied a strip of black silk around the red plaque he had flashed earlier and handed it to her. 'Keep this with you. It will ensure you smooth passage through the palace. When you're there, offer this in exchange for an imperial pass—'

'You're taking me straight to the palace?'

'Since you intend to see the emperor, our destinations are the same.' He surveyed her expression. 'You have nothing to fear, Desert Rose. This city may be daunting, but that depends on whom you've got behind you. Right now, I have your back.'

Out in the desert, she was safe as long as she belonged to a tribe—safe from predators, bandits, and even the supernatural. Here, she had to figure out how to survive on her own. Prince Meng had not only helped her enter the Capital, but he was also going to take her to the palace. He was all she had in this foreign land, and he was the biggest ally she could have on her side here.

'Thank you,' she said at last, ignoring the doubt nagging at the back of her mind. He smiled.

As they cut towards the heart of the Capital, narrow, cluttered streets expanded into broad, empty roads neatly lined with trimmed hedges topped with snow. They passed through two pairs of heavyset vermillion gates as massive as the ones at the Capital entrance. There, they emerged from the carriage and proceeded on foot, trailed by only a pair of guards from Prince Meng's entourage.

The journey through the palace seemed endless. Carved stone walls stretched alongside as they passed through courtyards and pavilions decorated by snow-topped bonsais and stone sculptures. Prince Meng supplied a cursory explanation of the palace grounds, but Desert Rose only half-listened as she eyed the new environment.

At last, they arrived at the Red Circle, the heart of the palace, where the imperial family's private quarters were located. It was a series of sprawling manors, each separated by bamboo and bonsai gardens, bordered by high walls, fronted by polished red doors, and guarded by a pair of stone lions. Overhead, perched at all corners of the roofs, intricately carved stone dragons cast their silhouettes against the night sky. Without the incessant comings and goings of maids and servants in the outer courts, the Red Circle was a world removed.

'Where are we going?' Desert Rose asked.

'I'm taking you to Matron first,' Prince Meng said. 'She oversees the court maids and all the domestic affairs in the Red Circle. After you've settled in, we can arrange a way for you to meet the emperor.'

'Settled in?'

'You can't possibly hope to meet the emperor now, and I presume you have nowhere else to stay.'

He was right. The Capital was too large to find her father in a day, and she had nowhere else to go.

They walked in silence. Desert Rose tried to memorize her surroundings while keeping pace with Prince Meng, but it was hard to keep track of how many turns they had made or how deep in the palace they were now. A lone gust of wind trailed after them wherever they went, their only companion.

Frenzied footsteps ahead made them slow to a stop. A figure burst out of the gloom, shattering the silence as he cried, 'The Crown Prince is dead! The Crown Prince is dead!!'

The news-bearer was a male servant dressed in a deep-blue tunic, his forehead glimmering with sweat. He came to a halt and bowed low when he saw Prince Meng, but his brows remained creased.

'What is going on?' the prince asked calmly.

The servant took a shaky breath. 'Th-the Crown Prince. I f-found him in his chamber—*dead*!'

Prince Meng frowned. 'My brother is dead? When did this happen?'

'He seemed fine at dinner time. But when I returned after, he was already lying on the floor, purple in the face.'

'Take me to him,' Prince Meng ordered, ready to dash off until he noticed Desert Rose still by his side. He waved over a pair of court maids who had been whispering between themselves behind a pillar.

The maids bowed when they approached and greeted in unison, 'Your Highness.'

'Do not breathe a word of this to anyone. We don't need to send the palace into an uproar. Am I clear?'

'Yes, Your Highness.'

Prince Meng gestured at Desert Rose. 'Now, take this lady to see Matron.' He turned to Desert Rose. 'My apologies, I must leave you for now. Show Matron what I gave you earlier. She'll know what to do.'

He hurried away with the servant, leaving her with the maids who were back to whispering between themselves. They straightened when she turned to them.

'This way, please,' they said, and turned to lead the way.

Matron lived in the Hall of Virtuous Happiness, separated from the imperial bedchambers by a maze garden and a lotus pond. Though considerably less extravagant in furnishing and architectural detail than the imperial quarters, the Hall stood as a dignified four-storey manor, where at least fifty maids milled around at the ground and second level, finishing up their chores for the day. The pair of maids led Desert Rose through the common area, dodging other maids carrying empty dinner trays.

News of the Crown Prince's death had already spread to this part of the palace. Desert Rose picked up snatches of conversation as she passed.

'Poisoned, I heard.'

'Not strangled?'

'He was having dinner when he suddenly collapsed.'

'How is that possible? We always taste-test the food before sending it out.'

'Who were the ones who prepared his meal and delivered it to him?'

Fear rippled through them like a silent draught.

'They're lucky if they survive this,' someone said.

An imperious voice cut in. 'Are we all done with our duties? Because I still see trays lying around. If I see one person idling about gossiping, she will have her privileges suspended for a month.'

The maids scrambled apart and filed into two rows facing each other, their heads bowed. 'Yes, Matron,' they murmured.

At the front of the line, between the two rows of maids, stood the mistress of the Hall of Virtuous Happiness. With a stare that quailed everyone into silence, Matron appeared much taller than anyone present. Not a hair was out of place, and her stately gait made barely a ripple in her dark green court dress as she strode down the line. Her hawkish gaze swept past every girl, narrowing when it landed on Desert Rose.

'And you are?' she asked.

One of the maids who brought Desert Rose in spoke on her behalf, her head still bowed. 'Prince Meng brought her in, Matron. He left her in our care when he heard the news of . . .' She risked a glance up but ducked her head again when Matron silenced her with a warning glare.

But Desert Rose couldn't help herself. 'The Crown Prince was killed?'

Matron's glare was a frost-tipped arrow aimed at her. 'You will speak only when you are spoken to.'

Desert Rose pursed her lips. Matron reminded her of Anar Zel, the official matriarch of the Dugur tribe who used to teach the girls in the tribe social etiquette, except that she wore a fancier robe and held a straighter back.

She stepped closer to Desert Rose. 'A desert girl,' she murmured, her eyes skirting down Desert Rose's sun-browned face and dishevelled hair to the men's garb she wore. 'Prince Meng must have a reason for bringing you to me. Can you sew? Do domestic chores? Pour tea? Play a musical instrument? Read and write?' Her gaze grew narrower every time Desert Rose shook her head. 'Can you fight?'

Desert Rose exhaled at that. 'That I can.'

'Dance?'

She thought of the times she had danced with the clanswomen at gatherings and ceremonies. Her father had always encouraged her to dance more and fight less.

'That too, I suppose.' She remembered the red plaque Prince Meng had given her and pulled it out of her robe. 'Prince Meng told me to offer this in exchange for an imperial pass.'

At the sight of it, Matron's back stiffened even further. Behind her, the maids broke into feverish whispers, which Matron silenced with a single look before turning back to Desert Rose.

'Very well. Follow me.' She turned to leave. 'The rest of you, return to your chores.'

The maids scurried back to work, though their curious, wary eyes remained on Desert Rose as she wove through the crowd. She kept her gaze straight, watching as Matron unhooked a lantern at the door and stepped out through the double doors.

They headed back out into the snow-covered courtyard, down a path undisturbed by footprints. Lanterns became sparser and the gloom grew deeper. Finally, there were none altogether, save for the one in Matron's hand.

They walked in silence, Desert Rose following three feet behind Matron and trying to pick out the slightest sounds in the darkness. The crunch of snow under their feet. The muted call of a lone bird.

Within these high stone walls, there was a stillness that Desert Rose had never experienced in the wild, wide desert. It muffled her senses, made her as good as blind and deaf.

The air rippled, parting for a figure that swooped down towards them. The glint of a blade was the only warning they had. Desert Rose pushed Matron aside and ducked out of the way just as the sword skimmed her shoulder.

What sort of palace was this if the Crown Prince could be murdered in his own chamber and assassins could break in?

She was about to pull out her knives when Matron commanded, 'Novice, still your hand.' She paused. *Novice?*

The masked attacker straightened and withdrew her weapon. Her blade, now by her side, glowed orange under Matron's lantern light.

'You would do better to identify your target before launching an attack,' Matron said.

The girl dipped her head and raised her clasped hands. 'Forgive me, Matron. I was not expecting you at this hour.'

'Where is the housemistress? I need to speak with her.'

The girl led them through what appeared to be an impenetrable hedge that in fact hid a narrow door fit for one person to slip through at a time. Beyond that lay an expansive court bordered by rows of single-eave chambers.

Across the courtyard, the housemistress stood silhouetted by lamplight at the entrance of the main chamber, addressing three girls all slightly older than Desert Rose. Dressed in identical fitted black tunics and standing at attention, hands behind their ramrod straight backs, the older girls nodded in unison at the housemistress. Upon noticing Matron and Desert Rose, the housemistress dismissed the girls, who disappeared into the shadows like smoke.

The housemistress dipped into a curt bow. 'Matron,' she greeted. She looked every bit like how Desert Rose had always imagined Capital women to look, with delicate but austere features and her hair pinned up into a tight bun. Her gaze slid to Desert Rose, but she waited for Matron to speak.

'I understand this is not the most convenient time, housemistress, but . . .' Matron glanced at Desert Rose, a flicker of curiosity in her eyes, 'Prince Meng has brought to the House of Night a new protégé.'

Eight

Wei

The desert girl was gone before dawn.

Just as well, Wei thought as they set off. At least she had some sense of self-preservation.

But thoughts of her continued to pervade his mind. Had she made it to the Capital on her own? It was a half day's ride from the inn, but walking could take a day—perhaps longer with her injuries, although she seemed to heal abnormally fast. She also didn't seem to know the ways of the Capital. Even if she managed to find her way there, she would have little to no chance of surviving.

Wei shook the thoughts out of his head. Desert Rose was no longer any of his concern.

After making a detour around a desert town to throw the scouts off their back, the crew now sat at a corner table in another inn a few hours away from the Capital. It had been a long time since he last stepped into The Travelling Horse. The place remained unchanged, with its carved wooden horse at the centre and familiar aroma of smoked meat jerky sweetened by a hint of snow custard pudding.

News about the disturbance they had caused the previous night in the Dragon's Head Inn had spread, so they kept their heads down and voices low as they plotted their entry into the Capital.

Wei had sworn he would never return to the place that had cast him out. He told himself he never wanted to live there anyway, with its stifling borders, pointless caste system, and a father who despised him. The Capital might be the trading hub of Oasis Kingdom, but Wei now knew there was a vast, wild world beyond its walls—one that was far richer than what the Capital had to offer.

Yet, here he was, back again.

The inn was starting to get busy with campers who had stayed the night and travellers who were preparing to set out. But when a young man in Wood Caste tunic burst through the front door, everyone stopped what they were doing.

'Did you hear?' he announced to no one in particular. 'The Crown Prince was found dead in his chamber!'

Wei froze, not sure if he heard him right. Voices erupted around them, some laced with doubt and others with morbid fascination.

'They say he was poisoned,' someone said.

'No, I heard he was stabbed.'

'That sounds rather messy.'

'But don't the servants taste the food before serving it?'

'Does that mean . . . a servant was complicit?'

The crowd in the tavern gathered around the messenger, hungry for more details. It took Wei everything he could to remain where he was, although he realized he was gripping the edge of the table so hard his knuckles were turning white. Zeyan shot him a glance, all pretence of indifference gone. The rest of the men exchanged tense looks, but they held their tongues.

It had been less than a year since the news of Yong being officiated as Crown Prince had travelled across the desert. After the eldest prince Han was exiled for suspected treason, the emperor had wasted no time in appointing his next heir. Wei sighed. Had his mother heard the news already? As if it wasn't enough that she was imprisoned. Now her elder son was murdered while her younger one was in exile.

Wei hadn't seen his brother in years, but he had never felt like they were apart. He recalled the time when he was ten and his father had declared to him and his brothers—Han, Yong, and Meng—that the Crown Prince would be the bravest and smartest of them all.

Han, the eldest, had feverishly tried to brush up on his studies, while Meng had approached General Luo to learn sword-fighting. Instead of trying to sharpen his edge to become worthy of the crown, Yong had spent his efforts coaching Wei instead.

'But I don't want to be Crown Prince,' Wei had protested.

'We all should take a shot at it.'

'But I don't *want* to. Doesn't that mean I'll be competing with you?'

'Listen to me, Wei,' Yong had said, his voice tight with urgency. 'If Han or Meng gets the title, you can count on Queen Wangyi to try every means to chase you and me and Mother out of the palace. Becoming Crown Prince—be it you or me—is how we will survive.'

Wei had opted out, but Yong had played by the rules of the game. He had learned to survive.

Until now.

'Wei, I know what you're thinking,' Zeyan said, interrupting his thoughts. 'But we need to plan our way in.'

'To hell with the plan,' he said. 'I'm going in now.'

Beihe, one of his Snow Wolf Sect brothers, protested. 'You won't make it to the palace in one piece.'

They were right. The emperor was not known for his sentimentality, Wei knew that. Yet, a stubborn, foolish part of him hoped his father would wish to see more of his sons alive than dead. Han was as good as gone, exiled to the brutal Northlands; Xiong, the youngest, had died in the womb; and now Yong had met an untimely end too. He and Meng were the only ones left.

'I have to,' he said.

'What I mean is, you can't go in alone,' said Beihe. 'So we're going with you.' The others nodded grimly.

Wei frowned. 'No.'

'There's no time to debate on this,' Zeyan said. 'We're coming.'

On the day after he had been inducted into the Snow Wolf Sect, Wei's mentor had made him and the other novices go into the forest in Palamir Mountain to observe the native wolves. They had stayed there for a whole week, but unlike the time his father had taken him out to the desert and left him to die, he hadn't been alone on the mountain. By the time he left the mountain, he had found a new family among his Snow Wolf Sect brothers.

He looked each one of them in the eye. There was no question that he would be willing to risk his life for them too. 'All right,' he said at last.

*

They wasted no time in making their move, arriving at the Capital gates in half a day. It was almost dusk by the time they arrived, the encroaching darkness offering some cover. Still, Wei pulled his mask higher as they rode towards the front of the line, with Zeyan alongside him and the other four behind them in two pairs.

'Damn foreigners,' a Steel Caste man said to his companion as they were let through the gates. 'Think they can bring in their filthy magic and corrupt the Capital.'

Wei found his thoughts drifting back to Desert Rose. Had she even managed to enter the Capital? Even if she had, the Cleansing would reveal her identity and she would be listed as a threat. Worse—the Cleansing might even have killed her.

Cleansing was a process that turned magic into poison. It made the magic dusted on your skin burn and the magic living under your skin turn against you. Regular people might experience some discomfort from Cleansing, but if what he had glimpsed the other day was true, the desert girl carried magic in her bones. And the stronger her magic, the more lethal the effect of Cleansing would be on her.

He shook the thoughts of her out of his head. He couldn't worry about her now.

The crew inched closer on their horses after the guard waved in a group of locals who showed their identity passes. None of them in the crew had those, but their plan did not require a pass anyway. They only had one chance to get in, a brief window, before the Capital gates closed.

The guard frowned up at them. 'Dismount, travellers, and lower your masks.'

Wei eyed the line next to him. Two other guards were preoccupied with checking the identity passes of a pair of Capital citizens while the old scribe recorded their details.

The guard came up to him for a closer look. 'Dismount and lower your mask,' he repeated, his tone sharpening. The other guards and scribe glanced over as they waved citizens through.

Wei unhooked his mask from behind his ear and shot the guard a grim smile. 'I'd appreciate if you could keep this short. I'm in a hurry.'

The guard's eyes widened. 'It . . . it can't be.'

Behind him, the scribe dropped his brush with a clatter. Whispers broke out around them and people started craning their necks.

'The bastard prince! He's back!' someone cried.

Before any of the guards could call for backup, Wei reared his horse. 'Now!' he roared.

They careened through the gates, clearing everyone in their path and leaving behind the screams that pierced the thunder of hooves. Wei zeroed in on the row of sentries guarding the path that led to the Cleansing pavilion—the first obstacle.

Under his rein, his horse gave a huge lurch and hurtled past the pavilion, knocking over several guards in the way.

He ventured a glance back. The gates were sliding close, trapping him in this city. He was past the point of no return now. Close behind him, Beihe and the rest already had their swords drawn as the guards rounded in on them.

'Wei!' Beihe called. 'Go!'

'Come on, Wei!' Zeyan called, appearing next to him. 'They can handle a few guards.'

The crew kept the guards busy enough, but things were trickier now that he and Zeyan had entered the Capital. Sentries were ready for them, and they had been trained for an offensive like this. They charged at them from all directions, weapons drawn, but Wei knew the real attack came from above.

He glanced up at the sentries at their watch posts, their steel-tipped arrows aimed at them, and shared a look with Zeyan. They rode helter-skelter until they were beyond shooting range, past the cleansing pavilion and out of the fray.

Bells clanged as they raced through streets, reverberating across the town and shattering the peace. The invasion warning.

Along the main canal, Wuxi Market was a familiar hub of activity, with vendors and shopkeepers hawking their wares, fishermen peddling the last of the day's catch from their boats, grocery shoppers with their loaded baskets, and errand boys whizzing about with parcels of goods.

Their approach sent everyone scrambling, screaming, and tripping over wagons. It wouldn't take them long to realize that the rogue prince was back. Nor would it take long for the rumours to start flying: The

Third Prince, scorned son and traitor to the kingdom, was back to seize the throne.

Wei glanced back. At least six guards were on their tail and gaining on them. He leaned low against his steed's back and flicked the reins.

They sped forth, heading straight towards the palace.

Wei exchanged a glance with Zeyan as they arrived at the Meridian Gate. They split up, Zeyan exposing himself to the guards on the watch tower while Wei headed towards the secret gate at the far end of the wall.

The bells had stopped clanging, but everyone had been alerted by now. The palace guards were far more relentless than those at the city gates. They formed a near-impenetrable line of defence, attacking both him and his horse. Wei wrapped the reins around his wrist and reared back. His horse let out a whinny and crashed down on the guards.

He barrelled through the secret gate before the guards could slide it shut.

More guards jumped into the fray the deeper he dived into the palace. He could easily take down the soldiers here, but they were only two against the entire Imperial Army that his father could easily call upon. He held back on the offensive, only fending off their attacks, but they proved to be more ruthless. One slashed his horse's legs, sending it crumpling to the ground with a shriek. Arrows rained down on him.

They're not here to spare you, Wei, he heard his mentor say in his head. *Listen to your instincts.*

Wei rolled off his horse and leapt to his feet, cleaving his way through a pair of soldiers coming at him before whirling around to stab one of them in the gut.

He fought through the storm of attacks until the rest of the crew reappeared from all corners of the courtyard, coming to his aid. They slipped into their practised pattern of striking and defending, moving as one body, until at last Wei alone was racing down the path leading to the Hall of Harmony, where his father spent most of his days listening to counsel and ruminating alone.

He ignored the calls of the servants stationed at the entrance of the Hall, charging straight for the doors.

'Your Highness,' they cried. 'The emperor is currently engaged with the Grand Council. You mustn't . . . '

Wei laid the tip of his sword against one of the servants' jugular. 'Tell me again what I mustn't do.'

The servants faltered. Threatening them wasn't the best way to improve his reputation around here, but he had a feeling it wouldn't matter either way.

The Grand Council was gathered in the Hall, all ten council members split into two rows facing each other, headed by the emperor on his dais at the far end.

The men were neck-deep in an argument among themselves when Wei barged through the double doors, sword swinging by his side. News clearly hadn't travelled to this part of the palace.

Voices died as everyone turned to stare at him. With his hair matted against his face and his blood-stained black tunic, he looked more unkempt than a member of the Untouchable Caste, out of place in the gleaming, gilded hall. He couldn't have looked more like an outsider if he tried.

Wei scanned the faces of everyone in the room. Still the same bunch of them, the same ex-general, secretariat, and advisers who had whispered amongst themselves while eyeing him sideways years ago. He knew what they had seen then and what they saw now—the emperor's most abhorred son, a black horse, wild and unfathomable, more a criminal than a prince.

And then there was Matron, who stood by the emperor's side, almost hidden in the shadows. But Wei knew better than to dismiss her importance. He also knew better than to group her with the council members.

Matron broke into a small smile after getting over her shock at seeing him. But the smile disappeared almost immediately as she checked herself and folded her expression back into her usual frosty indifference. Good old Matron. At least she was still around.

Finally, someone broke the silence. 'Huwei.'

Wei's gaze slid to the adviser who spoke. Not Prince Wei or Third Prince. To them, he had always been Huwei, who took his mother's family name instead of Emperor Zhaode's. It suited Wei just fine.

Two of the remaining guards caught up with him at last, spluttering their excuses as they came to a halt before the doors of the Hall.

'You fools let a wanted man break into not just the Capital, but the palace?' ex-General Sun roared. The guards knelt in apology. 'Have you all gone soft? Seize him—now!'

'Hold it.' The emperor's voice rang across the hall.

'With all due respect, Your Majesty, we mustn't let this interruption waylay our plans,' High Adviser Mian urged from the emperor's side.

Wei's lip curled. *Still as slimy as ever.* He had detested the High Adviser ever since he was a child—the way he leaned close to speak into the emperor's ear, the way his smile crept up his face like he ate secrets for lunch, the way he calculated Wei with sidelong looks.

But most importantly, he hated how the High Adviser had claimed, right from Wei's birth, that one of the emperor's sons would one day betray his father and steal the throne. He and Meng had been born on the same night, but it was Wei whom Mian had singled out as a threat—never mind that Wei had never cared for the throne.

Mian claimed to be able to read anyone's fate in the stars, but as far as Wei knew, all he did was feed lies and plant seeds of madness in the emperor's mind. Ever since the emperor had latched on to the idea of harnessing—no, monopolizing—the magical spring, Mian had been stoking his obsession and made it all he could think about.

'We can spare some time for this unexpected visit,' the emperor said. He leaned forward on his seat, sizing up Wei like he would an uncaged beast.

Wei approached him on his dais, ignoring the whispers that followed, the slant of his father's gaze. Nothing had changed since the last time he was here.

'What happened to Yong?' he demanded, sheathing his sword now that the guards were put on hold.

'Impudent boy,' the emperor snapped. 'Have you lost your manners out in the wild?'

A beat passed. The last thing Wei wanted to do was bow before his father—seeing him again reminded him of his life in the palace before he found freedom beyond the Capital gates—but this was not the time to cling to his pride.

Wei sank to one knee and raised his clasped hands. 'Greetings, Your Majesty,' he said, allowing a hint of sarcasm to creep into his voice. 'Your third son Wei boldly seeks your audience.'

The emperor was silent. The courtiers seemed to be holding their breaths too. Wei kept his head bowed, a million thoughts racing through his head. Would his father order for his execution right away?

Would he ever get to find out what happened to Yong? What would become of his mother if he were sentenced too? *Bit late to start regretting this, Wei.*

At last, the emperor said, 'Rise.'

'Thank you, Your Majesty,' he said, shoulders unclenching as he returned to his feet.

The emperor reclined in his seat and raised a lofty brow. 'Bold of you to return, knowing that you are wanted for treason—for the years you have turned your back on the country, and for the contact you have made with the outside world and its magic . . .'

'Father,' Wei said. 'Is it true?'

The emperor's face twitched with fury. He turned to the ex-general. 'See to it that those who let out the news prematurely are punished.' He turned to Matron. 'You too, Matron. I will not have ill-disciplined tongues wagging in this palace.' Matron bowed.

'Is it true, Father?' Wei asked again.

He glanced back at Wei. 'What happened to Yong is . . . unfortunate.'

'Unfortunate,' Wei echoed. 'Your son's death is *unfortunate*.'

'We are in the middle of investigations.'

'Maybe your alliance with the desert clans could provide some insight.'

A palpable chill settled in the hall. Matron shook her head almost imperceptibly. If every alleged crime Wei had committed up to this moment hadn't pushed the emperor to have his head, this would be the tipping point. But to sentence him now would raise the question of what the emperor had to hide.

Wei held his father's gaze, watching as his expression shifted from restrained anger to shrewd contemplation. Wei kept his face blank. He had seen the way his father read people's minds just by studying their faces, and he was not about to give him any leverage.

'Council dismissed,' said the emperor. 'I wish to speak in private with Huwei.'

'Your Majesty, we cannot delay this matter any further,' the Councillor Yuan said. 'The palace is already in upheaval. We need to come to a consensus soon or—'

'I am well aware of what needs to be done, Councillor Yuan.' The council member flinched at the emperor's tone. 'But the timing of Huwei's unexpected return is not to be overlooked and might shed some light on the Crown Prince's demise.'

Wei willed himself to keep his cool. It didn't matter now if his father made it seem as though his return was connected to Yong's murder. He had to pick his battles—a vehement denial now would only make himself appear defensive and therefore guilty.

All the councillors bowed and took their leave. Matron sent Wei a familiar look that warned him to behave (not that he ever heeded it) before retreating through the back exit. Mian was the only one who remained where he was.

Wei could tell the emperor was deciding what to do with him, but he waited to speak. He had more questions than answers at this point, but with his father he knew it was best to sound out his intentions before making his own move.

'You dare return to the Capital after being marked as a criminal?' said the emperor.

'My mother remains imprisoned and now my brother has been murdered. I wasn't going to remain hiding away just because you put out a death warrant for me. I have to say, though, it's a tad dramatic, even for you, Father.'

'What do you know about the desert clans?'

'Enough to know that you're making a big mistake colluding with them to find the spring. Do you really believe they will help—'

'I have been the ruler of Oasis Kingdom since before you were born. I am not naïve enough to think that the clan leaders will not turn against me as soon as a higher bidder enters the picture. I have leverage. In any case,' he added, 'this is no concern of yours. Why are you back, Wei?'

'I want to find out who killed Yong.' *And clear my mother's name that Yong hadn't been able to.*

The emperor narrowed his gaze. 'Are your intentions truly that simple? Or are you back to spread your radical ideology in my kingdom?'

'Radical? Let's not pretend that I'm the only one who believes in magic here, Father. Do you ratify magic only when it benefits you?'

His father's trust in the High Adviser was befuddling to everyone, but those in the inner circle knew how Mian had treated the emperor's asthma and ignited his obsession with the desert spring by telling him it contained the elixir of life.

'Things have changed since you last set foot in this kingdom,' Mian quipped.

Wei shot him his most scornful look. 'By change, you mean you've managed to convince the emperor that the kingdom's future hinges on us gaining control of a magical spring?'

The emperor slammed his hand on the table, sending Mian retreating backwards. 'I am safeguarding the future of our kingdom,' he snapped. 'We cannot let Yong's death distract us from finding the spring—'

'Your son was just murdered,' Wei said quietly. 'And all you care about is the spring?'

His father did not miss a beat. 'A good emperor is not ruled by his emotions.'

No, he is ruled by an adviser with his own agenda. Wei's gaze slid to Mian, who curved his lips into a smile as he nodded by the emperor's side.

'The Lettorians are planning to collude with the Sorensteins and develop magical weapons for what we believe would result in an unprecedented form of warfare,' the emperor went on. 'The spring is our strongest defence against our enemies.'

'I don't care what those people are up to,' Wei said. 'I'm just here to find out who killed my brother.'

'That,' said his father, 'is your biggest problem: you don't care. Yong would have cared. It shouldn't have been Yong who died.'

He wishes it were me instead. Wei had always known implicitly that if their father had to sacrifice one of his sons, he would be the first to go. And his father wouldn't even spare a moment to grieve.

He bit back against the sting of his father's words. 'How unfortunate, then, that you get your rogue son instead.'

'You are no son of mine. You're a disgrace to the imperial family.'

He should be immune to this by now. He had fought with wolves in the bitter cold mountains and bandits in the desert, brushed shoulders with death several times. But it seemed like a part of him would never stop hoping that his father would regard him as a son—and it was that foolish hope that hurt more than anything else.

'I found my family out there,' he said. 'One that doesn't judge me based on a measly star.'

The emperor raised his brows. 'Is that why you sent them here to die?'

Wei stiffened, trying not to reveal the fear that slid down his back.

His father caught it anyway. 'All those men who helped you enter the palace today—did you think they would be spared? I did say that whoever found abetting you would be punishable by death—without trial, I should have mentioned. But that's just a technicality.' A slow smile slid across his face.

Wei kept his clenched shaking fists by his side even as hate burned through his veins. If his father thought this was enough to deter him from staying in the Capital, then he was wrong. He was no longer that scared little boy sent out to die in the desert.

'If the killer could get to Yong, who's to say he or she won't come for you next?' he said.

'Are you threatening me?' the emperor snarled.

'Just pre-empting you, Father.'

'I could sentence you right now.'

'You could,' Wei agreed. 'But then you'd never find out who actually killed Yong. You would never find out who's really after the throne, who has the ability to send the palace into unrest.'

It was there in the curl of his father's lips that Wei saw just how eager he had been to get rid of him, how despite being related by blood, Wei was nothing more than an inconvenience at best and a threat at worst. In that moment, it was easy to believe that his father could send him to the most desolate corners of the earth to die.

Wei took a slow, measured step closer to the emperor. 'You're afraid, Father. Deep down, you know that you are losing control day by day. Enemies are invading from every corner, the famine's depleted most of our resources, and trade is slowing. The people are losing faith in you. They're wondering if there's a better life beyond these Capital walls.'

'You can't possibly know all this, having been away for so long,' Mian said.

'I have my sources, Adviser.' He turned his attention back to his father, who was watching him with his fingertips pressed against each other. 'Pretty soon, Father, the people are going to revolt. And now with Yong murdered, there's the question of whether you can even stay alive to protect your throne.'

'You're not the only one who can solve this murder,' said the emperor. 'Meng is as much of a liability, being next-in-line to the throne. And who else would have rightful access to Yong's private possessions aside from his next-of-kin?'

There was no way Wei would go quietly, even if his father sentenced him now. They both knew that. The smart thing to do was to keep Wei under close watch while he had him here.

At last, the emperor said, 'You have until the Spring Ceremony to find the perpetrator. Otherwise, you and your mother will both be executed.'

'I accept the conditions.'

The emperor leaned back in his seat, satisfied. 'Matron,' he called.

Matron arrived promptly enough for Wei to realize that she had been within earshot the entire time. She shot Wei an almost imperceptible disapproving glance. Like his mother, she had always said he was too impulsive for his own good.

'Your Majesty,' Matron said with a bow.

'Kindly see to new living arrangements. Prince Wei will be taking up residence in the palace until the case of the Crown Prince comes to light.' He flicked a glance at Wei. 'Don't get too comfortable.'

*

The palace dungeon was a draughty labyrinth of stone-walled cells, dimly lit by torches parked in brackets along the wall. Canal water leaking in from the ground left it perennially slick, and the stench of mildew and rot hung in the air.

Wei's mother had languished in this forsaken place for almost as long as Yong had been Crown Prince.

The outer cells—smaller and filthier ones reserved for those from the lower castes—were almost fully occupied. Upon his arrival, a few of the inmates scurried to the bars and stared at him as he passed by. Others watched from the dark recesses of their cells, all the light extinguished from their sunken eyes.

Wei wound his way through the narrow passageways, trailing after the pair of guards. What would happen if he knocked them out right then and stole the keys to his mother's cell? Nothing. It wouldn't achieve a thing, except add another crime to his ever-increasing list and put his mother in greater danger.

He tightened his jaw and kept walking, his helplessness a rein around his neck.

They came to a stop at last in a cavernous space. In front of them was a lone cell, larger than any other and padded with more straw on the ground.

Through the gloom half-illuminated by the guards' torches, Wei found his mother in a corner of the cell, near unrecognizable in soiled white prison garb. Gone were her silk robes embroidered with gold. Her hair, once perfectly coiffed and dripping with jewels, now hung loose and long, highlighted with silvery-grey strands. She sat on a straw mat, half-tucked under a rough hemp blanket, staring down at her hands.

Wei fought back a wave of emotions, stopping himself from rushing towards her. This was not how he had left her. How had everything taken such a turn since the last time he was in the palace?

He held up a hand, requesting privacy. But the guards were already gone. Instead, there was Matron standing behind him with a tray of food and water. She lingered at the back and nodded at him to speak to his mother first.

Wei turned back around. 'Mother.' His voice rang out in the wide, empty cell.

She snapped to attention, then squinted through the darkness. Wei shifted so that his face was illuminated. Recognition sparked in her eyes. She scrambled towards him, reaching for him. Her legs, weak from disuse, failed her and she stumbled to the ground.

'Wei? Is that really you?' she rasped.

'It's me,' he said, stooping down and grasping her hand through the cold metal bars.

She caressed his face with her thin, papery hand. 'You're okay. You're alive.' Her voice tightened with urgency. 'It's Wangyi. I know it is. This is all part of her plan. She means to destroy us all. First me, now your brother . . .'

Her voice cracked on the last word. News had obviously reached the dungeons.

'But you managed to return,' she said softly. 'How?'

'I made a deal with the emperor. I'm going to find out who killed Yong. And then I will get you out of here.' He leaned his head against the bars. 'I'm sorry.'

'For what, my boy?'

'For all this happening. For not returning sooner.'

She gave his hand a firm squeeze. 'None of this is your fault, Wei. Do you understand?' She waited until he forced himself to nod. 'The last time I saw him . . . Yong told me he found out something.'

'What did—' He glanced over his shoulder, but there was only Matron, steadfast and impassive like always. 'What did he find out?'

She shook her head. 'He didn't say much. Something about'—her voice faded into a whisper—'your father creating a secret guard or weapon. He said he would explain more the next time he visited, but then . . .' A tear slid down her cheek.

Matron stepped forward with the tray. 'Here, have something to eat, Your Highness.'

His mother reached for Matron's hand and gave it a grateful squeeze before picking up the bowl of water. 'I told you, you don't have to call me that any more. Call me Luzhen.'

'You've been visiting her regularly?' Wei asked Matron.

'Only when I can,' she replied. 'To avoid the empress's suspicion.'

'Thank you.' Here, where deceit and danger lay in every corner, it felt monumental to know that he had but one person on his side whom he could trust.

'Wei,' his mother said, setting down the bowl of water. 'You be careful out there, you hear me?'

Wei swallowed. 'Always am, Mother. I'll be back soon, I promise.'

'*Don't*. Don't promise.' A sob escaped her. 'That's what he said too.'

His feet felt like dead weights as he stood up. This was not how he had left her, and this was not how he wanted to leave her now. But he had work to do. And he was going to make the people responsible for this pay.

Nine

Desert Rose

The palace was a world in its own. Unlike the wind-whipped vastness of the desert, the palace was a labyrinth of courtyards, gardens, chambers and halls, and secret pathways that snaked into the gloom.

And right behind the Red Circle, obscured by a dense bamboo garden, snow-coated hedges, and stone walls with secret doors, the House of Night seemed like a secret wing.

This was clearly no ordinary court in the palace. *A novice*, Matron had said. Was this a school? Why had Prince Meng brought her here?

The housemistress led the way into a sparsely furnished chamber lit by a pair of candles on a wooden table in the middle of the room. She gestured to one of the chairs around the table.

'Have a seat.'

Desert Rose drew it out, careful not to make a sound. The housemistress slid into a seat directly opposite and fixed a piercing stare on her. Everything felt like a test, but Desert Rose wasn't sure what for.

'It's an understatement to say that you came at a bad time,' said the housemistress.

'I didn't plan to arrive on the night the Crown Prince is murdered,' she muttered. The housemistress narrowed her eyes at her. 'Madam,' she added.

'You may call me *shimu*.' She cocked her head. 'You're from the desert. Why have you come to the palace—and with the Fourth Prince as your guarantor?'

There was no way to skirt the question. 'I wish to speak to the emperor.'

If Shimu had more questions in response to that, she did not press further. 'Do you know what the House of Night is?'

Desert Rose shook her head.

'It's where girls come to dedicate themselves to the most noble cause in the Capital: serving and protecting the imperial family. Here, we train special forces for the Imperial Guard, and by extension, Oasis Kingdom.'

'You train assassins,' Desert Rose realized. That explained the assailant who had greeted them out front.

'We view it as the art of combat here,' Shimu said.

An assassin school. She, a desert girl picked off the street, was brought here by a prince to train as an assassin. *Why*?

'What is your name?' the housemistress asked.

Desert Rose hesitated before offering it to her. It sounded like coarse sand in this place with ornately carved roofs, stone sculptures, and tidy gardens.

Shimu did not repeat it. 'Here, you will be known as Mingxi, and you will join the Blue Cranes, the novices. Drafting was over months ago, and we are in the middle of training period. But since the Fourth Prince brought you here, I shall make an exception for you. You will sleep with the other novices tonight. Tomorrow, you will assemble in the courtyard at dawn with everyone else. Do *not* be late.'

The housemistress brought her to the bedroom, where four other girls were already sound asleep. A couple of them stirred as she settled in but did not rouse.

After washing up and changing into a fresh night tunic, Desert Rose crashed into her new bed, grateful to finally rest despite the worry that continued to gnaw at her.

Sleep was out of the question tonight. She lay staring up at the darkened ceiling. Apart from the soft breathings of her roommates, it was silent, too silent—the sort that made one alert and ready to bolt at the slightest ripple in the air.

Her thoughts churned like a desert storm. What should she do now? This was not how she had planned to enter the palace, and she had no clue what to expect from being a novice here. Should she sneak out and comb the Capital for her father? But if she left the palace, she would have no other way that would take her closer to the emperor or her father. Besides, how would she even find her father in this foreign city on her own?

The prudent thing to do was to stay put for now. It didn't matter how she made her way to the emperor, as long as she did. Because she wasn't just here to find her father; she was here to save her tribe.

The only way was to get to the root of the problem.

If the clan leaders were working with the Oasis Emperor, then she needed to get to him. And if that meant infiltrating the House of Night, then that was what she would do. She could at least get some answers out of him, if not coerce him into letting her father go.

What kind of deal had he made with the clan leaders? What had he done to her father and where was her father now? What did he plan to do with the magical spring if he ever found it?

Most importantly—and this was a question more for herself—how could she undo the damage already done to her tribe? The weight of her tribe's fate now sat heavy on her chest. She thought of Qara who had risked her life to help her escape, her tribemates who were now a collective victim of the traitorous clan leaders and one emperor's greed. When push came to shove, how far would she go to save her tribe?

Sleep must have eventually claimed her, because she was swept into a turbulent dream in which her father was claimed by the devil under the desert and she came face-to-face with Bataar sitting on the Oasis Emperor's throne.

Dawn could not have arrived sooner. Desert Rose caught the first smattering of conversation before first light filtered in through the windows.

'Shimu must have brought her in here at night,' someone was saying.

'Why is she joining us now? Drafting is long over,' came another voice.

'We're going to be late if she doesn't get up now.' A shadow loomed over her and someone shook her by the shoulders. 'Wake up, new girl.'

Desert Rose sprung upright to find the four girls peering at her. They were already dressed in identical dark blue fitted tunics—ones that Shimu had handed her the night before—and their hair were pulled into neat buns.

'Are you new?' asked a petite girl with flushed cheeks and wide eyes. Desert Rose nodded, still bleary from sleep. 'Welcome to the House. What's your name?'

'We don't have time for pleasantries, Xiyue,' another girl interrupted in a decidedly less genial tone. She had a sharp gaze and an imperious set of brows. 'Wash up and get dressed, new girl. We need to be out before seven bells.'

When the five of them reached the courtyard, there were already six other older-looking girls—clad in identical black uniforms and each with a sword sheathed behind their back—lined up in a row before Shimu. The housemistress, who was midway through addressing them, shot the new joiners a look as they lined up in a row behind the black-clad girls. Desert Rose copied their stance and stared straight ahead. Already, her scalp was hurting from her hair being pulled too tight, and her sleep-hungry mind struggled to catch up with her body.

'Late,' Shimu declared.

'Sorry, Shimu,' said Xiyue. 'We didn't want to leave the new girl behind . . .'

'Our apologies, Shimu,' said the bossy girl who had herded them out. 'It won't happen again.'

'We have a new joiner,' Shimu announced. 'Her name is Desert Rose. But here, she will be referred to as Mingxi.'

The name sounded like it was meant for another girl. Clarity and hope. Neither of those applied to her at all, especially at that moment. Her peers kept still, even as their gazes slid towards her. Desert Rose kept hers fixed straight ahead.

'There has been an incident last night,' Shimu went on. 'The Crown Prince was found dead in his chamber, believed to be a result of an intruder sneaking in and poisoning his dinner.'

A collective gasp rippled through the Blue Cranes, although the older girls remained stoic.

'The emperor will hold a kingdom-wide mourning ceremony within the week. In the meantime, the Black Cranes will be split into pairs and assigned to guard the imperial family.' The girls in the front row clasped their hands before them in unison, accepting the order. 'The Blue Cranes will guard the palace. No one is to leave her assigned post.' Desert Rose was certain that the housemistress's eyes lingered longest on her. 'Do I make myself clear?'

'Yes, Shimu,' the other Blue Cranes chorused. Desert Rose joined in a beat later, when the girl next to her gave her a nudge.

Shortly after the Black Cranes had been dismissed, Shimu ordered the Blue Cranes to head to the armoury and prepare for their training session.

She could do this, at least. She could fight. Despite the clanswomen's attempts to school her in the natural arts and her father's wish for her to hone a more conventional skill for girls, she had always felt more comfortable wielding her knives.

But her sort of training was done with the clan boys, who were rough and rowdy, and would toss you for a laugh until you learned how to fend for yourself. They didn't wear uniforms or bow to rigid hierarchy. In the fray, everyone was equal; everyone was fair game. There was something pure and unbridled about that. Here in her scratchy uniform and too-tight bun, she ached for that freedom.

But all that was gone now. Her clan brothers, her tribe. That was the reason she was here, lined up with the other girls, about to receive a different kind of training.

The armoury was a cavernous room heavily stocked with more forms of weaponry Desert Rose had ever seen—from sleek, gleaming blades of all shapes and sizes (she recognized the butterfly swords, ring swords, and hook swords commonly used by desert bandits or sold by traders) to long, sturdy halberds hung on the walls, knives, whips, pickaxes, and more types of armament she couldn't name.

The girls stood in the middle of the room, around a square wooden table wide enough to fit two large silk maps pinned down by miniature bronze markers. One featured the warring states surrounding Oasis Kingdom, and the other was a detailed map of the palace.

Desert Rose was surveying the maps when one of the girls proffered a hand, palm open. She stared at it, unsure of what to do. This was a customary desert greeting. Did Capital girls brush hands with one another like they did in the desert? She placed a tentative hand on the girl's and slid her palm over hers.

The girl didn't seem to find Desert Rose's gesture strange. 'Didn't get to introduce myself earlier. I'm Fengying, but you can call me Windshadow.' She said her real name in the desert tongue, although it was one Desert Rose was unfamiliar with. A different tribe, probably closer to the north.

So Windshadow was foreign too. It was somewhat of a relief to know that she wasn't the only odd one out, even if Windshadow looked far better adjusted than her.

Windshadow shot her a small conspiratorial smile as though she had heard her thoughts. 'Takes one to know one.'

The girl who had hurried her out of bed that morning elbowed her way to the front and introduced herself as Shuang. 'How did you manage to get in after the Drafting?' she demanded.

'Separate arrangement,' Desert Rose muttered. It was probably safer to explain less.

Shuang narrowed her eyes at her, as though debating whether to probe further. 'Welcome to the House of Night, I suppose,' she said at last.

The final girl introduced herself as Liqin. 'So what's your specialty?'

'My specialty?'

'Shuang got accepted because of her double swords. Xiyue specialises in the willow leaf sabre. Windshadow—well, you'll have to see for yourself.' Windshadow shot her a devilish smile but didn't elaborate further.

'What about you?' Desert Rose asked.

Liqin lifted her chin, smug. 'I was a court dancer. They said I have potential to develop my skills further.'

'Dancing?' Desert Rose asked before she could help it. 'The House of Night trains dancers?' Shuang and Liqin exchanged an exasperated look.

Shimu returned before any of them could offer an explanation. Everyone snapped to attention, arms crossed behind their backs. 'Last night's events are to remain strictly confidential. We will carry on with our training,' she said.

'Why is everyone so keen to keep the Crown Prince's death under wraps?' Desert Rose whispered to Windshadow.

'It's not good for morale when the one who's slated to take over the throne is murdered,' she whispered back.

Shimu arrowed them with a stare. 'Rule number one: do not gossip about the imperial family amongst yourselves. We are trained guards, not common maids.'

Windshadow muttered, 'Yes, Shimu,' but shot Desert Rose a smirk as soon as the housemistress glanced away. Shuang narrowed her eyes at them.

'Mingxi.' Shimu's attention landed on her. 'You were brought in under special circumstances. Prince Meng must have seen something in you.'

Windshadow snorted under her breath. 'I'll bet he did.'

'We shall see what you are made of.' The housemistress gestured around the room. 'Pick your weapon.'

The other girls watched as she deliberated. Shuang and Liqin had their brows raised, ready to be unimpressed, but Xiyue offered an encouraging smile. Desert Rose glanced at Windshadow, who urged her on with a nod.

She scanned the room and reached for the one weapon she was most familiar with. They were nothing like the double knives from her father—these were smooth steel, lighter than the carved bronze ones she had trained with, but the blades were just as keen. She swung them around in a few practised moves and gave them a twirl once she had grown accustomed to their weight.

'Very well,' Shimu said. 'Shuang, please address your opponent.'

The other girl reached for her double swords hanging from the wall and unsheathed them without hesitation.

'We're duelling now?' Desert Rose blurted.

'I need to assess your skills before we commence with formal training,' said Shimu. 'It would take more time to train someone incompetent, and we are bereft of time now. Out to the yard.'

The girls hurried out to the courtyard. Desert Rose had barely stepped out when Shuang launched one of her swords straight at her. It sliced through the air, skimming past her nose when she dodged and stumbled like a prey caught off guard.

'Follow your instincts,' Shimu said, as though it were completely natural for Shuang to launch an attack like that. 'Think on your feet. Be like water—adapt to your opponent.'

Desert Rose was used to fighting dirty. The clan boys did not follow rules either, unless they were playing in the official games each year where the entire tribe gathered to watch. In a regular brawl, they would undercut where one least expected, pull feints, and tackle when their opponent lowered his guard for a split moment. Bataar had taught her to observe before attacking, find her opponent's weakness (there was always a tell) before showing her hand.

But apart from sneak attacks, Shuang also seemed to be flawless in her sword work. She spun and charged, lashed and struck, her movements almost as mesmerizing as a dancer's but far more vicious. Shimu observed her with grim approval, then looked at Desert Rose as though inquiring when she was going to make her move.

Desert Rose barely managed to fend off another attack from Shuang before launching one of her own. They parried around the courtyard, neither of them yielding. Shuang was clearly well-schooled. Not once did she falter, pause, or retreat; her swords were a constant whirl. She moved with practised ease and her stances were perfect—the model student. She had none of that wild, rampant energy the clan boys had. But while her moves were precise, they were also, apart from the initial surprise attack, predictable. Even her feints followed a pattern after a while.

The key, then, was to interrupt her momentum. Desert Rose had learned that from her skirmishes with the clan boys, who went by their instincts, not the rules.

When Shuang aimed her blade at her, she ducked low and attempted to knock Shuang off her feet, but Shuang only leapt aside and struck her in the back. They spun and parried, lunged and skirted, until Desert Rose feigned an attack from the side and launched herself straight at Shuang, knocking her to the ground and sending their weapons clattering to the side. Shuang let out a grunt of surprise as they both went rolling.

They came to a stop near the entrance of the armoury. Shuang threw Desert Rose off her and shot her a glare, ready to strike back.

Shimu and the other girls hurried over. 'Off the ground, both of you,' Shimu snapped. 'This is not a common brawl.'

'That's how people normally fight,' Desert Rose argued as she picked herself off the ground. She offered a hand to Shuang, who ignored it and leapt to her feet.

'We don't fight with normal people,' said Shimu. 'Our charges are royalty. We protect them against highly skilled threats, those who can sneak into a heavily guarded private chamber to poison a prince. They are not going to get in a street fight with you. We do not engage in face-to-face combat unless forced to, and we certainly do not tackle our opponents like drunkards at an inn.'

Desert Rose tried her best to look contrite instead of protesting further.

'I never want to see such an uncouth form of duelling in my House again.'

'I'm sorry, Shimu,' Shuang said, dipping her head. She shot Desert Rose a filthy look after the housemistress turned to address everyone, splitting them into groups. Desert Rose was paired with Xiyue this time.

Shimu glanced at Desert Rose. 'You'll do,' she said, breezing past. 'For now.'

Shuang edged between Desert Rose and Xiyue. 'For now,' she echoed in Desert Rose's ear. From her lips, it sounded more like a warning.

*

Straight after training, the girls filed into a classroom behind the House of Night the size of Desert Rose's old tent she used to share with her father. A large square table took up most of the space in the middle, next to a rack of wooden scrolls, and shelves of books lined the side of the room. Shimu went to crack the windows open as the girls shuffled in.

Desert Rose had never sat in a classroom before, but there was something appealing about receiving formal education. Most of her lessons with the clanswomen were conducted in their tents, where everyone sat in a circle while the older women explained the essence of the natural arts or celestial history.

The girls took their seats. Windshadow gestured at a seat next to her on one side of the table, and Desert Rose settled into it gratefully.

'For the benefit of our newcomer, I will run through the basics again. The rest of you may regard this as revision,' Shimu began. 'As part of your House of Night training, you will be schooled in history, geography, politics, court etiquette, duelling, palace protocol, values, combat. And you will learn the flower dance.'

Desert Rose frowned. A dance. Did assassins *dance* too? Was that some sort of code?

'What's the flower dance?' she ventured.

'You will know in time,' Shimu said. 'Everything you do meanwhile before the Spring Ceremony will prepare you for the trials—from classroom lessons to regular patrols and, of course, duels. You are not trained to be one thing. The House of Night produces the best warriors, dancers, and strategists. Some go on to become councillors, generals, and advisers; others join the Imperial High Guard, which protects the imperial family. Specially chosen ones will become Nightwalkers, the emperor's personal spies.' Her gaze fell on Desert Rose. 'You will be placed according to your skills. But before that, you need to learn the basics.' She turned to the rest of the class. 'Now, who can tell me when and how the new Oasis Kingdom was born?'

Shuang's hand shot up. 'Nearly four centuries ago, a war broke out between magical and non-magical folk. To defeat the dangerous magical folk, our Great Father Zhaoshun—later known as the First Oasis Emperor—led a team of scholars to develop a concoction that could temporarily disable magical abilities, allowing our armies to defeat the outsiders. It was a breakthrough that freed our kingdom from our oppressors.'

Oppressors? We *are the oppressors?* Desert Rose glared at Shuang. How many times had she heard the older tribesmen talk about the Oasis War that had ripped them from their families and killed their loved ones? As though being persecuted for their practice was not enough, they had to be vilified too.

A response, tart and fiery, sat on the tip of her tongue. She was about to set it loose when Shimu said, 'That is indeed the story that has been passed down for generations, and the version you will be tested on. But your textbooks do not tell the full story.'

Shuang's smug smile dropped.

'The Oasis Kingdom had once been part of the greater empire of Hesui, which had been under the rule of magical folk, the Ling,' said Shimu. 'The Ling consisted of creatures who could wear different skin, shamans who saw the future and the past, half-mortals who could fly among clouds and live underwater.

'When the First Oasis Emperor seized control of the kingdom after driving out the magical folk into the desert, the first thing he did was massacre all the remaining ones within the city walls. Those who managed to flee made for the far borders of the kingdom. Some say that there are some Ling still living there in hiding to this day.

'The emperor then had a team of sorcerers purge all remnant magic from the land. After they had served their purpose, he ordered for them to be disposed of. The only one who remained was the High Priest, who had helped him create the Wall to protect the kingdom from magic. Finally, the First Oasis Emperor killed the High Priest, the last known practitioner of magic in the Capital. No other magical being or practitioner has been detected since then, four centuries on.'

An uncomfortable silence elbowed its way into the room.

'Yes, our history is rather unpleasant,' Shimu concluded. 'And our rulers would prefer us to stick to the polished version. But it is vital for you to understand the complicated history we share with those who remain a threat to the kingdom's safety.'

Desert Rose couldn't believe what she was hearing. Who could possibly think that the *tenshyo*, brave and loyal horse-human companions, or the rascally but kind *chi* goblins could harm anyone? The shamans and healers—some of them crossbreeds and magical folk themselves—were also the gentlest people she knew. Their souls had to be clean, their intentions pure, before they could draw on the elements for their magic. The thought of them as dangerous was laughable.

Of course, there were dark magic practitioners and creatures that the desert only revealed in the dead of the night, but they were rejected by most tribes too.

Shuang, Xiyue and Liqin shared a solemn look, which only made the rage in Desert Rose burn stronger. *How dare they?* How dared these Capital people paint themselves as the martyr when *her* people were the ones who had suffered.

Next to her, Windshadow kicked her leg, and only then did she realize she was glaring at the Capital girls while gripping the table edge so hard her knuckles had turned white.

'That is not true,' she blurted, ignoring Windshadow. 'Oasis Kingdom was founded by a power-hungry man get who sought to eliminate those who threatened his rule. He was afraid of magical beings and those who practised magic because he was woefully mortal, so he declared magic a threat and ruled by fear-mongering—'

Windshadow kicked her leg again, this time hard enough to make her wince.

Xiyue was staring at her as though she had just called a storm upon them, her eyes wide as moons. Shuang and Liqin sneered. Desert Rose turned back to the housemistress, whose piercing stare quelled her fury, but she did not relent. She would not apologize for trying to set the record straight.

The silence grew brittle with each passing moment. It shattered only when a messenger arrived at the doorstep with a silk scroll.

'I bear news from the Red Circle,' he announced.

Shimu broke her stare and turned to the messenger. 'Go on.'

He unfurled the scroll and read aloud: 'The emperor has announced that the mourning ceremony for the Crown Prince will take place today at one bell before last light. All are to gather at the Winter Court before the procession sets out across the Capital.'

Shimu nodded and the messenger hurried off to his next venue. Shimu divided them into teams—the desert girls in one, and the Capital girls in another—to guard different parts of the palace. She said nothing more about Desert Rose's earlier outburst, but Desert Rose could feel the housemistress's stare burning into her back as she left with Windshadow.

*

'You need to be smart about the way you behave around here or you're not going to last,' said Windshadow.

Desert Rose came to a halt just before they arrived at the corner tower, where she and Windshadow were to be stationed. 'What's wrong with what I did?'

The injustice still stung. She was still raring to give Shuang a piece of her mind. Perhaps later tonight in their dormitory . . .

'Listen to me, new girl,' Windshadow said. 'You're going to get into trouble running your mouth like that.'

'But did you hear what they said? How they made themselves look like victims and—'

'Yes, I heard them as well as you did. But that's not the point. Of course they're going to paint history in their favour. You need to learn to blend in. Whatever your reasons are for being at the House of Night, if you want to stay, you cannot call the wrong sort of attention to yourself by butting heads with those Capital breeds. That kind of behaviour can get you killed around here.'

Desert Rose looked at her askance. 'What is *your* reason for being at the House of Night?'

'I'll tell you mine if you tell yours.'

She fell silent.

Windshadow smirked. 'Didn't think so. You'll learn that it's best not to ask too many questions around here.'

Ten

Wei

Wei was twelve years old when he first noticed that people in the palace looked at him differently from his brothers. They bowed deeper before Yong and Meng, and sometimes they would even send Wei a look reserved for disgraced officials, even though they observed court etiquette by greeting him as well.

Empress Wangyi, Meng's mother, who had been just an imperial consort then, had made no disguise of her contempt for him. To her, he was nothing but a hindrance in Meng's path to success. 'You are not fit to be a prince,' she had told him once, as though her opinion mattered to him.

But his father seemed to loathe him too—and *that* he had not understood. When he'd asked Yong, his older brother had sighed.

'It's because of your birth-star,' he explained. 'The High Adviser had seen the Star of Chaos right next to your birth-star on the night of your birth. Apparently, that means you're the one who will bring chaos to the kingdom. But, you know'—he sent him a sidelong glance—'change isn't always a bad thing.'

'Does that mean I'll take over the throne?'

Yong shrugged. 'Who knows? Maybe you will. Maybe you'll bring disaster to the kingdom, like what Adviser Mian and Father believe. Or maybe you'll make this kingdom a better home for our people.'

'What about Meng? He was born on the same night as me.'

'His star glowed bright and pure, which makes him destined for greatness.' Yong hadn't seemed to believe Adviser Mian's theory, but he had refrained from voicing his reservations.

It seemed ridiculous that his fate would already be decided at birth because of a mere star. How could they treat him differently for something that had not even happened, for something that he might not even do?

'Do *you* think I'm a threat?' Wei asked. 'That I'll destroy the order and steal the throne?'

Yong grinned at him. 'I know you, little brother. You're a good seed, no matter what people say or think of you. And how others look at you does not matter as long as you know your intentions are faultless.'

As Wei walked through the hallways of the Red Circle now, his brother's words rang over and over in his head. Were his intentions truly faultless? Did turning his back on a kingdom that shunned him make him partly responsible for the way things were now? If he hadn't left, might he have been able to save his brother and mother?

Wei was used to roaming these halls alone. He had done that when he was younger—without his tutor, his brothers, or servants, and most of them were glad to leave him alone. The palace had always been the loneliest place in the world to him, but it felt even more bereft now, as though Yong's death had drained whatever life that remained in these grounds.

Soon after the emperor's announcement about the mourning ceremony, the palace was blanketed in rolls of white silk, draped over the balustrades, archways, and the roof of the Crown Prince's chamber. Wei watched it billow in the gentle breeze in the doorway of Yong's chamber, a stark reminder of the space his brother had left behind. Had he ever been happy here, living dutifully as Crown Prince, hoping to make a difference to the kingdom?

He was about to enter Yong's chamber when the doors swung open, revealing a stately woman dressed in an embroidered jade-green silk robe.

Empress Wangyi appeared no different from the last time Wei saw her. The same proud tilt of her chin, the same imperious gaze and perpetual sneer, especially when she laid eyes on him.

Wei gave a half-bow, the best he could manage. He would have remained upright and offered a dirty look if he had his way. 'Third Son Wei offers his greetings to Your Majesty.'

'Huwei, you have returned,' she said coolly. She always made sure to address him with his first name, just to remind him that he did not belong here. 'How unfortunate that it took your brother's death to make you come home.'

'Home is a place one chooses to be for love and safety. I found neither of those here. And neither, it seems, did Yong and my mother.'

Her lips tightened for the briefest moment before levelling into a cold smile. 'You are lucky to be alive until now. If you had any regard for your already disgraced mother, you would learn your place and return to the wild where you belong.'

Baiting, always baiting.

His younger self would have reacted to any comment Wangyi made about his mother. His reputation as a scorned, vengeful son had been sealed by the one occasion where he had pinned Wangyi against a pillar for making a derogatory remark about his mother. Now, however, he saw her for the jealous, insecure woman she was. More than anything, Meng was to be pitied for being her pawn in her bid for power.

He took a threatening step towards Wangyi, towering over her. She staggered backwards, already glancing around for the guards.

'My mother was framed, and you know it,' he said. 'Indeed, it seems "the wild" might suit us better.'

Her lips stretched into a smile. 'You think your mother was framed? Prove it.'

No one else here had an agenda like Wangyi to see his mother behind bars. Even though his mother had nothing to do with Han's exile, Wangyi had always resented her for the fate of her eldest son.

But this was all his conjecture—he had been out in the desert when everything happened, and thus had no way of proving his mother's innocence. Wangyi had him there, and she knew it.

'Congratulations,' he said instead. 'Your son is in the running for the throne again. How convenient that Yong's seat is made empty just as Meng returns from his assignment.'

This time, fury clouded her face. 'Are you insinuating that my son and I might be involved in Yong's death?'

Wei let his silence speak on his behalf.

'Don't you dare bring my son into this,' she spat. 'You have no proof that Yong was murdered, or that we had anything to do with it.'

The shallow triumph of seeing *her* rise to the bait this time made him smile.

'Rest assured, Your Majesty,' he said, 'that when I get to the bottom of this, I will find ample proof to present to the imperial court. And I will track down every single person who was complicit in Yong's death.' He took one last look at Yong's chamber before turning to leave.

'It's too bad that your mother gave birth to a prince so weak that he couldn't even defend himself in his own chamber,' Wangyi called after him.

His feet slowed. 'Then it's too bad that I will do whatever it takes to find out who poisoned him, even if it means getting up on that throne myself.' He gave her a casual wave, the kind that desert folks would give one another, and left before she could say another word.

*

The last memory Wei had of his older brother was when he was about to leave the palace and Oasis Kingdom for good. He had just turned sixteen, and his heart was filled with a raging desire for escape. He was ready to ride straight through the Capital gates and never look back.

He'd had it all planned out. He would ride to the first desert town on the map, acquire a fresh set of civilian clothes, blend in with the locals to shake off his father's guards who would undoubtedly come tracking, and from there head for the mountains. *The* mountain. The one where the Snow Wolf Sect lived in isolation as they were trained to be warriors, called upon by those in need of protection, regardless of where they were from. He would leave the palace life behind, devote himself to a cause, make a difference, and explore the world beyond the Capital gates.

Yong was waiting for him at those very gates the night he snuck out, lone horse and single baggage in tow. He was alone, which Wei took to mean that his older brother wasn't there to expose him.

'You know that once you leave, you'll be branded as a traitor to the kingdom,' said Yong. 'Father will have you tried like a common criminal if he catches you.'

'Oh, he certainly will. It'll be a convenient way to get rid of me like he always wanted. This way is better. He won't look like a heartless father exiling his son, and I get to leave this place on my own terms. *If* he ever catches me, I hope I would have left a mark in the world by then.'

'Why are you risking your life just to get a taste of what's out there?'

'It's not just about wanderlust, Yong. Look at us, are we truly happy here? Me trapped in a place that never wanted me, and you with a role you never really wanted, always having to fear for your life because of the title you wear.'

'It is my duty to—'

'I know that, and I respect that you wish to serve our people. But we're different. Your destiny is already laid out for you. I'm just seeking my own, one that I know lies beyond these walls. Mother used to tell us about the northern mountains. Maybe that's where I'm meant to go.'

Yong sighed. 'Will I ever see you again?'

Wei shot him a grin. 'If you don't die before you succeed our father, I might just return for sentimentality's sake.'

Yong cracked a reluctant smile.

'Don't tell anyone about tonight,' Wei said. 'You're the Crown Prince, you're not supposed to be abetting a rogue brother in his escape.' On impulse, he pulled Yong into a hug. Yong lurched forward in surprise, but he wrapped his arms around Wei too.

'Promise me you won't do anything stupid out there and get yourself killed,' Yong said.

'Promise me you'll have more faith in me if I return.' Flashing him one last grin, Wei pulled up his mask and leapt onto his horse.

That was the last time Wei had seen his brother.

Now, it was all he could think about as he watched the funeral ceremony from his usual hideout in the bell tower (no one missed his presence anyway). In this part of the palace, there was only one lone sentry roaming around the roof of the adjacent building.

From his vantage point, Wei could see the massive jostling crowd that had gathered in the sprawling courtyard just outside the palace gates. They were organized by caste—Silver at the very front guarded by rows of guards, followed by Steel and Wood making up the bulk,

Stone—worst hit by the famine—looking sunken and resentful, and finally the Untouchables at the far back waiting to pick someone's pocket. Closer to him, in unobstructed view, was the terrace where his father sat with Wangyi and Meng, flanked by two pairs of guards, and the court officials who settled into their orderly rows behind them.

Wei could hardly remember a time when he sat together with them as part of the family. Of course he didn't have a seat at public events next to the emperor. He had long given up on the notion of being regarded as his father's son, as legitimate as Meng or Yong.

Where *did* he belong then? In none of the castes because they only saw him as the rogue prince, nor with those people on that terrace. Only the world beyond this kingdom would have him now, and it was there that he longed to roam again.

At five bells sharp, High Adviser Mian took his place at the podium with a scroll that he unfurled once the crowd below had settled down.

'Dear people of Oasis Kingdom,' he intoned. 'We are brought here today by the demise of our beloved Crown Prince, Zhaoyong.'

Some among the crowd were already weeping, some clutching one another for support. Some held baskets of white chrysanthemums, ready to toss at Yong's casket when it was paraded around the Capital. Others fixed their sombre gazes on Mian.

'Zhaoyong was a kind and brave prince, a devoted and dutiful son. At just twenty years of age, he shouldered the immense responsibility as Crown Prince, preparing to take over our great kingdom one day from our esteemed Fifteenth Emperor Zhaode.' He paused to let the crowd's attention drift to the emperor, who let out a heavy sigh on cue.

Wei scoffed. Yong would have hated this fanfare, this public display of grief and exaltation. He had never enjoyed the spectacle that came with being Crown Prince. During his coming-of-age ceremony when he was sixteen, he had struggled not to squirm in his sedan as he was paraded through the streets and tried not to flinch when the people tossed fresh flower petals and sprig leaves at him for blessing.

Now, from the main chamber at the back of the terrace, the guards carried out Yong's casket—a sturdy, polished redwood draped in white silk and topped with chrysanthemum and lotus petals—and laid it on the white marble dais in the centre of the terrace. Wei couldn't help but wonder how uncomfortable Yong must be, lying in there as the whole capital gawked.

Unlike the elaborate mourning rite Wei had once witnessed during his stint with the Aranya tribe in the highlands, the Oasis way of sending off the dead was far more unceremonious. There was no priest to perform any religious ritual, no calling upon the heavens or underworld deities to ensure a smooth passage into the afterlife. Notions of magic and spirituality had died in Oasis Kingdom long ago. There was only the imperial orchestra playing a melancholic tune as a troop of soldiers performed a solemn march around the dais.

The orchestra fell silent when the emperor rose from his seat and approached the podium.

'The emperor, His Majesty,' the High Adviser announced before stepping aside to let the emperor take his place.

'My people, it is with a grieving heart that I address you today,' the emperor began.

His demeanour was nothing like it had been yesterday, when he had threatened to sentence Wei and called Yong's death unfortunate. Now, he looked like a father mourning his beloved son.

'My son was found murdered in his chamber,' he declared. 'Poisoned.'

The crowd drew a collective breath before breaking out in a buzz of chatter and whispers.

'You may be wondering,' the emperor went on, raising his voice to be heard, 'how can someone slip into the palace, into the Crown Prince's private chamber? The Red Circle has the tightest security in this entire kingdom. And yet . . .'

How indeed, Wei thought. One would have to get through at least three lines of defence to get into the Red Circle, and then slip past Yong's personal guards. There were also magic detectors that would raise an alarm if anyone did try to use magic to break in. This had to be an inside job. His gaze drifted to Empress Wangyi. Could she really have orchestrated Yong's death? She might be ambitious, but would she really dare to kill the Crown Prince?

'What this means,' said the emperor, 'is that our security has been breached. The kingdom is no longer safe from that which we have fought against so valiantly for centuries. What this means is that the threat of magic is very real and very near. We have every reason to believe that the Crown Prince, my beloved second son, was the victim of an act of terror—against the imperial family, against the kingdom, against everything we stand for.'

The murmurs grew louder. Wei snorted. Of course his father would seize this opportunity to bring up foreign invasion and magical security breaches. Nothing like some old-fashioned fearmongering to keep the people in check. Whatever resentment that the famine might have bred would fade in the face of this immediate and more violent threat.

A scoff behind him made him whip around. He scanned every inch of the roof, but no one was there, just a fine dusting of sand in a corner that stirred in the gentle breeze.

Could it be one of the House of Night guards? They were the only ones (well, other than him) who would be up here during the ceremony. If so, this one wasn't doing such a great job of staying invisible.

But he could almost swear he caught a glimpse of a figure on the rooftop of a lower adjacent building. Someone who looked very much like Desert Rose.

Wei shook the thought from his mind. There was no way she could be here now. He needed to stop thinking about her once and for all—they had parted ways long ago.

'We will not let this incident quail us,' the emperor said, his voice rising with conviction. 'My son's death will not go to waste. We need to shore up our defences against the growing threat of invasive magical forces beyond our walls.'

A cheer erupted from the back of the crowd where the lower castes stood.

'No more magic! No more terror!' a group of burly Steel Caste men shouted, pumping their fists in the air.

The chant spread like wildfire. By the third reiteration, the entire crowd had joined in the rallying cry. Soon, even children perched on the backs of their fathers were chiming in—a new generation taught to fear and hate magic.

Wei had been so close to becoming like them, had it not been for that experience out in the desert when he was twelve, and all those times he had snuck into the restricted section of the imperial library to read about the world, wild and vivid and teeming with magic. And had it not been for the songs his mother had sung to him when he was a child, forbidden ones about mountain gods and earth deities, he might have been led to believe that humans were the makers of the world, second to nothing else.

The people here would never know what lay beyond these walls, nor did they want to, it seemed.

No one saw the fire coming.

It broke out amid the spirited chanting, somewhere between the Wood and Steel Castes. The chorus disintegrated into shouts and cries as people began jostling each other to get to safety.

But Wei saw it coming. He saw the petite girl with a mask in the middle of the throng, pressed close against a burly man with a hat pulled low over his face. He saw her set down the woven basket she was carrying and drop a lit match into it, setting it in flames within a heartbeat. He saw her slip away from the man as soon as the chaos started, blending into the crowd and disappearing from sight.

As the human tide dragged him away from the scene of the crime, the man glanced around wildly for his companion, but she was long gone.

The fire burgeoned, reaching further into the crowd and sparking fresh screams.

Out of the flames, a group of masked people emerged. All twenty of them were dressed in identical white robes and black masks that revealed only their eyes. They raised their lit torches and roared in unison, their voices carrying across the din, 'Denounce magic, denounce life! Magic is our being! Magic is our blood!'

People around them scrambled out of their way as they advanced, tight as a pack of wolves, through the throng of civilians. Flames leapt around them, as though protecting them.

Wei turned back to the emperor, who was already issuing an order to the imperial guards to capture the group. Below, patrol guards split into two groups—one swarming in to surround the masked protestors, the other attempting to control the hysterical mob.

But no one could tame the fire that was now taking on a life of its own.

No, Wei thought, watching the mayhem unfold. *Not at Yong's funeral.* After all he had sacrificed for the kingdom, his brother deserved at least a proper send-off, not this.

He was about to head down to stop the disruption himself when he felt droplets of water pelt his head. He paused and glanced up.

Rain? In winter?

The deluge seized them, cascading in copious sheets. On the terrace, the pall-bearers scrambled to move Yong's casket back under the awning. Wei watched until they managed to get it to safety. By the time he turned his attention back to the fire, it had been extinguished by the rain.

The rain left as abruptly as it came, dissipating as soon as the last ember died, as if its sole purpose was to douse the flames. This could not be nature's doing. But who in the kingdom had the ability to conjure rain? All their sorcerers were dead long ago, and the Cleansing made sure no magic could enter the kingdom.

An unnatural calm settled upon them like a silk blanket. In the bated air, they braced themselves for more. Even the masked group paused in response to the phenomenon, their obscured faces upturned. The sky had returned to its original winter grey, still and heavy, as though nothing out of the ordinary had just happened, but the ground, previously coated with snow, now bore the stains of the downpour.

The emperor emerged from under the awning, flanked by a pair of guards, and crept back onto the podium. He surveyed the sky, then pointed at the rebels. 'This is witchcraft!' he cried, breaking the silence. 'Seize them—all of them! Leave none alive!'

The rebels scattered faster than the guards could react, weaving through the crowds, shoving people aside and abandoning their robes along the way. Wei tracked their movements, the fastest ones fleeing as far as Dongmu Market five streets away.

The guards nabbed only two in the end. One of them—a stout, broad-shouldered man—put up a fierce struggle as he was dragged towards the palace, but the other—a slim younger woman—complied with dignified calm, not even flinching when her mask was ripped off. Wei couldn't tell which caste she belonged to. She had an air that suggested a noble background, but she was as unadorned as the next member of the Wood Caste. The man, however, bore the rough-hewn edges of the Stone Caste: tattered rags, days-old scruff, and a scar atop his right brow.

The male protestor spat at the ground, narrowly missing the guard's foot. In return, the guard gave him a sharp wrench in the arm.

'Remove them,' the emperor ordered. 'I will not have my son's funeral interrupted by terrorists.'

There was no telling what would happen to them next. If they were lucky, they would be locked up before being interrogated. Otherwise, executed without trial.

'These miscreants are a threat to our kingdom, our home,' the emperor proclaimed once the captives were dragged away. 'We will not tolerate antics of their kind.' He gestured for the casket to be brought back out.

'As night falls over this woeful day, Oasis Kingdom bids goodbye to its beloved son,' Mian intoned. 'Farewell, Prince Zhaoyong. You have served the kingdom well.' He bowed his head.

The people followed suit, but a palpable fear lingered in the crowd, suffocating as a second skin. Music filled the air again when the moment of silence passed, heavy and swelling as the guards pulled the white silk completely over the casket. Some people wept as they placed their hands over their hearts.

The pall-bearers lifted Yong's casket off the dais and mounted it onto a gilded platform, which they shouldered as the procession set off. They made their way down from the terrace and out of the palace gates. The people surged forward as soon as the gates opened, eager to have one last look at the Crown Prince.

Wei leapt off the parapet of the bell tower. The procession was going to last until sundown and watching it wasn't going to change anything—he might as well get started on his investigations.

He combed the bell tower, just to make sure he had imagined Desert Rose after all. The sounds of the funeral march receded into the distance, leaving behind a hollow silence. There was nothing out of the ordinary here, save for a fine dusting of sand sprinkled atop the parapet in a trail that led nowhere.

Sand again? When everywhere else was covered with snow? It wasn't the hard-grained variety or coarse gravel, but sand as fine as that from the Khuzar Desert. Who could have left sand behind, and why would they be on the parapet?

With just about everyone out of the palace to send off the Crown Prince, Wei was free to roam the grounds. He headed down the deserted hallways to Yong's chamber, trying to brush away the memories that came rushing back at every turn.

To find out how someone could slip into a heavily guarded chamber, he needed to understand all the defences that had been in place. The House of Night would have the best answer to that, but how did one even begin to locate that elusive House?

Yong's chamber was now, for the most part, unguarded. Wei stepped through the main doors and stood in the middle of the room, surveying every corner. Everything seemed intact, even pristine, as though his brother might just be sitting there in his study, practising his calligraphy. Nothing here indicated that he had been murdered. Then again, nothing was ever what it appeared in the palace.

Wei started with the obvious places like cupboards, desks, the bed, not knowing what exactly he was looking for. Even the secret compartments under the bed, along the wall, and in the ground yielded nothing. Yong had always held on to his thoughts, airing them only when he was asked.

Perhaps I'm too late, Wei thought. Perhaps the culprit had removed all the incriminating traces by now.

No, there had to be something he was missing.

He was making his fourth round of the room when he spotted it. There, at the foot of the dining table, so inconspicuous he had overlooked it several times while combing the chamber.

He went closer, reached out to touch it. It was loose and dry and almost as fine as dust.

Sand. Just like the one he had found on the roof earlier.

*

When the sun cast its final rays across the palace grounds, Wei heard the lament of distant music again. Back at his spot at the bell tower, he watched as the casket returned, now covered in more flowers, sprigs, and rice grains that the people could spare. All the blessings that Yong would never receive in person.

The emperor made his final speech in the dying light of day.

'People of Oasis Kingdom, remember today. Remember how we lost the Crown Prince. Remember how we were terrorized by rebel factions among us who seek to disrupt our peace and tear us apart. Remember that this threat is pervasive and to let your guard down is to allow it to infiltrate your homes. We must not take our safety and prosperity for granted.

'If you witness any use of magic, or discover any magical beings or practitioners lurking among us, do your part as a citizen of this kingdom and protect your loved ones. Hand them over to the Imperial Court before they become the next threat.'

An uneasy murmur rippled through the crowd. People glanced askance at their neighbours, fresh doubt in their eyes.

'The time of magic is over,' the emperor proclaimed. 'We must not allow it to rule over us. We are intelligent beings capable of free thought and wielding weapons. We do not need to cower in fear in our own kingdom!'

The crowd roared in assent. 'No more magic, no more fear! Free from magic, free of fear!'

Wei felt his fingers dig into his palms. This was what Yong's death had been reduced to—merely a convenient occasion for his father to rally the people and fortify his agenda.

As the mob kept up its boisterous chant, Wei caught a final glimpse of his brother, trapped in a box until the very end.

Eleven

Meng

Meng surveyed the crowd, despair mounting within him as the chanting reached a fever peak.

They did not understand. They were mere pawns in his father's game. He would send their sons and brothers to die out in the desert for a mythical spring. He would put in place reforms that took away their land and livelihoods for the benefit of the kingdom. He would strip the lower castes of more rights to keep them under his control. He would make the people hate and fear magic so that they would remain blind, voiceless, and none the wiser.

They did not understand that they were fighting against the wrong enemy.

But Meng could only swallow his frustration and watch as his father stepped off the podium, satisfied with what he had incited below.

Later that evening, as he headed to his father's study, Meng prepared a carefully worded speech in his head. He would tell him, this time with more conviction and persistence, just how far off the mark he was.

All that conviction dissipated, however, when he crossed paths with Wei just outside the Red Circle. Was this really the best time to challenge his father now that his brother was back? Wei never had any qualms about butting heads with their father, and it got him nowhere. If Meng questioned their father's decisions too, it would only make the emperor raise his guard against both his sons.

Back when they were all teenagers and Wei would run his mouth with their father, Yong would be the one who stepped in as mediator. Now that their diplomat was gone, Meng was the only one left hovering at the door like he had arrived too early for a banquet.

He and Wei believed in the same things, but there was too much inherited enmity between them for them to ever stand on the same side. He hesitated now, his feet slowing as he and Wei neared each other. It had been years since he last saw his half-brother. Wei was as good as a stranger now.

He was lost in thought, frowning at the ground as he walked. Before Meng could turn back, Wei looked up and locked eyes with him.

Meng offered a civil smile. 'Brother. You're back. I must have missed you at the ceremony earlier.'

Wei replied with a withering look, seeing right through his lie.

'I heard you are investigating Yong's death,' Meng tried again. 'We've searched Yong's chamber. The murderer left no trace behind.'

'You must have missed something then.'

They eyed each other in the curdled silence. In the time apart, the wall between them had grown as impenetrable as the magical barrier around the kingdom. What was the point in trying to tear it down now?

At last, Wei brushed past him to leave. Meng, already late to meet his father, hurried off in the opposite direction.

In the study, his father was seated before the High Adviser with a pot of tea brewing on a low table between them. After making his greetings, Meng seated himself at the tea table upon his father's request.

'You said you have news to share with me, Meng,' said his father.

Meng glanced at Mian.

His father waved a dismissive hand. 'It's all right, speak. Mian is almost family.'

Mian thanked the emperor and urged Meng with a nod.

'I found a girl at the Capital gates last night,' said Meng. 'A desert girl. She was drinking from the well.'

A gleam appeared in his father's eyes as he understood at once. 'I remember the lengths you went to find the other one. Does this one have . . . abilities?'

'If she does, she does not seem to be aware of it. I will continue to observe her.' His father nodded. 'She said she wishes to speak with you. I let her join the House of Night.'

A frown crept between his father's brows. 'You let her train as an assassin?'

'Given the climate in our kingdom now, I thought it would make more sense for her to earn your audience than for you to see a desert girl out of the blue. The trials would test her tenacity too.'

His father took a sip of his tea, mollified. 'We shall see. In the meantime, I'd like you to also keep an eye on Wei. I want to know his true intentions for returning.'

'Yes, Father.'

'That would be wise, Your Majesty,' Mian agreed. 'Prince Wei is . . . volatile. His star has been bright ever since his return. There is also the question of where his loyalty lies. Perhaps we should find out the sort of alliances he has been making in the time he has been away.'

The emperor nodded. 'See to that,' he told Meng. 'What intel have you gathered on the Lettorians?'

Meng's undercover visit to their western neighbour had showed him just how out of depth they were. Lettoria gave him a glimpse into the future, with its magic-fuelled machines and cinder block edifices called factories in which things were mass-produced at rapid speed. Magic wove through the city, kept it blazing bright even at night. Far from fearing it, the people had full rein over it, controlling it as if it were no more than a tool.

'They are far too advanced,' he said. 'Father, we cannot afford to place all our hopes on a magical spring, not when the kingdom is still reeling from this summer's drought and famine. Even if everything goes according to your plan—even if we do find the spring and monopolize international trade—the Lettorians would already have devised a thousand ways to counter our attacks.'

Silence stretched out between them.

'I see,' said the emperor at last. His gaze fell upon his teacup on the table. Meng recognized that pensive look. The last time he saw it, his father had launched a surprise attack on the Lettorians after sealing all their trade routes.

'Tell me,' his father said, looking back up at him. 'Have they prepared anything to counter biological warfare?'

'Biological . . . warfare?' Meng echoed.

His father smiled. 'My boy, there are many possibilities you have not considered. When we control the spring, we can control the desert. Plus, the people can stop grumbling about the famine. But we don't have to stop at monopolizing the spring. It's better to disable your enemies before they strike.'

Realization crept over him. 'You mean to poison the water supply.'

His father raised his teacup to his lips. 'Magic is meant to serve us; it is our weapon to wield.'

'But there's no time to look for the spring, Father. We are wasting manpower on this quest that has no end in sight.'

The emperor paused, then set down his cup to survey Meng.

'You know I am fully in support of your search for the spring, Father,' Meng added hastily. 'But perhaps we can better deploy our men in the meantime, so that we can be ready for the Lettorians when they attack.'

At last, his father conceded, 'Your judgement is sound. At least one of my sons has a sensible head on his shoulders.'

Meng felt his shoulders loosen in relief.

'Indeed, Your Majesty,' said Mian. 'Prince Meng shows greater potential in following in your footsteps than anyone else. His birth star has always shone brightly over the kingdom.'

'Brighter than Wei's?' the emperor asked.

'Certainly.'

Meng held back an exasperated sigh. 'If there's nothing else, Father, I will take my leave.' He bowed.

'Pay our new prisoners a visit, will you? See that they are well hosted in our cells.' He bared his teeth in what almost passed for a smile. 'They might be feisty at first, but give them a few days and they'll crack. They always do.'

Meng swallowed and bowed again. 'I will inform you of anything I learn, as always, Father.'

He got up and took his leave, catching the High Adviser's measuring stare as he retreated. Even after he left the chamber, he still felt it lingering on his back.

Twelve

Desert Rose

The next day, the palace was in an uproar again—not merely because of the riot during the funeral procession, but from an unexpected homecoming. News of the rogue prince's return tore through the grounds, reaching even this remote corner of the palace.

Xiyue was the one who brought the news after collecting their breakfast from a maid. She sat down at the dining table with the rest, wolfing down her porridge, her eyes wide as twin moons as she reported, 'They said he stormed in on a black horse and killed at least twenty guards along the way.'

'The Third Prince does have a reputation for being violent,' said Liqin, bringing her spoon to her mouth daintily. 'I heard he trained with wolves up in the mountains and joined a gang of desert bandits that slaughtered villagers after robbing them.'

Xiyue gasped. 'Did you know why he was exiled by the emperor in the first place? He was caught plotting a rebellion and threatening the empress. Plus, we all know'—her voice fell to a whisper—'his mother is in jail now for attempted regicide.'

'The apple doesn't fall far from the tree, I suppose,' Shuang said as she brought her spoon to her mouth primly.

The Capital girls shared a scandalized look, giggling. Windshadow rolled her eyes at Desert Rose.

'Well, what did you expect from the bastard prince?' Liqin went on. 'He's probably sore that his mother's not the empress any more.'

'He's not actually a bastard, though,' Shuang pointed out, waving her spoon for emphasis. 'He's a legitimate son, except that the emperor disowned him.'

'Which probably explains his rage issues,' Liqin countered. 'I don't recall seeing him at the mourning ceremony yesterday. Do you?'

'Maybe the emperor doesn't want him in the public's sight, given his history,' Shuang said. 'It *was* the Crown Prince's funeral, after all. Wouldn't want the black sheep of the family to upstage that.'

Windshadow tipped her face to the heavens, as though she couldn't take any more of this conversation, but Desert Rose edged closer to listen. Why did the Third Prince try to stage a rebellion? How was he foiled? And why was he back now?

'As if it wasn't upstaged anyway,' Liqin said, pushing her bowl away in disgust.

Shuang's upper lip curled. 'I'll bet you anything, those masked creeps are from the Wood Caste, or maybe the Untouchables. They're a disgruntled lot. Actually, I wouldn't be surprised if they were linked to the Third Prince. He's always had rather radical ideas.'

'And that rain,' Xiyue added with a shudder. 'Where did *that* come from?'

Desert Rose glanced away from them and shovelled porridge into her mouth.

Calling for rain was her first response when she saw the fire. But she couldn't possibly have called upon that deluge on her own. The elder clanswoman and head shaman of her tribe, Dil Mura, had always said she was the worst at natural arts.

But Desert Rose doubted even Dil Mura could have summoned that downpour so quickly. That was far beyond the skill of any natural arts practitioner. And yet . . .

'If you are this capable at retaining hearsay, I trust you will have no problems with today's lessons,' Shimu said from behind them.

The girls dropped their spoons and scrambled to attention, murmuring a collective greeting.

'You have until seven bells to finish up your breakfast and gather at the classroom,' Shimu said. 'Look sharp,' she added, pointing at Xiyue's messy topknot, before leaving the dining room.

After their previous lesson on the history and geography of Oasis Kingdom, Desert Rose was not looking forward to more today. As she took her seat in the classroom, Windshadow leaned over and whispered, 'No outbursts today.'

Shimu retrieved a blue-covered rope-bound book from the cupboard at the back of the room and handed it to Desert Rose. On the cover, the title read *The Art of Combat.*

'While the trials serve as your practical test,' Shimu said, 'you will be taking a written preliminary theory exam on the art of combat.'

Desert Rose balked. A written test? No one mentioned anything about that. She flipped through the book, frantic. With the amount of Oasis language she had managed to learn from her father, she was as good as illiterate. More than half the book was unintelligible to her.

Shimu nodded at Desert Rose. 'For your sake, the test will be postponed to next week. Be sure to read this manual from cover to cover.' She glanced around the room, her gaze settling a beat longer on Xiyue. 'Having witnessed the energy you spend on gossiping, I expect perfect scores from all of you.'

All but Shuang and Windshadow squirmed in their seats.

'Every test you take, every practice you undergo, will prepare you for the trials, where only one of you will be selected to be part of the Imperial High Guard. Whether you receive the honour of serving the emperor himself depends on your daily performance.'

Desert Rose snapped to attention. The winner of the trials would have direct access to the emperor? Was this why Meng had brought her to the House of Night? So that she could legitimately work her way towards the emperor?

Three more months. Could she last that long? Could her father wait that long? What would happen to her tribe during this time?

Then again, even if she did manage to leave the palace, where would she even begin to find her father? Her odds of winning the trials might actually be higher than finding him in this kingdom.

Shimu's voice broke into her thoughts. 'So I expect all of you to regard every lesson and training session with due seriousness.'

Desert Rose glanced at Shuang, her strongest competitor so far. The girl, too, was surveying each of them out of the corner of her eye, no doubt deciding on her biggest threat.

After they were dismissed for self-study, Desert Rose stayed behind in the classroom to buckle down on the manual.

I can do this. This is just another hurdle to leap over.

The book stared back at her, taunting. She flipped it open. Despite Shimu's brief explanation of the manual earlier during class, there was too much to absorb. The characters swam before her eyes, blurring into an incomprehensible jumble.

She sighed and banged her head on the desk. 'What am I even doing?' Her father could be dead now, for all she knew, and here she was, struggling to read a war manual.

'Right now, it appears you are about to crack your head open on that desk,' said a voice behind her.

She jumped in her seat and spun around to find Prince Meng standing outside the window, his lip quirked in a smile. 'P-prince Meng,' she greeted as he stepped into the classroom.

'Don't stop on my account.' In his pristine silk robes, he looked too exquisite for the spartan classroom. He peered at her face. 'I'm guessing you're not settling in very well.'

'It's very different from tribe life,' she admitted.

'It certainly takes some getting used to. I apologize for sending you blind into something you didn't ask for, but it was the only excuse I could find to help you enter the palace.'

'I never got to ask this before, but . . . why *did* you help me? You knew nothing about me. I could have been one of those troublemakers during the Crown Prince's funeral.'

An uncharacteristic shyness settled in his gaze. 'It's not every day you come across someone with so much fire in her eyes. I wanted to be part of your journey, in whatever way I can.' He gestured at her books. 'You look like you could use some help here.'

'Are you offering me your help?'

'Always that tone of surprise,' he said with a wry smile. 'I wonder what your impression of Capital people is that makes you doubt my intentions every time.'

She shook her head. 'That's not what I meant.' Why would he spend his time coaching her when he had his own princely duties? What *did* princes do anyway?

'I brought you in here, after all. It would be terribly irresponsible of me to leave you here to perish before you've accomplished what you came for.' He settled into the seat next to her, where just moments ago

Windshadow had nudged her and cautioned her to watch her back. 'Can you read the Oasis language at all?'

'Just a little. My father taught me what he knew.' The mention of her father made her stomach twist into the familiar knot of worry again.

Prince Meng misread the frown on her face. 'Don't worry, it's not too difficult. You should be able to pick it up in a few days.' He traced a finger down the first line, reading in a slow, clear voice as he went along. The words rolled off his tongue in a smooth cadence, almost melodious. 'The art of combat is often mistaken for weaponry prowess.'

She repeated after him, once to test the words on her tongue and once more to understand their intent. Prince Meng continued with the next line, then the next, explaining its meaning whenever Desert Rose stalled. They worked through line by line, page by page, until they reached the end of the third lesson.

She looked up with at him with a triumphant grin—*she had read a third of a book!*—and found herself staring straight into his eyes.

A heartbeat passed. Then another.

They pulled back at the same time. Desert Rose hoped the sunlight streaming in through the window was enough to disguise the heat rising in her face. Was she allowed to be in such proximity with a prince?

Prince Meng cleared his throat and smiled as he straightened. 'Let's stop here today. You've made good progress.' Desert Rose busied herself with gathering the books. 'We'll continue tomorrow. If you'd like,' he added.

'Y-yes.'

Prince Meng gave her another smile before turning to leave.

Her face still warm against the icy wind, Desert Rose watched him from the doorway, staring at the trail he left behind him in the snow after he was out of sight.

*

That evening, Shimu sent them out for their first stealth training. It felt like the first breath of fresh air Desert Rose had taken ever since she entered the Capital.

Dressed in nondescript civilian clothing, under which they hid their weapons wherever possible, they were to blend into the crowd and locate each of their marks before tailing them to their abodes.

Desert Rose's mark was a merchant named Geshao, one of the Capital's most wanted criminals. Behind his innocuous-looking apothecary business, he was suspected of having ties with the southern colonies for smuggling magical blood-shade root into the Capital. Blood-shade root was known for its ability to reverse the effects of *ticha*.

At first, the name Geshao meant nothing to her. But then she saw the portrait of him.

She had seen that face in her tribe when she was a child. Golsha had been a member of Blackstone's clan, but he left the tribe after Blackstone was chosen as clan leader instead of him.

Years in the Capital had changed Golsha. Not only did he have a different name now, his lean, brow-beaten look was gone too. His sun-browned skin was now fair, and his scraggly beard had been trimmed to a coiffed moustache.

With his face in mind, Desert Rose now navigated the streets of Wuxi Market with the other Blue Cranes. It was just before sunset, and everyone was still out and about, trying to make the most of daylight hours. Perfect for blending in.

Swerving to avoid a drawn pushcart, Desert Rose didn't notice the Capital girls sidling up to her until Liqin seized her arm.

'What did you do?' Liqin demanded, her eyes gleaming.

Desert Rose inched away, only to find Shuang on the other side, trapping her between them. 'Excuse me?'

'What did you do to capture Prince Meng?' Liqin asked again. Behind Liqin, Windshadow gave a subtle shake of her head.

Desert Rose squirmed out of Liqin's grasp. 'Capture . . . what? I didn't do anything.'

But Liqin kept her hand clamped on her arm. 'Well, you obviously did something, if he's spending his precious time to teach you how to *read*.'

'It's a good strategy, but even Prince Meng won't be able to get you very far,' Shuang said. 'The trials are fair and just—only those worthy of protecting the imperial family are qualified.'

Indignation surged through her. 'I'm not . . . Prince Meng and I—'

'It's okay, Mingxi,' Xiyue quipped earnestly from behind them. 'We do whatever we can to get ahead. There's nothing wrong with getting some help.'

'Especially for a foreigner like you, it's harder.' Liqin shrugged. 'You have more to prove, especially your loyalties.'

'I don't have anything to prove, nor am I using Prince Meng to get ahead,' Desert Rose snapped, tearing out of Liqin's grip.

'Oh, leave her alone, all of you,' Windshadow said at last. She reached for Desert Rose's hand and pulled her away from the two girls. 'Worry about yourselves. You'll have a far better chance of making it to the trials than being jealous twits.'

Liqin and Shuang shot her identical sneers before flouncing off together. With an apologetic glance at Desert Rose, Xiyue headed off in a separate direction.

'Children,' Windshadow muttered. 'See if they survive beyond the Capital gates with their tiny minds.'

'You're not curious why the prince is helping me?' Desert Rose asked.

Windshadow shrugged. 'He's the prince. He can do whatever he pleases. Shuang's right on one thing, though—we qualify for the trials based on our own merit.' She flashed a smug grin. 'And I'm fairly certain I'm far ahead of all of you right now.'

Desert Rose smirked. 'Is that so? May the best girl complete her assignment first, then.'

The evening chill was starting to settle in, but inns were still receiving their final customers for the day and vendors made their last desperate cries about their wares from pushcarts lining the snow-coated pavements and the frozen canal. Pedestrians huddled close in their fur coats as they hurried home.

Desert Rose longed to linger at each stall and explore every shop along the way. This was her first proper look at the city, and it was almost exactly as her father had described. Papa would have loved it. She recalled the look in his eyes, uncharacteristically wistful, whenever he told her about the Capital.

'Do you see yours?' Windshadow muttered, pulling her out of her thoughts. 'Mine's a tubby, middle-aged man with a penchant for tacky purple robes.' She sniggered. 'I guess all that money he got from money laundering can't buy him good taste.'

Desert Rose shook her head. *Focus, Rose.* This was not the time to get distracted, not if she wanted to make it to the trials. She scanned each face she passed by, searching for a moustached middle-aged man in the crowd—

'Found him,' Windshadow murmured. She pulled her arm out of Desert Rose's, a predatorial smile working across her lips. 'You're on your own, *azzi*.' They might come from different tribes, but the word for *sister* was common in the desert.

Windshadow was gone the next moment, like smoke dissipating into the breeze, leaving Desert Rose alone in the middle of the street.

According to the records, Geshao was a nifty one who managed to keep evading the law because he covered his tracks impeccably. He had no wife, but a steady rotation of women from whom he derived pleasure, so a likely hangout at this hour might be a pleasure house.

It was no good being on the streets. The other girls already had a head start in tracking, having lived in the Capital longer than her, and even Windshadow seemed confident of her mode of operation. But *she* was practically thrown out into the wild without a compass. She had neither vantage point nor geographical awareness that would help her navigate the city with native ease.

She slipped into a dark alley, making sure she was alone in the shadows before stripping off her civilian clothing, pulling her hair into a firm bun, and tying on a mask over the lower half of her face. She bundled up the clothes and tucked them behind a discarded wooden crate in an alley, glad to be in a more comfortable tunic for now.

The buildings here—mostly two to three stories high—looked scalable, despite their snow-topped sloping roofs. Desert Rose clambered up to the roof of a three-storey teashop and studied the lay of the land.

Strings of lanterns dotted the neat rows of houses and shops, spilling their crimson glow onto the streets. It was a tidy grid, a predictable pattern, with shops along the canal and residences further down each street. In the distance, on a hill where almost all roads ended, the palace was silhouetted against the night by flaming torches lit along the outer border.

Desert Rose made a mental note of the city's layout, identifying the places with the heaviest flow of human traffic and squinting to make out the dimly lit signboards, committing the names to memory.

She was about to leap over to the next building to get a better view when she spotted him.

There, on the second floor of the Million Blessings Inn diagonally across the street, sitting around a private table by the window with two other men and a young boy who hovered behind him like a dutiful servant, was Golsha.

The ex-clansman looked more Capital-bred than desert-born now, as though he had completely buried his past under the layers of tailored fur coats he was wearing. His companions raised their wine bowls to him, and he obliged by doing the same. Later, he paid the waiter two taels of silver and parted with his company at the entrance of the inn. The boy trailed in his wake as they stepped into a horse-drawn carriage waiting for them at the doorstep.

Desert Rose got to her feet and teetered across the rooftops, keeping her steps as light as she could while pressing close to the shadows. The moonless night was deepening, but she didn't want to take any chances.

The carriage travelled seven streets away from the inn, deep into the residential district. They were four streets in before the houses started looking distinctly more ramshackle than those closer to the city, with cracked walls and chipped tiles the owners hadn't bothered to mend, and faded roofs buckling under the weight of snow.

At last, they came to a stop in front of a manor that seemed far too shabby for someone as extravagantly dressed as Geshao.

It was a nondescript abode, much like the others in the vicinity, with four rectangular buildings surrounding an open courtyard. But unlike the other residences, the wooden board above the front door was blank where the name of the manor would be. Shrivelled weeds peeked half-heartedly through the foot of the fractured walls, and a pair of faded red lanterns hung by the doors, extinguished.

The courtyard was empty, though a warm fire lit up the living area. The manor's interior was decidedly the opposite of its façade. Although not extravagant, it featured utilitarian furniture that saved it from looking spartan.

A man dressed in a simple ivory-coloured tunic sat in a wooden armchair facing the window in a corner, nursing a steaming cup of tea on the table before him. Desert Rose mentally willed him to turn around and reveal his face, but he remained unmoving, in deep thought.

Geshao's servant rapped the rusty brass knuckle thrice, and a slim figure clad in a dark hooded winter coat let Geshao and his servant in. When they approached the living area, the man in the armchair gestured at his guests to take a seat. Geshao settled into an ornate wooden chair opposite him, but his servant remained hovering at the back.

Desert Rose crept closer, close enough to hear their conversation. She sent a fervent prayer for the freezing tiles under her feet to not crack and shatter onto the ground. A snowflake drifted onto her shoulder, and she glanced up to find that a gentle snowfall had begun.

'The *shouren* are preparing the draught as we speak. I expect you to hold up your end of the bargain.' Geshao's voice was barely audible, but there was no mistaking the threat laced in his words.

The other man's reply was low, muffled and indiscernible, as though caught behind a mask.

Geshao slammed a hand against the table between then, making the hooded figure next to the gentleman jump. 'I did my job,' he snarled. 'I ordered the draught like you wanted, and I have the item you asked for. Do you know how far I went to acquire it? I had to steal from the chieftain—'

'Ousted chieftain,' the man corrected him calmly, his voice low and smooth. 'You have nothing to fear about the Dugur tribe. Their chieftain is no longer in our way.'

No longer in our way. Desert Rose felt a wave of fear wash over her. What did that mean? And what had Golsha stolen from her father? Was he involved in the uprising against her father too?

The rest of the conversation was drowned out by her thoughts, but a noise near her—a soft shuffling of feet—made her whip around, praying that it was just her imagination.

But no, a figure appeared out of the gloom, creeping closer. Desert Rose squinted, recognition dawning on her when she saw the well-cut features, strong brows, and eyes dark as sand hound blood.

'Wei?' she whispered. Wei froze, staring straight at her. She removed her mask, revealing her face.

'You're alive.' His eyes widened as he took in her outfit. 'What in heaven's name are you doing here?'

'I thought you people don't believe in heaven.'

'My people, not me,' he said. 'And you haven't answered my question.'

Below, the hooded figure turned in their direction. Wei reached over to press Desert Rose back against the roof so that they both lay flat on their backs, facing the sky. Desert Rose peered down, trying to make out the person's face, but he had turned back to Geshao. She and Wei both let out a breath.

'I could ask the same of you,' Desert Rose muttered.

'Answer my question,' he said. It was the threat in his voice that gave her pause and remember why she decided to leave his crew. He might have saved her out in the desert, but now that they weren't both fighting for their lives in the wild, he was just another stranger she was better off keeping her distance from. 'Why are you really here?'

'My business is none of your concern,' she replied, already planning her escape.

The figure turned again in their direction, this time stepping out of the living area for a closer look. The men, too, paused their conversation and peered out.

Wei grabbed her hand. 'Run.'

He yanked her to her feet before she could respond. As Geshao and the other man came out to investigate, Wei and Desert Rose dashed across the roof, not bothering with stealth any more.

The hooded person was right at their heels, climbing up onto the roof with unnatural speed and agility. Desert Rose and Wei leaped off the roof in tandem and rolled onto the ground on the other side of the wall.

Footsteps rushed to the door. Desert Rose and Wei shared a look, then picked themselves up and ducked around a corner just before the doors were flung open. Darkness settled like a cloak around them, but their breaths echoed in the silence. A chilly breeze wafted by.

Wei tugged on Desert Rose's hand, leading her down the darkest alley.

Snow and dim lighting aside, the alley was an obstacle course riddled with potholes, uneven cobblestone, and random debris discarded out front. They could only go by their intuition to navigate their way down alley after alley.

She had failed in her task. This was her first stealth training and she had already alerted her mark, possibly putting her behind in the running for the trials. And the person to blame was holding her hand right now as they fled. His pace was unfaltering, although he paused a couple of times when she stumbled into potholes.

The path became smoother the closer they got to town. Alleys were aglow with lanterns that hung before abodes with polished façades, guarded by stone lions.

Lights in the distance indicated that they were nearing the marketplace. Noises crept in—the sounds of life. Desert Rose shared a look with Wei, and they hurtled down the alley and out into the main street at last.

They took a moment to collect their breaths, pretending to observe the trinkets on sale at a pushcart next to them as they peered behind them. But the alley was empty—no one was on their tail.

'Thanks very much,' Desert Rose snapped, pulling her hand out of his. 'I failed my task because of you.'

Wei glared at her. 'And I was so close to finding out who—wait, what task?'

Desert Rose pursed her lips.

'Hair pins for the lady?' the pushcart vendor suggested, gesturing at her display of cheap jewellery.

Sending Wei another scowl, Desert Rose turned to leave. Now that she had failed tonight's mission, there was no point in lingering on the streets. How had the other girls fared? Had they already gathered intel and reported back to Shimu?

Wei caught up with her and blocked her way. 'What were you doing up on that roof?'

'Like I said, it's none of your business.'

'I see you've brought your mistrust of people with you to the Capital.'

'Just my mistrust of you,' she said, sidestepping him.

'I did save your life before,' he pointed out. 'There's a restriction on foreign entry now. How did you get past the gates?'

'You wouldn't believe me if I told you.'

'Try me.'

'Prince Meng, the Fourth Prince. He found me at the gates.'

Wei froze. 'Tell me you're not training at the House of Night.'

'I—' She frowned. 'How do you know about the House of Night?'

Who *was* he? One moment, he was the leader of a motley crew, well versed in the magical geopolitics of desert tribes, and now he was aware of a top-secret House in the palace.

'Are you?' he pressed.

'So what if I am?'

His jaw tightened. 'So it *was* you I saw on the roof during Yong's funeral.'

A familiar face flashed by the corner of her eye, and whatever else Wei said next was drowned out by the roaring in her ears. Cold fear slipped down her back, paralyzing her in a heartbeat.

It couldn't be. What was he doing here?

But there was no mistake about it. Less than twenty feet away was Bataar, with his brawny, slightly sloping shoulders and resolute jaw. He stood before an inn in the company of three other men, dressed in a heavy wolf-skin coat and boots, a stark contrast to the fur robes and gleaming leather boots that two of the men sported.

Memories of that night came surging back, along with the sting of Bataar's betrayal. The wound in her thigh throbbed with a phantom pain even though it had healed completely by now. She could still see Bataar's cold, dark eyes when he shot her down like an animal. But there was none of that cruelty now—Bataar was laughing and clapping Bezo, son of the Komur clan leader, on his back, as though he hadn't helped to overthrow her father, as though he were still that boy who had taught her how to ride and shoot, back when they were wild and free in the desert.

Wei's voice cut through her thoughts, dry and humourless. 'Hungry?'

Desert Rose snapped out of her thoughts, only then noticing the smell of barbequed meat and rice wine that wafted out from the inn. A sharp pain in her palms made her realize she was clenching her fists so hard her fingernails were digging into skin.

'What's wrong?' Wei said, his attention shuffling between her and the group of men. 'Someone you know?'

Words abandoned her as dread coursed down to her feet and her heart thundered in her chest. Were they here for *her*? Where were Blackstone and the other clan leaders? Did that mean her father had managed to escape?

Bataar and company made their way down the street, heading in her direction. She whirled around, starting to shake. If Bataar or Bezo caught even a glimpse of her, they would catch her before she could take another step back to the palace. It would be over before she could even meet the emperor or find her father.

Wei frowned, peering at her. 'What's wrong?'

'Nothing, I need to go.' Her breaths came fast and shallow as she pushed past him.

The street was emptier than before, but stares followed her as she hurried down the street with her head dipped.

Wei caught up with her and took her hand. 'Follow me,' he said, leading her down the street away from the men.

She kept pace with him, but as soon as she ventured a glance back, she found herself locking eyes with Bataar. Her breath leapt to her throat.

'Rose?' Bataar called. The timbre of his voice, once reassuring, now sounded like a threat.

Wei squeezed her hand as a signal to start running. They sped down the street, avoiding people and pushcarts, on the run once more. But as long as they were out in plain sight, there was no way Bataar could miss them.

'This way,' Wei said, tugging her towards the right. They ducked behind a pushcart that rolled by, its elderly owner oblivious to them as they slipped into the second alley they came by.

They wound deep into the deserted lane, keeping to the shadows and avoiding the murky glow of lanterns hung out on door fronts. Two sharp left turns and one right. Straight all the way, and then another right turn.

It was only when they were safely blanketed by the dark again that they slowed to a stop.

Desert Rose peered behind her, fear thrashing in her chest and the roar of adrenaline in her ears blocking out any sound. Chilly night air hit her lungs as soon as she caught her breath. She stifled a cough.

Wei's hand was warm around her shaking one. She let go and sank back against the wall, taking deep breaths to calm her racing heart. The stone wall against her back was cold but sobering. Wei propped a hand against the wall, shielding her from view. They peered down the alley, their ears pricked for the sound of footsteps, voices, anything. But there was only the whistle of cold wind and then . . . silence.

'I think we threw them off,' Wei said at length.

The proximity of his voice, deep and slightly ragged from exertion, made her jump. She turned to face him, and this time her breath caught in a way that made all the heat rush to her face. In the encroaching darkness, she saw only his silhouette. Her gaze trailed down the ridges of his cheekbones, his jawline, before snapping back to his eyes.

He was staring right back at her, his gaze wandering across her face, as though she were a book he could not comprehend. As though he wanted to drink in every word nonetheless. A snowflake rested on his eyelashes and slipped off when he blinked.

They were now close enough for her to feel his breath on her cheeks. If she tipped her toes, her lips would meet his.

The air in the alley suddenly felt too thin.

It occurred to her that she should feel afraid. Of him, of being alone in a dark alley with him. After all, she had seen the way he killed the soldier and the sand hound without blinking an eye. She had almost been at the receiving end of his ruthlessness too.

But she had also seen the way he nursed her fever and helped her purge poison from her wound. She had seen the sadness collected in the corners of his eyes and the loneliness that sat on his shoulders.

For some reason, too, he smelled of the desert, as though he hadn't quite left it behind. It was sharp and rough, like the hide of a wolf, but mixed with the musky scent of campfires and sweet mulled wine. In him, she caught a whiff of home again, and the ache in her chest grew so large it could have cracked her open then.

'I . . . I think we did,' she said. Her shaky voice reverberated between them like a shared breath.

He pushed away from the wall—slowly, carefully—as though trying not to shatter this strange, fragile moment. His eyes lingered on her, and she found herself unable to look away either.

Frigid air rushed in to fill the space that now lay between them. She shivered. Night was chasing away the remnant warmth of the day, and her tunic, though padded, was a poor defence against the raw winter cold.

They walked back in silence. It felt strangely comforting, wending through the quiet alleys with someone in the aftermath of danger. They were careful not to brush against each other in the narrower parts, Wei always taking a step back and letting her through first.

When they returned to the entrance of the first alley at last, Wei gestured for Desert Rose to stay behind him as he scanned the surroundings.

'They're gone,' he reported.

Desert Rose peered out, half-expecting Bataar to be standing right before her, ready to shoot her down like he had in the desert. But there was only the empty street lying wide before her. Shops had boarded up for the night, and the only people in sight were a pair of patrol guards chasing the homeless off the street.

She inched out of the alley, her heart easing back into a normal rhythm. She was safe, for now. Whatever Bataar's business here in the Capital was, she wouldn't have to face him as long as she was in the palace.

'Thank you,' she said to Wei.

Looking at him again brought back the dangerous rush she had felt in the alley. She turned away and started walking, trying to ignore the jumble of emotions she felt from seeing Bataar and that indefinable moment in the alley with Wei.

Wei's voice tailed her. 'Who was that?'

She paused, allowing silence to stretch between them, hoping it would be enough for Wei to drop it.

But he went on. 'The same person you were running from in the desert?'

She slowed to a stop by the canal. Willow trees dangled their ghostly, snow-dusted arms by the canal, caressing the skin of the water. Lanterns posted along the canal and hung along the rows of shops cast their crimson glow on the water. She watched the light dance upon the ripples, as she tried to find the words.

'You wanted to know what I'm doing here in the Capital,' she said. Wei waited, expectant, but she couldn't bring herself to explain more. 'He's one of the reasons. He's my enemy now.' She cut him off before he could ask any more questions. 'I have to get back.'

It was a long walk back, and there was always the chance that Bataar was still lying in wait for her. But the sooner she returned to the palace, the sooner she could put an end to this disastrous evening. It didn't matter that she still had no idea what Wei was doing on that roof. It hardly even mattered that she had failed her assignment now. All she wanted was a warm bath and some sleep.

'I'll give you a ride,' Wei said. She started to protest, but he cut her short. 'Trust me, we're going the same way.'

She understood only when she saw his horse.

It was the same steed that he had ridden on the way to the Capital, ebony and well-muscled, except it now wore the imperial saddle. Imprinted on the brown leather was the garish gold and red emblem that she had seen all around the palace.

She stared up at him, trying to see all the things she hadn't noticed before. His air, his dressing, his possessions—none of that had suggested that he might be royalty. 'You're . . .'

His reply was wry. 'I believe they call me the bastard prince around here.'

Thirteen

Wei

The House of Night had always been a mystery to Wei. He didn't know who belonged in it, had never seen anyone drafted, didn't even know where exactly it was hidden in the palace. All he knew was that it existed somewhere, and that it trained assassins.

So if he wanted to learn how someone could sneak into heavily guarded private quarters, this would be the place to do so.

Desert Rose had insisted that they parted ways at the palace gates, but Wei was not leaving until he managed to speak with the housemistress. At last, she conceded, muttering, 'Well, who am I to defy a prince now?'

'If it helps, everybody in the palace hates me.'

She only responded with a sulky silence.

'Would you have believed me if I told you I'm a prince?'

She whirled around to face him. 'No. And I don't care that you're a prince. Your lot was responsible for destroying my clan. You're lucky if I don't kill you in your sleep.'

He smirked. 'Give it your best shot. Just don't group me together with that lot.'

'Mingxi.' A sharp voice made them both jump. Wei straightened, turning to find the housemistress standing at the doorway of the manor. 'Prince Wei. How kind of you to return me my student.'

'I'll admit it was not an entirely altruistic gesture,' he said. 'I wish to speak in private with you, Housemistress.'

Without another word, she led them into the common room, where three other girls in identical blue tunics were already gathered before a fire blazing in the corner. They stared as he walked in—one of them was even slack-jawed. It was only when he came to a stop in centre of the room that everyone remembered their manners, bowed and greeted him in unison.

The housemistress regarded Desert Rose. 'Mingxi. You exceeded the time limit. For that, you have failed this assignment. But I will speak to you shortly. The rest of you are dismissed.'

'Yes, Shimu.' Desert Rose snuck a final glance at Wei before disappearing behind the back door with the other girls.

'Prince Wei, please have a seat,' said the housemistress.

Wei tore his gaze away from Desert Rose to meet the older lady's penetrating stare. He settled into the rosewood chair before him as the housemistress did the same from across the table. 'About Desert Rose—I mean, Mingxi—we—'

'With all due respect, Prince Wei, I hope you and the Fourth Prince will stay away from my charges. Your presence serves as a distraction for them, and they need to focus on the trials.'

'I understand.'

'Furthermore, with the palace in its current state of unrest, they are being deployed for patrol and security duties sooner than they are supposed to. They need to be training more intensively.'

'That's what I came to speak with you about, actually. I've surveyed every inch of Yong's chamber. The guards said they saw no one approach that night, and there is no way anyone can slip in unless they can become invisible or enter the gap between the windows that Yong left open, no wider than a finger. My father is adamant that this is the work of a supernatural being. I would like to hear *your* theory on this.'

'Going by his hypothesis, the first suspect would be'—she hesitated for a beat—'the *shouren*.'

Shouren. The shape-shifting beast-people had fled to the northern mountains after the great purge centuries ago. Everyone knew they still lived in the kingdom, but they were so good at evading capture that eventually the emperor gave up. That was until Wei's half-sister Qiu eloped with one of them from the fox clan a couple of years ago, creating a scandal that overshadowed Wei's exile. A *shouren* could easily shift into an ant, crawl through the window and shift back to human form to murder Yong in his chamber.

But Wei shook his head. 'No. The *shouren* are too weak and outnumbered to attempt something like this. Whoever dared to murder the Crown Prince must have powerful backing.'

'Perhaps. But it is one possibility to consider.'

'One more thing. Geshao—Desert Rose's mark tonight.' The housemistress stiffened. 'I'd like to see his dossier.'

'I'm afraid that's confidential, Prince Wei.'

'The emperor has given me permission to investigate my brother's death, Housemistress. I have reason to believe he is related to the case, whether directly or otherwise. Your assistance would be very much appreciated.'

The housemistress pursed her lips, but conceded. 'I will have it sent to you in the morning.' Her attention snapped to something over his shoulder. 'Fengying. What are you still doing here?'

The shadow lurking by the back door revealed itself to be one of the girls from earlier. Wei knew a desert girl when he saw one, and this one had the sharp, feral gaze of a desert fox and a faint sardonic air when she bowed in apology.

Another desert girl? Wei thought. Having one in the palace would cause enough of a scandal if word got out. Why did the emperor allow two of them in here?

'Sorry, Shimu. Left my clothes behind,' said the girl. She grabbed her civilian rags from the chair in front of her before leaving through the back door.

'Clearly, your charges require more disciplining,' Wei said, getting up. 'I shall leave you to it, then. Thank you for your time.'

The housemistress rose and bowed as he headed out the front door. He searched for a glimpse of Desert Rose, but she was nowhere in sight. Instead, he caught the other desert girl watching him leave, still lingering behind the back door, a fine dusting of sand at her feet.

*

Zeyan's letter came at dawn.

Wei had had no way of knowing where the crew was until his pet eagle tracked them down in the desert several days ago. How many of them had managed to escape after storming the palace with him? Zeyan's letter, now delivered by the eagle, didn't reveal that. It contained only four rows of words scribbled in urgent script.

Sandstorm imminent.

Steel enemies await opportune timing.

The well runs dry.

Beasts of the north stir the pot.

Wei read it thrice, then burned the letter.

Beasts of the north. Could the *shouren* really be behind the latest riot? Would they dare? If so, who was backing them?

There had to be something he was missing, a crucial link that would lead him to the answer. Even if each day brought them no closer to finding the spring (*the well runs dry*), the answer he wanted was somewhere among Geshao's late-night meeting, the impeccable timing of Yong's death, the dissolution of the desert clans (*sandstorm imminent*), and the ever-looming threat from the west (*steel enemies await opportune timing*).

Wei rushed down to the dungeon, only to find their cells empty.

'They have just been sent to the emperor,' the prison guard reported. 'For interrogation.'

Wei cursed under his breath. One step behind his father.

At the Hall of Justice, he found the emperor with the last few people he wanted to see—Mian, Empress Wangyi, and Meng. They were seated on the podium, Meng and the empress on either side of the emperor and Mian hovering in the back near the empress. Before them were the two prisoners on their knees, their hands and feet chained. The man growled, but the woman remained unnerved, staring straight ahead at the emperor. Despite her matted hair and tattered prison garb, a stark contrast against the gaudy lavishness of the hall, she seemed poised, almost regal.

'Oh, good. I'm not too late,' Wei said.

The emperor and his company stiffened at the sight of him. Wei sauntered in and stood next to the prisoners. They glanced at him and shared a look between them, like they weren't sure what to make of his sudden arrival.

'Wei,' the empress said with a tight smile. 'This is a private interrogation.'

Wei directed a pointed stare at her. 'My apologies. I presumed we're all family here.'

'It's all right, he can stay.' The emperor gave her a placid smile. 'He shall learn about protocol for prisoners. Adviser, please.'

Mian stepped forward with a bowl of water and a few leaves floating in it. He fished out the leaves—bright green with jagged edges—and pressed it to the male prisoner's neck. The leaf sizzled almost instantly, smoking at the edges and turning dark green. The man squeezed his eyes shut and gritted his teeth, but as the effect of the *ticha* leaf wore on, he let out a cry.

When he opened his eyes again, they had turned into the striking gold hue of a tiger's. He bared his canines as black stripes flickered on his orange-hued skin. A guttural moan escaped him as he began to shake from head to toe.

'Stop,' the woman cried at last. 'You'll kill him.'

Mian continued to pin the *ticha* leaf against the man's neck as the others watched on, silent and impassive. Wei caught Meng's eye, but his brother turned away from his accusing stare.

This time, the man let out another agonized cry that sounded more animal than human in nature. His companion pressed close to him. 'Stay with me, Bo,' she pleaded.

Wei reached over and grabbed Mian's hand, dragging it away from the man's neck. 'You heard her.'

Mian dropped the charred, smoking leaf, recoiling from Wei. With a huge shudder, the *shouren* reverted to human form and slumped forward on all fours. His chains clinked as he trembled, shoulders heaving, and his breaths escaped short and heavy.

Mian bowed to the emperor. 'Your suspicions were correct, Your Majesty. *Shouren.*'

The emperor's expression darkened. Next to him, Meng and the empress exchanged a tense glance. After Qiu's scandal two winters ago, Wei heard that the emperor had gone so far as to hunt the *shouren* down in the Yeli mountains, but to no avail.

The emperor leaned forward in his seat. 'You dare instigate a riot on my turf? How many more of you are there? Who organized the riot?'

'Bite me,' the man growled.

The emperor nodded at Mian. A cry ripped through Bo again as Mian pressed the leaf to his neck.

'We can do this all day, beast,' said the emperor. 'Or you can cut short your suffering and answer me truthfully.'

Bo spat on the marbled ground. 'I'd rather die. You're only trying to beat us down because you're afraid of our magic. You will never—' His ashen face twisted into a grimace. His skin flickered, shifting into the striped fur of a tiger, as he took a shuddering breath. The *ticha* leaf was destroying his human form.

The woman wrapped an arm around him. 'Stay with me, Bo.'

When she looked up at Wei, her once stoic gaze was now blurred by a sheen of tears. 'Please, help him.'

'Who organized the riot?' the emperor demanded.

She pursed her lips, torn. Next to her, Bo let out a growl, glaring at Wei. 'Don't tell them anything, Shaoxi.'

'Perhaps you would prefer to watch your home burn? I wonder how many of your kind will be driven out of Yeli mountain if I have it razed.'

'You can kill us both now, but you will never find the rest of us,' said the woman.

'Very well.' The emperor nodded at Mian. 'Prepare for execution.' Wei barely managed to protest before the prison guards dragged the *shouren* away. This time, Shaoxi did not look back at him. 'And send a team to Yeli mountain. I want no bodies left.'

'This is a little extreme, even for you,' said Wei.

'They've lived on *my* land for long enough. I should have had them all killed before . . .'

There had been no news of Princess Qiu ever since she was last spotted in the Yeli forest, but Wei took that to be good news. It meant his younger half-sister was well hidden, living her best life with the fox clan.

'So you're going to wipe out an entire race of people based on a personal grudge?' he said.

'This is *my* kingdom. And this is more than a personal grudge. They are threatening the peace.'

'You mean they're threatening your rule,' Wei said quietly.

'Perhaps you should leave the decision-making to the actual ruler of this kingdom, Wei,' said Empress Wangyi.

The emperor knew his own daughter was with them and he was going to burn the mountain anyway. What did he care about the rest of the *shouren*?

Wei tightened his fists. This was how his father meant to punish him—for stepping out of line, for standing up to him, for helping the 'outsiders'. This was how his father meant to show him how powerless he was and would always be as long as he was not the ruler of Oasis Kingdom.

Sometimes, Wei actually considered getting on that damn throne himself.

Fourteen

Desert Rose

Ever since her first duel with Shuang, Desert Rose had been looking forward to another round of combat training. Restless energy rattled inside her, and a good duel was what she needed to get it out.

But when she came blade to blade with Shuang again, she found herself distracted by thoughts of the previous night.

What had Golsha taken from her tribe that the other man wanted? What hand did they have in the tribe rebellion and what were they planning? What was Wei doing on that roof?

Thoughts of *that* moment in the alley with Wei also kept crossing her mind as she fended off Shuang's blows.

What was it about him that took her home to the desert? It was, for some reason, comforting, in a different way from Prince Meng's tea. If Prince Meng was a gentle ripple in a pond, Wei was a desert storm. His eyes flashed like both a warning and a beacon, and his hand was as warm as the air in the prelude to the storm.

A shriek of metal yanked her back to the present, just in time for her to register Shuang's sword. She spun aside as it whistled past her ear, then rolled to the ground, ready to throw her leg out to trip Shuang—but found herself pinned to the throat at sword point. Shuang's lips curved into a slow, victorious smirk.

'Desert Rose,' Shuang taunted, dragging out her name. 'I know you think you can saunter in here on Prince Meng's back, get a couple of princes to fall for you, and cheat your way to the trials. But I see right through you, desert girl. You are nothing but a fraud, and you will bring shame to your people.'

Rage burned white-hot in her. How dared this Capital girl presume anything about her people? Shuang was born and bred within this walled city—what would she know about shame? Shame was not being able to save her tribe when it fell apart before her eyes, shame was running like a coward when her father was being captured.

Desert Rose knocked Shuang's blade aside and flipped to her feet. Her own pair of knives had been strewn across the courtyard beyond her reach. How had she allowed her opponent to render her in such a wretched state?

Windshadow, who had been sparring with Xiyue at the other end of the courtyard, shot her a sympathetic glance.

'Mingxi.' Shimu's face was taut with disapproval. 'If you have neither the aptitude nor the desire to be here, I suggest you save us all the time and effort and take yourself out of the running,' said the housemistress. '*Again.*'

Desert Rose collected her weapons and turned back to her opponent. Shuang stepped forward, twirling her swords in a showy pattern before settling into her fight stance. Her lips curled into a smirk. Desert Rose held out her knives before her, tracking and mimicking Shuang's footwork. She would not slip this time.

They crashed into each other in a flurry of steel.

Desert Rose went on the offensive, pouring all her rage and frustration into every attack. Her knives whirled in a blur around her, throwing shards of reflected sunlight across the training ground. Shuang struck back with her usual fervour, leaving no room for Desert Rose to think, only act on instinct.

They parried back and forth with their blades until Desert Rose spun around and aimed a swift kick at Shuang's back. Shuang stumbled towards a pillar. By the time she whirled around, Desert Rose already had her backed against the pillar with an arm pressed against her jugular. Shuang's gasp of shock turned into a struggle for air.

'Maybe I *am* a fraud,' said Desert Rose, leaning close to her. 'Maybe I didn't earn my place in this House. But we'll see who's the last girl standing at the trials.'

Shuang's glare was fiery, but she could only gurgle in response.

As Shimu strode towards them, Desert Rose slowly released Shuang. 'Good work, Mingxi,' said the housemistress. 'But your consistency needs work.'

'Yes, Shimu,' said Desert Rose.

'Fengying,' Shimu called. Windshadow paused in her sparring with Xiyue and came over to join them. 'I would like you to duel with Mingxi.'

Liqin, who had been practising with her fans by the side, sidled over to Desert Rose with a smirk. 'Wait till you experience this one. You won't know what hit you.'

The other girls stepped aside as Windshadow and Desert Rose stood facing each other.

Crouching low with her lone dagger, Windshadow bared her teeth in a smile. 'Let's see what you've got, *azzi*.'

She pounced. But in a flash, she was out of sight. Desert Rose whipped around, every muscle tensed for a surprise attack, but her opponent was nowhere to be seen. Then, quick as the wind, Windshadow reappeared right before her with a dagger aimed straight for her heart.

Desert Rose leaped out of the way, but not before the blade caught her tunic and ripped down her sleeve. Desert Rose did a double take at the blood oozing from a gash in her right arm. Shuang's attacks seemed tame in comparison to Windshadow's vicious one.

'I did say I'm far ahead of all of you,' Windshadow said before dissolving into a blur and vanishing from sight again. Her next attack came as a swift kick in Desert Rose's back, followed by a slash to the waist.

Desert Rose sprawled onto the ground, clutching her side. Blood leaked past her fingers. She grunted in frustration as she got to her feet, ignoring Shuang and Liqin sniggering by the side. Shimu only watched in silence, lips pursed.

Focus, Rose. She scanned the ground, the walls, even the sky for any sign of her opponent's shadow. But all was quiet, and there was no sign of Windshadow. Perspiration streamed down her face, but she kept still and let her senses take over.

A cool rush of air whipped past her neck. She spun around, but immediately received a kick in the chest. The ground slammed against her back, knocking the air out of her lungs.

And then Windshadow's dagger was at her throat.

How did she do it? How was she able to move like that, so swift and undetectable? Where had she trained to fight this way? Desert Rose had seen the northern *tsalkhi* warriors in combat—they relied on speed and precision to wear out their opponents. She had witnessed the best fighters in her tribe battle with inexorable stamina and flawless technique.

But nothing she had encountered came close to this.

At the end of the session, Shimu instructed Desert Rose to get her wounds seen to by a court healer. But as the other girls left to wash up before dinner, Desert Rose lingered behind in the courtyard with Windshadow.

'The wound's not too deep, so don't worry,' Windshadow said, reaching over to pat her good arm. 'It'll heal within—'

On reflex, Desert Rose pulled her arm away. Her father had always told her the rate at which she healed was a little faster than normal—possibly because of all the holy *mukh* water the tribe healers fed her when she was a child. Her tribespeople didn't think much of it (there were far more unnatural things in the desert, after all), but here in the Capital, they just might stone her for being abnormal.

But Windshadow only glanced at her already healing wounds and said, 'Well. Looks like you're ready for another duel, then.'

Desert Rose mirrored Windshadow's hungry grin and readied herself without hesitation.

They were about to dive in on each other when Windshadow's attention shifted to something over Desert Rose's shoulder. She straightened and bowed. 'Your Highness.'

Desert Rose whirled around to find Prince Meng standing at the entrance of the courtyard, dressed in a royal blue robe that brightened up the austere setting. He strode towards them, serene and purposeful, his gaze pinned on her even as he said to Windshadow, 'My apologies for interrupting. I would like a word with Mingxi, please.'

Windshadow bowed. 'Of course, Your Highness.' She turned to leave, but not before shooting Desert Rose a meaningful smirk.

Desert Rose tugged at her tunic to straighten it, aware of how dishevelled she looked after sparring with Windshadow.

'You're injured?' he said, gesturing at her blood-stained clothes.

She shifted her arm out of his sight. 'Just a scratch.'

He surveyed her wounds and torn clothing but did not press further. 'Desert Rose.' It was the tightness in his voice that made her heart pick up speed. 'I'm here to talk about your previous mission.'

'You mean with Ge—'

He shushed her sharply, but his voice was gentle when he spoke. 'You were spotted spying on Geshao. Your mark has been alerted.'

Shimu had already driven the point home the night before, when she detailed the ways Desert Rose had failed her assignment.

But instead of rebuking her like Shimu did, Prince Meng said, 'I brought you here because you wanted to speak with the emperor. I would hate to be the one who put you in harm's way.'

'You might have brought me to the House of Night, but I chose to compete in the trials. I chose to take part in the trainings. And Geshao was my mark, my assignment. I want to see it through.'

'Why?'

She paused. Shimu had asked the same question, when she had requested to keep Geshao as her mark despite failing her assignment. Under the housemistress's interrogative stare, she hadn't been able to answer, not without revealing the past she had been trying so hard to hide.

But there was neither distrust nor wariness in Prince Meng's eyes. He wasn't already expecting a desert girl like her to betray him, and he had come to her when no one else cared.

The truth slipped out of her lips before she could think twice. 'That night, I overheard his conversation. He might have news of my father.'

'That's the reason you came to the Capital? To find your father?'

She nodded. The familiar unease and worry started gnawing at her again.

'Is he in danger?'

She nodded again, her throat tightening. Prince Meng reached out and laid a gentle hand on her shoulder. He didn't push for an answer, but the sympathy in his eyes made her words spill out.

'My father was overthrown at the turn of winter. Last I saw him, he was taken by the clan leaders. We were supposed to meet here in the Capital.'

This was the most she had revealed to anyone in the Capital about her situation. The palace seemed like the last place she should let her guard down, but it felt like a relief to finally unload all the anxiety sitting on her chest. And Prince Meng had been nothing but kind to her since she came to the Capital.

'So you're the princess of the Dugur tribe,' he said.

She cracked a smile. 'We don't go by princes and princesses. I'm just the chieftain's daughter. My father's daughter.' The lump in her throat made her choke on the last part.

His hand fell away from her shoulder and he turned away. 'As far as I know, the clan leaders have already appointed Blackstone as the new chieftain, and they have allied with the emperor to find the spring.' His gaze crept back to her. 'Last I heard . . .'

Dread crept into her heart, but she needed to hear it, whatever it was he was holding back. 'Tell me. Please.'

'Last I heard, the emperor has killed the leader of the Dugur tribe.'

To conquer your enemies, you must first understand them.

—Snow Wolf Sect teaching

Fifteen

Wei

As he wandered through the palace grounds, Wei's thoughts churned up a storm in his head. The sun had relinquished the last of its feeble rays for night to settle in. Snowflakes drifted down from the indigo sky, and Wei found his thoughts drifting to Desert Rose in the alley that night, snowflakes in her hair and fear in her eyes. She couldn't have been the one who killed Yong. The timing did not match up. Besides, what motive would she have for doing so?

He wandered through the gardens, past the snow-capped bonsais and frozen obsidian pond, around the Hall of Valour . . . and found himself at the House of Night.

In this remote part of the palace, the carpet of snow on the pavement was thick enough to mute the sound of his footsteps.

The housemistress would loathe seeing him again. So instead of entering through the double doors, he went round the back, where he had discovered a narrow door obscured by bramble the last time he was here.

The door inched opened with some coaxing, revealing a hedge-lined path that led to the courtyard, where Wei found Desert Rose practising with her double knives despite the falling snow.

She was alone; the housemistress and the other girls were nowhere to be seen. Why was she training alone out here at this hour?

She moved like a blizzard, swinging her knives at an invisible opponent. Snow danced in a flurry around her, and her figure shifted in the gloom along to the ringing of her blades.

It was then that he saw, with sudden clarity, what he had been blind to all this time.

He thought he would never see her again, the desert girl who had saved his life all those years ago, offered him shelter and warmth on that freezing night, chasing away the fear that he would die out in the desert alone. But there she was, that once chatty little girl now focused and iron-willed.

Wei was about to call out to her when he realized her eyes were red-rimmed, her movements too unrestrained, almost reckless. Twice she stumbled and skidded on the frosted ground, panting heavily as she righted herself.

How long had she been going at it? Probably far too long, given her flushed, sweaty face and the way she winced every time she thrust and struck. Something was wrong. She moved with wild abandon, technique be damned, throwing too much strength into her moves. Her feet made erratic tracks across the snow as she skirted around the courtyard.

Wei snuck past her and headed down the corridor into the armoury, where the door was left ajar, and reached for the nearest sword hanging on the wall before dashing out to join her.

She didn't notice him until he drew his sword and their blades clashed. The scream of metal rang out in the muted night. Her fury seemed to intensify at the sight of him. She shoved him back, swiping her other knife at him, but he dodged with little effort—she wasn't catching him off guard with such predictable moves.

'What's gotten into you?' he yelled.

She didn't reply, just continued charging at him with the fervour of a wild cat. He ducked and deflected blow after blow, never once attacking, even though he could easily have disarmed her, given how blindly she was going.

'Rose, talk to me!' he roared.

But nothing could get through to her. Around the courtyard they went, until at last she threw her arm out too hard and lost her balance. She let out a cry as she crumpled to the ground, her knives clattering by her side.

It wasn't until he went closer that he saw the tear tracks on her face and her heaving shoulders.

He set down his sword. 'Rose.'

'The emperor killed my father. Prince Meng told me.' Her voice was ragged as a fresh scar. She looked up at him, her eyes brimming with fresh tears. She seemed far from the feisty desert girl who had battled a sand hound and fought alongside him against the imperial soldiers. In that moment, she was simply a girl who had lost her father, the man who had saved Wei's life years ago.

He struggled for the right words, but none came. There was nothing he could do for her. He could make Meng pay for upsetting her with the news. He could even storm into his father's chamber and demand to know what exactly he had done to the chieftain.

But none of that would change a thing. Nothing he did or said now could lessen her pain, helplessness or frustration. He saw in her eyes everything he had felt at Yong's funeral and in the prison before his mother's cell.

All he could do was wrap an arm around her, making sure to not aggravate her shoulder, and help her to her feet. 'Come on, let's get you out of the cold.'

She remained where she was. 'You once told me not to group you with your family. But will you stand with them in the end? Because I won't let my father die in vain.'

He understood what she meant to do. In her gaze was the same fire that had fuelled him after Yong's death. But her killing the emperor would mean Meng ascending the throne. And there was no way his mother would be pardoned once Empress Wangyi became empress dowager.

As much as he wanted his father's rule to end, he couldn't let Desert Rose do it now without risking both his mother's life and hers.

'The wars of my father are not mine to fight. But if you kill him, my mother will suffer a worse fate. I cannot let you.'

Her eyes flashed. She shoved him away. 'You cannot *let* me? You can try and save your mother, but I'm not supposed to do anything to avenge my father?'

'If you kill the emperor, you will be charged for the highest crime in the kingdom and executed without trial.'

'I don't care. He needs to pay for what he's done to my tribe.'

'If you die, there will be nothing more you can do for your tribe!' he roared.

Her shoulders sagged, the fight seeping out of her. It made him want to pull her to him, but he only laid a hand on her shoulder and said softly, 'I'm sorry.'

And he was. He was sorry she had to go through all this, losing her home and her family. He was sorry for not being able to help her, for not recognizing her sooner and helping her find her father, for getting in her way of revenge.

'I'm not saying there's nothing you can do,' he said. 'I know you want revenge, but now's not the time yet. But I can promise you this: the ones who robbed us of our family, we will make them pay.'

She made no response. But when he picked her up the second time, she did not resist. He led her back to the common room, where the housemistress stood watching them from the doorway, stone-faced and silent.

'She needs some rest,' he told the housemistress. 'And see that her shoulder is tended to.' With a final glance at Desert Rose, he turned to leave before the housemistress could raise any questions.

*

Two things arrived the next morning.

The first was the news from an unknown messenger: the desert tribes had found a fresh lead to the spring.

This would be a new spring of hope that revived a long-parched dream, one that Wei knew the emperor would seize. And with any luck, it would take the emperor at least a month to realize he had sent his men on a wild goose chase, buying Wei the time he needed. And sure enough, the emperor immediately deployed a troop of soldiers to follow up on the lead that Wei had planted.

The second thing that arrived, almost fully formed, was his plan to find the *shouren*. He had lain awake in bed for the better part of the night before finally drifting off into a shallow sleep. At first light, he leaped out of bed and craned his neck for his eagle's arrival.

Of course, he wasn't naive enough to think he could take up conditional residence under his father's roof and not be under surveillance. But as soon as he stepped out of the Red Circle, he could already feel eyes on him—

'Are you going somewhere, brother?'

Wei let out a sigh. He turned around to find Meng less than five feet behind him, watching him with his curious, placid stare that for some reason always irked him. Meng, the model son with perfectly pressed robes and perfect scores in the imperial exams, never had to fight or beg for his place in the world. His destiny was there within reach, as bright as the star that rose on the night he was born. How was it that the two of them, born on the same night, could have such vastly different fortunes?

'Half-brother,' Wei corrected him. He continued walking out of the Red Circle, heading for the stables.

'Father wanted me to keep an eye on you.'

He snorted, not breaking his stride. 'Well, that's new.'

'You know I have to inform him that you're leaving the palace,' Meng called after him. 'You won't go far before the imperial scouts start tailing you.'

'Don't you ever get tired of doing his bidding?'

'It is our duty to—'

'Give me a break.' Wei whirled around. 'We both know you don't give a damn about your duty to him. Whatever you and your mother are planning serves only you both. I always thought you were just weak, but I never knew you were this cruel. You're going to do exactly what the old man tells you to, even if it's wiping out a whole people, including Qiu?'

'Our sister chose her own fate when she joined the *shouren*.'

Wei shook his head. 'If you're not careful, you'll turn out just like him.'

His eyes flashed. 'Maybe so,' he said. 'But at least I have a place where I belong.'

He didn't understand. Anywhere was better than here. Wei would rather wander in the wilderness forever than belong in a place like this.

'That's not belonging,' he said. 'That's hiding.'

'Perhaps you're not the only one trying to survive here. You and I just have different means of doing so.'

Wei raised his brows. 'I suppose your means involves putting others in danger.' He didn't have to say it out loud; they both knew he was referring to Desert Rose.

Meng stiffened. 'What does that have to do with—'

'Why did you bring her into the palace? Why did you send her to the House of Night? What exactly are you planning, Meng?'

Meng tightened his jaw and looked Wei in the eye. 'All I'm planning is to save my family and this kingdom.'

Regardless of who gets caught in the crossfire.

Wei was the last person who could change his brother's mind, and he wasn't going to waste his time trying. 'Well, then don't stop me from saving mine.'

In another life, they might have been brothers in arms. But their fates had set them on diverging paths from the moment they were born, and there was no hope of them ever standing on the same side.

'Tell the emperor not to wait up for me,' Wei called over his shoulder as he turned to leave. It was time to pay the *shouren* a visit.

Sixteen

Desert Rose

Days flew by. Weeks. And before any of them realized it, they were only a month away from the trials.

Desert Rose kept to a daily routine that saw her waking up two hours before dawn to memorize her well-thumbed textbooks, attending classes and completing assignments (often coming out top of the class), duelling with Windshadow (occasionally defeating her), and finally squeezing in some more time with her books by lamplight before going to bed.

Even Windshadow remarked one evening as they practised, 'Rose, calm down. You're starting to scare me. And that's a feat.'

There was no room for her mind to drift, no time to dwell on her sorrow. All that mattered was getting through the trials, making it to the Spring Ceremony, and meeting the emperor.

And then she would make him pay.

If the housemistress and the other girls noticed a marked shift in her behaviour, they neither commented on it nor probed. Shuang and Liqin whispered behind her back and cast sidelong glances at her as usual, and Shuang continued to toss barbed remarks at her, but those rolled off Desert Rose's back like water. Anything that didn't get her closer to the emperor was irrelevant.

Ever since he found her in the courtyard that evening, Wei had not visited the House of Night—nor had she ventured beyond those grounds. But she couldn't shake the feeling that something was brewing beyond the palace walls—perhaps even beyond the Capital gates—that would soon catch up with her.

Prince Meng, however, came by a couple of times, each time under the pretext of checking on their progress, until Shimu told him that the girls needed to train in isolation.

One evening, he finally found Desert Rose in the draughty classroom alone, after the Blue Cranes were dismissed for dinner. She rose from her seat to greet him as soon as he stepped into the room, but he held out a hand to stop her, then gestured for her to sit. She did so gingerly, observing him.

'I want to apologize for upsetting you the other day,' he said, pulling out a chair next to her and settling into it. 'That was not my intention.'

She shook her head. 'Thank you for telling me.'

'Will you continue to compete in the trials then? Serving as the emperor's personal guard is probably the last thing you want to do now.'

'I will.' She offered nothing more, keeping her face as blank as possible when he searched it for answers.

He glanced down the books scattered on the desk before her, then gave her a smile, gentle as the snow that drifted against the window. The sight made the manic, restless energy in her quiet down for the first time in weeks.

'A word of advice?' he said, motioning to someone at the door. 'It never helps to study with a frazzled mind.'

A maid entered, bearing a tray of tea for two. She set the tray on the table and served them both before retreating.

Prince Meng handed Desert Rose a teacup filled with a steaming, fragrant blend. It smelled floral, tasted a little sweeter than she expected, and reminded her of the brew her father used to make for her whenever she fell sick, only less bitter. As soon as she took her first sip, tension slipped from her body and a deep calm washed over her.

She nursed the cup in her hand, grateful for its warmth. 'Why do you keep helping me? I am just a desert girl you found at the gates.'

He fell into a pensive silence. Desert Rose took a sip of her tea, trying not to stare at his profile.

'Maybe because I secretly wish I were as brave as you,' he said at last.

He must be joking. He, a prince, calling a girl chased out of her tribe brave?

'You came all the way here to find your father, to fight for your tribe.' He brought his cup to his lips. 'I think you're stronger than you realize.'

Heat rushed to her cheeks. She hid her face behind her teacup and took another sip of tea. 'Is there nothing you'd fight for?'

His brows pulled together, the first hint of distress she had ever seen him reveal. 'This kingdom is crumbling. The riots during the Crown Prince's funeral are an indication of the growing dissent among the people. I will do what I can to save it.'

'By your definition, that makes you brave too.'

He shook his head. 'After Wei, I'm the next in line to be Crown Prince. Father has decreed that I will take on the title.'

She cocked her head. 'You don't sound very happy about it.'

'It's not something to be happy about. A Crown Prince is just a figurehead; there's not much I can do in that position that would bring about any significant change. Worse, I would be under greater scrutiny, with a tighter rein around my neck.'

'It must be tiring to carry around a title like that and its responsibility.'

'This is the life we were born into. You could say it's our destiny. We live to fulfil what's written in our stars.'

A snort escaped her. 'I don't believe in destiny. I believe we are the makers of our own lives and are only as free as we allow ourselves to be.'

'Maybe.' He smiled, but somehow seemed sadder. She hadn't realized it before, but there was a weariness in his eyes that she had seen in Wei's too. Were they both living under the weight of their so-called destinies?

Prince Meng set down his tea. 'I like to believe I can change some things while I'm here though.' His voice was charged with renewed conviction. 'My father's ideals are outdated and impractical, and it's hard to change his mind once it's set. But what good does it do for us to hide behind our walls against our magic-wielding neighbours? In these troubled times, regardless of how strong we are in trade and commerce, we will perish.'

'Your history books don't quite agree with that view.' She eyed her textbook splayed out before her, the text written in tight rows of script, characters packed together in a condensed version of the truth. 'They seem very critical of the magic that my people, and the rest of the world, practise. Apparently, we're the villains who threaten your borders and safety. I can't believe I'm getting tested on this garb—' She caught herself and snuck a nervous glance at him.

He laughed. 'It's okay. Don't censor yourself on my account.'

She had never heard him laugh before. It reminded her of campfire nights in the desert during winter, when she felt warm inside despite the bitter cold. A smile worked its way to her lips, slow and easy, like letting go of a bated breath.

'Tell me about the desert,' he said, pouring her more tea. 'Your gods, demons, magic, lore, rituals, customs.'

It felt good to think about home again. Talking about it made it feel closer, like there was no Wall in between, like the past few months were a bad dream she could chase away, one story at a time.

She told him about Khasov, the Ghost Festival where they prayed for harmony between spirits and humans, and Tsagen Sol, where they gave thanks to the gods for light and wisdom in the new year. She told him about the shamans who called upon the elements to aid them in their healing rituals. She told him about Anar Zel, the official tribal matriarch who once said, with no little amount of exasperation, that Desert Rose would much sooner leap into a skirmish with the clan boys than lead the tribal dance like the chieftain's daughter was supposed to. She told him about how they communicated with the heavens by reading the stars and lighting bonfires in a pattern. She told him about their magic, what her tribe called the natural arts, where they drew on their internal energies and the elements to destroy and heal, make and unmake. She told him how she once got lost in the desert for a week and almost died before she found her way to a water source that led her back home.

Prince Meng was a rapt audience, leaning in when she described the magic that the Kingdom had deprived him of. He drank in every detail like a parched wanderer in the desert. In him, there was none of his father's contempt for magic, only a keen scholarly wonder.

By the time they had finished their tea, the candle next to them was burning low, their last defence against the encroaching night. An icy breeze whistled through the ajar window. She had more stories to share, but Meng told her they had time the next evening. And the evening after that.

'Thank you,' she blurted.

Surprise flickered across his face. 'For what?'

'For . . . being a friend.' She wanted to say more, but this would do for now.

His face was unreadable. Had she overstepped the line? Was she being too presumptuous?

But a smile broke upon his face, reaching up to his eyes. A moment stretched between them. A glance turned into a gaze. The silence spoke more than they did. He reached over and laid his hand over hers. Over her callused knuckles, his skin felt comparatively smooth.

He leaned closer, his head tilted as though he might kiss her. Her breath caught. She willed her fluttering heart to calm down, but it did not obey. He had always kept a polite distance from her, but now that space between them had never been narrower.

Just as she was about to close that gap, he pulled away. A frown appeared between his brows. Cool air rushed in, filling the space where he had been a moment ago. Desert Rose blinked and straightened.

Prince Meng retracted his hand and kept it by his side. 'I'm sorry,' he said. But instead of explaining, he offered a wan smile and said they should call it a night.

They packed up her books in silence, lost in their own thoughts.

Meng walked her back to the common room and lingered at the door. 'I'll—I'll see you tomorrow.' He looked like he meant to say more, but seemed to think better of it. He brushed her cheek with a hand and turned to leave before she could respond.

Shimu was waiting in the shadows at the back of the common room, blocking her way to the dormitory. 'As long as you are at the House of Night, your duty comes before anything else. Any unbecoming behaviour will not be pardoned.' She narrowed her eyes at Desert Rose. 'Do I make myself clear?'

'Perfectly, Shimu.'

The housemistress stepped aside to let her retire to the dormitory.

But even Shimu's warning could not chase away the warmth that lingered in her. It could have been the tea, or the softness of Meng's touch, but for the first time that night since she received the news of her father, she fell asleep like falling into an embrace.

Seventeen

Meng

He had shared too much with her. The first thing that *The Art of Combat* taught was to never let your guard down, whether against a friend or a foe.

But why did it always have to be a combat? Why did everyone have to be a foe? Meng couldn't remember the last time he had spilled his heart open to someone. He felt, more than usual, tired of measuring his every step, taking care to never slip up.

And he had slipped up tonight. For the first time in his entire life, he had allowed himself to entertain the thought of a life without the weight of his destiny on his shoulders, where he could live and love as freely as he wished. And it took a girl from the desert to make him dream of a life as someone other than the Fourth Prince.

But that was not a dream he could afford. His fate was written in the stars. He was an arrow launched at birth, and he could not miss his mark. He had come too close to telling Desert Rose that. Would she still think he was brave then? Would she understand?

Meng shook his head. Of course she wouldn't. She was foreign to the ways of the palace. She didn't understand that every move had to be well calculated if one were to survive. She wouldn't understand that everyone had to play the game, whether or not they wanted to. Wei had turned his back on this, and all he did was stab himself in the foot.

Still, it had felt like a relief to just be free of all the secrets and lies that grew inside him like diseased roots—if only for a while.

Desert Rose was nothing like the giggly handmaids and Capital girls, or the foreign princesses who bored him with their incessant questions and shallow conversation. Those girls were flowers in a manicured garden, waiting to be plucked. Desert Rose was a storm, one that pressed closer each time he was around her. And tonight, he felt closer to the eye of the storm than he ever had. What would he have done, had he not stopped himself in time just now?

He was approaching his private quarters when two figures appeared before him, dimly lit by a feeble lamp one of them was carrying.

'Mother. Adviser Mian.' Meng tried to even out the surprise in his voice. 'What calls for an unescorted visit at this hour?'

'Clearly, it's not too late for you to be out either,' his mother countered.

'I got carried away in the library. Nothing like some tea and a good book to make one lose track of time. But let's not stand in the cold. Please, come in.'

He walked behind them, mentally running through a list of possible reasons for their unannounced visit but coming up short. *Does she know I went to see Desert Rose?* He was certain she didn't, but here she was, for whatever reason.

In his chamber, his mother settled into the chair next to the bookshelf while Mian hovered behind her. Meng remained standing across the desk from her.

'You need to spend more time preparing to be Crown Prince, not with your books,' his mother said. 'The ceremony is in spring. That should be your top priority now.'

His priority now was to make sure the nobles didn't instigate an uprising among the lower castes and upset the precarious peace in the kingdom. His priority now was to learn as much as he could about what lay beyond the kingdom and prepare for the imminent attack.

The last thing he cared about was his title.

But he said, 'Yes, Mother.' There was no sense arguing with her now, not when he was still disorientated by his conversation with Desert Rose.

'Geshao's position has been compromised,' his mother said. 'It's time we cut off some loose ends.'

Meng suppressed a sigh. It always came to this—loose ends that needed to be cut off with each manoeuvre. Each time, it got trickier. Geshao was their strongest link to the desert tribes, their eyes and ears to make sure the clan leaders stayed in line. They had already been caught off guard by the riot during Yong's funeral ceremony, a move undoubtedly instigated by the clan leaders, even if the *shouren* prisoners refused to confess.

A brave person would be better than this. If he were as brave as Desert Rose thought he was, he would walk in the light, try to make a change as honourably as he could, instead of relying on night-time meetings and dealings with mercenaries. If he were Wei, he might storm out, declaring he wanted no part of this.

But as noble as those options were, they would accomplish nothing. The kingdom's borders would still be threatened, and the people would continue to be at the mercy of his father's greed and paranoia.

'Meng?'

He blinked. 'Yes, Mother.'

'Is there going to be a problem?'

'Must we get rid of Geshao? I mean,' he hurried to add as his mother's gaze sharpened, 'he is a strategic ally. We might put ourselves at a disadvantage if we remove this middleman.'

She rose to her feet and managed to pin him under her stare despite her smaller stature. 'We must not be implicated in this. If the emperor learns that we have been working with the clan leaders behind his back, he will most certainly rescind his decision to make you Crown Prince.'

'Everything must go according to plan,' Mian urged from the side. 'The emperor's position is shaky now because of the famine—the people are losing faith in him. This is the best time for you to ascend, Fourth Prince.'

'We have worked so hard to arrive at this point,' said his mother. 'Are you going to let your conscience hold you back now?'

'No, Mother,' Meng said. 'Of course not.'

Her eyes softened. 'Remember what we are doing all this for, Meng. I've already lost Han and Qiu. We are the only ones left.'

How could he forget, when all she talked about was piecing this family back together again and bringing Queen Luzhen to her knees?

'Luzhen will pay for what she did,' she said. 'Her little stay in prison now is nothing compared to the exile Han is enduring. In the meantime, we need to keep fighting, and we can't do it unless you have the power to.' She laid a hand against his cheek. 'You are my biggest hope, Meng. The kingdom needs you. I need you. You have to finish what your father started.'

'That will be your greatest legacy, Fourth Prince,' Mian said. 'The star you were born under remains bright, outshining all others.'

His mother took his hand. 'This is the destiny you were born to achieve. Do you understand?'

His jaw tightened. His destiny felt like an anchor he could never be free of, but someone had to save this kingdom. He pushed all remaining thoughts of Desert Rose to the back of his mind. There was no room for dreams in his life.

'I understand,' he said.

His mother peered into his eyes. 'So will Geshao be a problem?'

He shook his head. 'I'll see to it.'

Eighteen

Wei

A long time ago, before the Wall was erected and magic was purged from Oasis Kingdom, the *shouren* had lived in peace with everyone else, walking among non-magic folk as equals.

But after the first Oasis ruler sealed the kingdom's borders against the warring neighbours, the *shouren* were declared as 'dangerous and volatile' and 'a threat to the values we uphold'. The persecuted shapeshifters then fled the city and headed for the northern forests.

Before the riot at Yong's funeral, no one had seen a *shouren* in years. The last sighting was on a blood-moon night many springs ago, when one of the wolf-men was reported to have lost control and shifted, killing three villagers in the forest. The emperor sent troops to hunt them down, forcing them deeper into hiding.

Further and further they retreated, until they reached the boundaries of the kingdom and could only go underground. Some said they had burrowed so deep into the heart of the earth that their calls could only be heard on a rare blood-moon night when they ventured above ground.

Never mind that there were more than one tribe and species among the *shouren*. Never mind that not all of them were wolves or predators. Never mind that they were not all bloodthirsty or violent, or that they only shifted when they were threatened or injured. The emperor needed to single out a clear villain, a target for the people's fear and anger.

Wei's own knowledge of the *shouren* was limited to what his useless history books had taught him. It didn't help that no one was willing to even utter their name. He had been riding undercover out of the Capital for days now, close to a week. And each time he stopped to ask about the *shouren*, he was flatly turned away.

As he made his way towards the Yeli mountains, Wei considered all the places the *shouren* could be. High up in the mountains, where the terrain was far more treacherous, the conditions less conducive, but where they would be safer? Or in the deep, dark heart of the forest, where they could shift whenever they pleased?

Where would the *shouren* be that his half-sister Qiu would willingly follow? In childhood, she had always, to Wei's memory, loved big open spaces where she could tumble around. He couldn't imagine her cooped up underground, spending her days fearing capture.

When he finally arrived at the mountain, he did the calculations. He had left the nearest town behind for three days, and now had a few more daylight hours to head up the mountain before night fell. If he got lost or trapped, his supplies would not be able to last him until he found his way back to civilization again.

Zeyan would advise him not to take the risk, to stock up on supplies before continuing or at least wait till first light tomorrow. But there was no time to waste, and Zeyan wasn't here to be the voice of reason.

Wei forged ahead, his senses peeled for any stir in the woods. He almost missed the set of bear paw prints near the tree on his left, but once he started looking out for it, the trail was apparent. He nudged his horse's flank, heading in the apparent direction.

The trail took him past a frozen ravine and down a narrow path lined with bare trees. As he wound further up the mountain, going on nothing but paw prints, he had to dismount his horse and navigate the trickier paths by foot. Snow grew thicker the higher he went, and the trail became fainter.

As he arrived at the last set of paw prints, the back of his neck tingled. Someone—or something—was behind him. His hand slid to the hilt of his sword. He turned around slowly, scanning every inch of the woods.

The trees whispered around him, giving away none of its secrets—until a rustle came from behind a wizened tree a few feet to his right. Snow crunched. Whatever it was, it was moving, creeping closer. Wei tightened his grip on his sword. Not far off now, bit closer . . . *there.*

He whipped around, unsheathing his sword and pointing it in the direction of the sound, and came face to face with a young lady in a grey fur coat.

Her eyes widened and she dropped the basket she was carrying. She was petite, but had the strong features of a desert girl. She seemed a little younger than Desert Rose, although, unlike Rose, she looked much warier with a sword held to her throat. Wei could have sworn that he had seen her before somewhere, but he wasn't sure where.

'I'm unarmed,' the girl said in a shaky voice.

Wei did not lower his sword. It wasn't always easy to distinguish a *shouren*, and the girl revealed no clue as to what animal she might shift into.

'You shouldn't be in these parts,' she said, revealing her Dugurian accent, stronger than Desert Rose's.

'What's a desert girl like you doing here then?' Wei said.

If she was surprised that he had guessed her origin, she didn't show it. Instead, her eyes flicked to the basket she had dropped.

Wei surveyed the devil's ear mushrooms that had spilled out of the basket. Magical herb for a magical tonic. 'You know where the *shouren* are?'

She shook her head, a little too adamantly to be convincing.

'I still have you at the tip of my blade,' he reminded her.

She bit her lower lip.

'I'm not going to hurt them. I just need to talk.' He lowered his sword to prove his point.

The girl released her breath. Whatever she meant to say next was cut off by a third voice calling out for her.

'Qara.' Another young lady dressed in a white fur robe stepped out to join her. 'Is everything o–?' She froze at the very sight of Wei.

It had been years since Wei last saw his half-sister, but she still sported the soiled dress, rumpled hair, and bright gleam in her eyes. There was a tinge of solemnity in her now, but that disappeared as soon as she saw him.

He grinned. 'Forest-living suits you well, Qiu.'

She rushed forward and threw her arms around him. 'Wei!' Behind her, Qara stared at them, rooted where she was. 'It's okay, Qara,' Qiu said, holding out a hand to her. 'This is my brother, Wei.'

'Your brother . . .' The desert girl inched a step closer and took Qiu's hand, eyeing Wei. 'So you're . . . a prince?'

'In theory,' Wei said with a shrug. He nodded at the contents of her basket. 'Your mushrooms are turning to frost.'

Qiu bent to gather the mushrooms back into the basket with Qara's help. 'Did you know, Wei? Magic still lingers in these parts. The devil's ear mushroom is one plant that managed to withstand the purge, retreating underground until the winter cold forces it to grow out of the ground.' She straightened. 'There is no sense in trying to beat down what exists naturally. They just grow back stronger.'

'I'm not here on our father's orders, if that's what you're trying to get at,' Wei said, sheathing his sword. 'In fact, I'm here to warn you.'

*

Contrary to popular belief, the *shouren* did not live underground. Instead, if Qiu's house was any indication, they lived in caves carved into the mountains. Obscured by snow-capped boulders and trees out front, the caves were nondescript enough to miss, unless one knew where to look.

Qiu led them to a granite cave hidden by a huge outcrop. The narrow opening, which fit one person at a time, opened up into a spacious interior, replete with a fire blazing in the corner, fur rugs, and an oak dining table in the centre of the room, atop which sat a jug of milk and a plate of dried figs.

Qara disappeared behind a stone wall at the back with her basket of devil's ears before re-emerging a moment later. She sank into a chair and helped herself to a fig, observing Wei in silence as he lingered at the door.

Qiu waved him in. 'Well, don't just stand there.' She pulled off her coat and threw it over a chair by the door. 'Would you like some tea? And something for your horse too?'

'Sure,' Wei said, scanning the abode as he entered. This was where Qiu had made her home for the past few years, where she had managed to survive despite their father's ruthless persecution.

When Wei first heard the news of his sister's elopement with the fox-man she had rescued, he had barely been surprised or concerned. Like him, Qiu had always dreamed of a life beyond the confines of the palace.

But to see his little sister living another life with the *shouren* now filled him with awe. She seemed more self-assured now in a place she belonged. Her palace breeding showed through in the way she moved as she prepared the tea, and her graceful motions stood out against the rustic surroundings, but Wei had never seen her more at ease. Out of all of them, she was the only one who seemed to have carved out the perfect life for herself here and shed her past as royalty.

'What are you smirking at?' she asked, glancing at him.

'Just marvelling at you, little sister.' He turned to Qara. 'And what are you looking at?' He didn't mean it in a malicious way, but she turned away quickly and stuffed her face with another fig.

Qiu poured floral tea into two clay cups and handed one to Wei and another to Qara. 'Heyang should be coming home soon, so you'll get to meet him and his brother Zhong. But until then'—she settled into a chair opposite him—'I want to hear your story. I thought you left the kingdom for good.'

'I wasn't going to let Yong's death go unanswered,' he said. 'It's what I came to tell you, actually. The emperor blames this on, well, the *shouren*.'

Qiu's eyebrows shot up. 'Right. We're supposed to have gone all the way to the palace, snuck in, and offed Yong. The emperor has indeed gone mad.'

We. No longer did she consider herself part of the imperial family. Her family was the *shouren* now.

'I'm home, love,' a voice called from outside, proving the point.

Qiu leapt up from her seat, grinning. 'The boys are back.'

Qiu's husband, Heyang, and his older brother Zhong lumbered in and shed their coats, revealing blood-stained tunics underneath.

Qiu eyed Heyang's clothes. 'Rough hunt?'

He gave Qiu a hug. 'The creatures are restless. There's disturbance in the mountains. Outsiders.'

'I'll bet it's this one,' Zhong said, noticing Wei. 'Who are *you*?'

Qiu went over to Wei's side. 'This is my third brother, Wei.'

'The Third Prince?' Heyang said.

'The rogue prince,' Zhong quipped. 'Black sheep of the family.'

Wei shot him a grim smile. 'It seems my reputation precedes me. Just call me Wei.'

'Not sure who the black sheep of the family is, though,' Qiu said with a laugh. 'Considering we both ran away from home and disgraced the family.'

Wei smirked. 'Please. You were just following in my footsteps.' But he didn't bother disguising the pride in his voice.

'How did you find us?' Zhong demanded. Qiu shot him a warning glance.

Wei nodded at Qara. 'Not very hard once I realized I was being followed.'

'Wei has . . . news.' Qiu poured two more cups of tea. 'Maybe it's best if we all sit down and talk over tea.' Neither of the fox-men moved. 'Please?' Heyang obliged, plodding towards the table and downing his tea in one gulp. He set his cup back on the table and looked up at Wei, expectant.

'The emperor is hunting all of you down,' Wei said. 'He means to kill all the *shouren* for allegedly murdering the Crown Prince.'

Heyang let out a bark of laughter. 'Just when you think he can't get more insane.'

'You think it's funny, Yang?' Zhong snapped. 'This. *This* is why we need to fight. I'm sick of hiding up here, scurrying like rats in a hole, when we've done nothing wrong. I'm sick of being blamed for everything that goes wrong in the kingdom—famine, wars, and now, apparently, the Crown Prince's death.'

Qiu exchanged a look with her husband, who shook his head and handed Zhong his cup of tea. 'Calm down, brother.'

Zhong stared down at the cup, then back at his brother. 'Don't tell me to calm down, Yang. We've already lost Bo and Shaoxi during the riots. How many more are we going to lose under this wretched monarchy?'

'Actually, we lost them *because* we went through with the plan,' Qiu said.

In that moment, Wei understood. 'You were the ones behind the masks, the riot during Yong's—oh, Qiu.'

'Not all of us,' his sister protested.

Zhong shot Wei a withering look that told him to stay out of the conversation. 'I say we follow through with the plan.'

'What makes you think the Dugur clan leaders can be trusted?' Qiu said. 'They claim that they can set us free, but so far I only see us blindly doing their bidding.'

'The Dugur clan leaders?' Wei said. 'You're working with them?' He should have known better than to trust that they would work with the emperor without a secret plan. And whom better to ally with than the oppressed, exiled magical community in Oasis Kingdom that needed a leader?

Zhong shot Qiu a look. 'Can we not discuss this in front of outsiders?'

'My brother is not an outsider,' Qiu said.

Wei shook his head. 'Of all people, you choose to fall behind the clan leaders?'

Zhong directed a scathing glare at him. 'Should we fall behind you then, Prince Wei? Should we let you in on our plans so you can run off to tell the emperor that the *shouren* are trying to throw him off the throne?'

'So setting fires and terrorizing people is your game plan?'

'There's a point to it all. Far be it from you to understand it, of course. You turned your back on this kingdom years ago. You know nothing about what's been happening—'

'Enough,' Qiu said. She drew herself up, looking, in that moment, more like a princess than Wei had ever witnessed. 'My brother wouldn't have come all the way here to look for us if he didn't intend to help. I won't have anyone maligning him.'

'If I may,' a small voice ventured. Everyone turned to Qara, who was nursing her cup of tea by the corner, looking far younger than any of them. She glanced at Qiu, who gave her an encouraging nod, before straightening in her seat. 'I come from the Dugur tribe. I *know* those clan leaders.'

Wei squinted at her, realization settling in. He *did* recognize her. She was there in the crowd at Yong's funeral ceremony. 'You dropped the match,' he said. 'And then you fled as soon as the riot started.'

'The clan leaders made me do it. I used the fire as a diversion,' she said, 'to escape from them.'

'Qara sought refuge with us after escaping from them,' Qiu explained. 'We found her after the ceremony. They don't know she's with us.'

'And yet, you're still working with them,' Wei pointed out.

'Not all of us,' Qiu said again. 'Some of us just want peace.'

'There can *be* no peace as long as we are in this position,' Zhong insisted.

Heyang rubbed his nose bridge, sighing. 'So you think storming the palace and wreaking havoc during the Spring Festival ceremony is the way to go? Can we even be sure the Dugur clan leaders will have our backs?'

'They won't,' Qara piped up. 'Blackstone won't think twice about sacrificing a few *shouren* as long as he remains on the winning side, whichever that might be.'

'So you'll basically be walking into the tiger's den,' Wei pointed out.

Zhong threw him a dirty look. 'I'm not going to stand here and take advice from a bunch of runaways who know nothing about loyalty. I've picked a side and I'm seeing the plan all the way through.' He threw on his coat and stormed out.

They sat in silence in the wake of Zhong's exit, until Qara exclaimed, 'The mushrooms!' She leapt out of her seat. 'Prince Wei, can you give me a hand in the kitchen?'

Wei tried not to let his surprise show as he followed her into the kitchen, a wide sub-cavern packed with woven baskets of dried herbs, pots of thick medicated paste and pungent-smelling ground herbs. It looked less like a kitchen than an apothecary.

Qara went over to her herbs simmering in a pot over a low fire. She stirred them in slow concentric circles. Wei watched her work, waiting for her to speak first.

'It's about the girl who snuck into your camp back in the desert,' she said at last.

Wei raised his brows. 'Desert Rose? Were you from the same tribe?'

Qara nodded. 'We broke into your camp together that night. By the time I woke up, she was gone. I went back to my tribe to find my family. Then I learned that it was your tent we had broken into.'

'We only saw Desert Rose out cold on the ground, so I took her back to my tent. She was hit by a poisoned dart, I believe.'

Qara bit her lip. 'Word on the street is that she was seen out at Wuxi Market one night with the Third Prince. Is she safe?'

Wei cursed inwardly. He should have known better—they had drawn too much attention that night. 'For now,' he said.

Qara's voice tightened. 'Now that Blackstone has usurped the seat, his son Bataar is next in line. Bataar was the one who hurt Desert Rose with a poison dart.'

Wei thought of Desert Rose shaking and whimpering in cold sweat that night in his tent, how she had panicked when she saw him that evening at the market. His fists clenched. Even now, Bataar still struck terror in her heart.

'He knows that Rose is in the palace now and he wants her back,' Qara went on. 'He means to steal her from the palace during the Spring Festival ceremony and take her back to the tribe.' Qara paused in her stirring and turned to regard him. 'I don't know what it's like between you and Rose, but . . . will you help her?'

There was no question about it. He owed his life to Desert Rose. They had crossed paths and crossed swords, and their fates had led them both to the palace. He couldn't leave her to fend for herself now, after everything.

He thought about how far she had gone to find her father, how she had fought her way to where she was now, and how she had broken down the other day when she realized she had failed to save her father. She was brave and brash, willing to go to any lengths to save the people she loved. They were, he realized, more alike than he had thought.

'With my life,' he said.

If Qara was taken aback by his conviction, she did not question it. 'Thank you,' she said. 'And now my mushrooms are really burning.'

As she scooped them out and laid it on the table, Wei surveyed the kitchen. 'What's with all the herbs?' he asked.

'They sell them,' said Qara. 'That's how the *shouren* make a living aside from hunting. Their biggest client is this merchant called Geshao, who runs several apothecaries and businesses in the Cap—what?' she asked when Wei's attention snapped back to her.

'Did you say Geshao?'

Qara nodded. 'He acquires rare herbs from the desert and gets the *shouren* to make concoctions to sell. Medicines, ointments . . .'

'Poisons?'

'Anything can be poisonous in excessive doses,' Qiu said, appearing at the kitchen entrance. 'Why do you ask?'

'Because our brother was poisoned.' Wei explained everything he had found out about Yong's death—from the poison to the sand—and what he had overheard that night while tailing Geshao, omitting Desert Rose's involvement.

Qiu's expression turned grimmer as he went on. 'You think Geshao provided the poison that killed Yong?'

'There's only one way to find out,' Wei said. 'When is he coming by next?'

Guard your back against those who offer help too freely. The enemy is often disguised as a friend.

—Snow Wolf Sect teaching

Nineteen

Desert Rose

As the trials loomed closer, the girls grew quieter and more solemn by the day. Xiyue started talking in her sleep, while Shuang and Liqin huddled close and went off on their own more often. Even Windshadow's fingers grew restless, tapping a frenzied rhythm that would in turn put Desert Rose on edge. When they gathered, the girls simmered in a collective silence where the slightest noise made them snap like frayed threads.

The last phase of their training—the sword dance—turned out to be the most difficult of all. Sure, she had danced with her tribe during Tsagen Sol and other festive gatherings. But the sword dance was a complex interplay of strength, technique, grace, and rhythm that fell beyond her abilities.

But this was a crucial segment, according to Shimu. 'You will be performing the sword dance at the Spring Festival ceremony, where the emperor will usher in spring and bless the kingdom. Esteemed guests will be present, and the emperor himself will pick the best dancer as the winner of the third trial.'

The dance, Desert Rose learned, was how a Black Crane had assassinated a Lettorian duke several years back. No one had expected a dancer, even a sword-wielding one in a private performance, to be able to slit throats.

'Whether or not you win the trials, performing at the ceremony is a huge honour,' Shimu said. 'I expect no student of mine to regard this lightly or bring dishonour to the House of Night.'

As soon as training ended for the sword dance, the exams began. Over the course of a week, the Blue Cranes were tested on a range of critical skills—from combat technique to stealth, geography, history, and combat theory to smell and taste test for poison detection. They were tasked to break into a locked chamber and slit a dummy mark's throat, battle each other to shoot a moving target through the woods, demonstrate their ability to wield an array of weapons to kill their mark—from sabres to spears, from knuckle blades tucked in their palms to poisoned needles disguised as hairpins and tiny blades hidden up their sleeves.

At the end of the week, Shimu announced the first trial.

'Tomorrow morning at six bells sharp, gather outside the Hall of Valour with your weapons,' she said. 'Latecomers will be disqualified.'

With none of them able to sleep, the girls were up before the crack of dawn the next day. They shuffled into line after breakfast, weapons by their sides, silent and pinch-faced, except for Windshadow, who yawned as soon as she fell in line.

'We've had exams all week. They won't even give us a break,' she said. But Desert Rose was just glad to be done with those—every test she completed took her a step closer to the emperor.

At six bells, they gathered at the Hall of Valour and waited in a row before the podium. Shimu arrived with Prince Meng and the emperor, the latter trailed by a pair of handmaids, and High Adviser Mian in his saffron and blue scholar's garb.

'Don't tell me they are the judges,' Shuang muttered under her breath. Desert Rose glanced at her. The Capital girl was already wound tight—a permanent frown had worked its way between her brows over the past few weeks, and she snapped at anyone who broke her focus for the briefest moment (Xiyue often bore the brunt of her annoyance). The sight of the emperor and the fourth prince now made her clutch her double swords hard.

Desert Rose's own grip on her weapons tightened too, though not for the same reason as Shuang.

She had come face to face with the emperor at last. She could now look straight at the person who had destroyed her tribe and killed her father. She could imagine the look on his face when he had lured the clan leaders to his side, when they had plotted to dispose of her father. Her tribe had disintegrated, her father was most likely dead, and she was all alone now—and the person who had lit the match was standing right before her.

Her hands trembled. It took everything in her to remain in place. She could end everything right now. She could charge at him, slit his throat, and then take off. *Not yet, Rose. You need answers.*

The girls bowed and greeted in unison when the emperor and Prince Meng settled into their seats before them. Shimu stood next to the emperor, her back even straighter than usual.

'Rise,' ordered the emperor.

Desert Rose straightened and looked up into his eyes—narrow and cold—just as they had been when he sent his dead son off on his final journey.

'It is a commendable feat and a great honour for all of you present to train at the House of Night,' he said. 'My guards must possess a combination of skill, grace, and wits. Only the best will be worthy of protecting the imperial family.'

'The first trial will test your ability to survive,' Shimu said next to the emperor.

Desert Rose steeled herself. She was a desert girl. She would survive.

'We would like you to help us retrieve a long-lost manual at the bottom of a well,' said Prince Meng, leaning forward in his seat. 'For centuries, no one has managed to retrieve it . . . because it lies in the middle of the White Crypt.'

Someone drew a sharp breath. Shimu's lips thinned as she glanced at the offending person.

Prince Meng went on. 'The White Crypt, if you are not familiar with it, is a labyrinth heavily guarded by ancient magic that the old sorcerers had used to guard their valuables such as manuscripts, artefacts, and weapons. You are there to retrieve one specific manual. You are not to read it or decipher the contents on your own.'

'Find the manual and return before last light,' said the emperor, 'or perish in the cold.'

Later, as Shimu led them across the courtyard, Windshadow whispered in Desert Rose's ear, 'What fools venture into a magic crypt with nothing but some bits of steel?'

Desert Rose shrugged. Despite the buttery sunlight scattered across the snowy yard, the morning air still nipped at her skin. But she was all fired up and ready to go.

'I mean, *we* could always work the natural arts,' Windshadow went on. 'But the others might just die out there.'

Desert Rose glanced over her shoulder at the three judges still watching them from the Hall of Valour. Prince Meng flashed her an encouraging smile when their eyes met. He had helped her get this far, taught her how to read and write, and offered comfort when she felt most alone. She could make the rest of the way herself now. She had to.

The border that separated the palace from the White Crypt was a desolate expanse of land. Here, the snow was calf-deep and trees grew emaciated.

They trudged forward. Winds cried out in warning, as though deterring them from going further, but they kept close behind Shimu until she came to a stop before a narrow, ornately carved black metal gate.

'The trial begins at the toll of my bell,' Shimu said, pulling a small brass bell out of her coat. 'You will go through this gate and find your way to the well as quickly as you can. Do what you can to retrieve the manual, but understand that the old sorcerers had advanced methods of safeguarding their valuables that we are unable to outmanoeuvre. The bell will toll thrice when the winner returns. The rest of you are to make your way back as soon as you hear it.'

Shimu unlocked the gate. As soon as she opened it, a frosty wind rushed out like a beast unleashed, rocking the girls on their feet. Beyond it lay white nothingness, a world smothered in thick blinding fog.

'On my signal,' said Shimu.

The Capital girls drew a collective breath. Windshadow and Desert Rose shared a look. Xiyue gave Desert Rose a small smile which Desert Rose returned.

Shimu gave the bell a firm shake. The clang reverberated through the row of wizened trees and back, but along with it came another force, one that rippled through the ground and through the air. Desert Rose flinched.

Shuang took the lead, marching through the gate after a bracing breath. Once they had all entered the Crypt, the gate slammed shut behind them. Desert Rose pulled her hood low against the gale whipping snow into her eyes. Next to her, Xiyue squinted into the distance, but it was impossible to see beyond their outstretched hands. The vastness looked ready to swallow them whole.

'We're doomed,' Xiyue moaned. 'How many assassins-in-training do you suppose have died in here?'

'Don't be such a defeatist, Xiyue,' Shuang snapped. 'I'm not standing here, wasting time with you lot.' Swords by her side, she braved ahead. It took no more than three steps for her to disappear into the fog.

'Shuang, wait!' Xiyue called. 'Let's stick together.'

'Don't be a baby, Xiyue,' Liqin said, although her own brows were knitted close. 'This is a contest. Fend for yourself.' She ventured one step out, then another, and glanced back at them. 'Get moving,' she said before vanishing in the churning fog too.

Xiyue took off after her, leaving Desert Rose and Windshadow behind after bidding a quick, 'Good luck.'

'Typical Capital girls,' Windshadow said. 'Flocking into a situation before understanding it.' She nudged Desert Rose. 'We know better.'

Desert Rose held out her arm, feeling the strange ripple in the air cling to her skin. 'This is not like any magic I've encountered, though. Does this blizzard never stop?'

Windshadow waved away a snow flurry. 'It's just elemental, but much more potent. Doesn't your tribe practise the natural arts too?'

It had been too long since Desert Rose engaged her *zokhra,* that essence buried deep in her soul like a swallowed star. She might have evaded Cleansing at the Capital gates, but months of living in the sterile Oasis Kingdom had dulled her inner spirit.

Everything has life, and everything holds magic, Dil Mura, the head shaman, once said in her class. *It's about how you communicate with it. Those who do not believe in magic with all their being will never experience its power.*

But Dil Mura had spent years honing her craft and communicating with the elements, harnessing its blessings and studying its ills. She spoke the language of the universe, and it, in turn, gave up its secrets to her. She was its pupil and its friend. Desert Rose was but a clumsy protégé next to her, stumbling around with her half-baked skills and tepid faith.

But that rain. The deluge during the Crown Prince's funeral ceremony. Desert Rose could have sworn the elements had responded to her call back then. The fire had started to get out of hand and it was the only thing she could think to do. She had pulled at the skeins of vapour in the air, gathered what little moisture she could reach for, and prompted a freakish spring rain in the middle of winter. Nobody could have been more surprised than her.

Now, in the middle of this magical blizzard, she gave in to that power, the rush of adrenaline that had made her draw rain from the skies that day. The elements teemed with a life of their own, tugging her in different directions. But her grasp was tenuous, feeble, and the energy slid away from her time and again. What hope did she have of using the natural arts to navigate her way through this place?

Next to her, Windshadow had both hands outstretched and her eyes closed. The wind began to shift, parting around them like water streaming past a rock.

This wasn't the natural arts. The natural arts harnessed the elements to heal and soothe and restore balance in a body, not manipulate the elements like Windshadow was doing. This was magic—pure, unbridled magic.

Windshadow. Desert Rose understood at last. It wasn't just a nickname, just as she was no ordinary desert girl. It was her moniker, her supernatural ability, her mode of attack. She could control the wind, bend it to her will, wield it as her tool, her weapon. She *was* the wind, and she was shadow.

Desert Rose closed her eyes and tried holding out her hands to connect with the energy in the air. If Windshadow was manipulating the wind, then she could work on water. She reached for all the moisture in the air and concentrated on pushing aside the snow swirling around them. The element resisted at first, but she tightened her hold on it.

When she opened her eyes again, the snow had cleared before them to reveal three different paths flanked by overgrown hedges at least twice as tall as them.

Windshadow shot her a grin. 'Not bad, *azzi*.'

They picked the straight path ahead, but it turned out to be more confusing than they expected. With Windshadow diverting the wind and Desert Rose clearing the snow in their way, they rounded bend after bend, hit dead-end after dead-end, and doubled back more times than they could keep track of.

Desert Rose groaned when they faced yet another wall of unruly bushes. 'I thought the emperor purged every bit of magic from this land. Why does this place still exist?'

'Well, the old sorcerers were no fools. They probably kept this place a secret when they were alive until the Purge dried up all the surrounding magic. By then, there were probably no more sorcerers left who could get through this maze. Serves those emperors right, having to spend all this time trying to get to the good stuff.'

'Why does he care about some manual at the bottom of a well if he doesn't believe in magic?'

'Oh, he believes, trust me. He just wants everyone to think he doesn't—keeps him in power. If there's no magic, no religion, and no divinity, then he's the supreme ruler. But he's just like anyone else—mortal and scared. Why do you think he's so obsessed with finding that spring?'

'So the manual offers some answers that will lead him to it?'

Windshadow shrugged. 'Who knows? I'm just here to win that trial and then kill him in his sleep.'

Desert Rose stopped in her tracks.

Windshadow turned around, her brows raised. 'You didn't actually think I was going to spend one moment of my life in his servitude, did you?'

'But the one who wins the trial will have to serve the emperor.'

Windshadow's lips quirked. 'Who said I want to serve *this* emperor? I'm counting on the next one to bring about some change.'

She understood at once. 'Prince Meng?'

'I think he would make a far better emperor, don't you think?'

Prince Meng did seem to be poles apart from his father. Not only was his vision of the kingdom more inclusive of magical folk, he seemed to have a genuine desire to create a better future for the people. And unlike his father, he had compassion. Desert Rose tried to push down the memory of him bringing her tea on that freezing winter night to calm her frazzled nerves, but the heat rose to her cheeks anyway.

'That's what I thought,' Windshadow said, watching her with a smirk.

Desert Rose quickened her steps, sidestepping a gnarled root near her left foot. 'Does Prince Meng know you intend to kill his father?'

'I'm sure he'll appreciate me clearing the way to the throne for him. Don't you want a more stable future for your tribe, Rose? Don't you want peace again? As long as Oasis Kingdom is ruled by some warmongering despot who thinks he can erase magic from the world, there will never be peace. Our tribes will never be safe.'

What she wanted was to be home again, to be in her tent playing bone chess with her father. She wanted to have dinner with her clansmen, get stuffed on lamb stew, steamed dumplings, and warm mare's milk, and listen to fireside stories told by Dil Mura and the other clanswomen. She wanted to see her best friend Qara again, to regard Bataar as an older brother and not fear him as she did now. She wanted to go back to the way things were, when she knew whom to trust, when her sleep wasn't plagued by nightmares of her father being hunted and killed.

Windshadow was right. Peace was what she wanted. And as long as Emperor Zhaode was in power, there was no hope of that. He wouldn't go to war against the desert tribes; he knew better than to go head-to-head against them when the kingdom was already the target of its neighbouring countries. But manipulating and exploiting them was worse than an outright attack. He could destroy all the desert tribes, turn the leaders against each other, without lifting a finger. The only way to restore peace was to remove him from power and discover a new establishment.

'See? We're on the same side,' Windshadow said, interrupting her thoughts.

'I . . .' Desert Rose glanced around her. Something was wrong. The ground was trembling—just a faint tremor, but a movement beneath her feet nonetheless. 'Do you feel that?'

Windshadow stared blankly. 'What am I supposed to be feeling?'

Out of the silence came a gentle dripping sound. The air shifted, and the pull at her feet grew stronger, tugging her in the north-west direction.

'This way,' she said, leading the way.

The signs grew more obvious as they ventured further. Snowflakes, instead of falling to the ground, drifted forward. The sound of gently sloshing water echoed in her ear, and the tremor in the ground grew into a rumble, like the protest of a waking beast. Desert Rose's pulse leapt with each step she took, and soon she was running. They were close. She was sure of it.

Windshadow kept pace with her, following her lead. But a thick fog descended upon them, swift as a shadow, blotting out everything in sight. The wind swooped back in, its howls filling the silence.

Windshadow was gone.

'Windshadow!' Desert Rose called, glancing around wildly for her friend. But there was no sign of her anywhere.

A muffled shout came from the distance, though it was impossible to tell, over the wind, where it originated. Figures loomed in the distance. Desert Rose struggled to stay upright against the squall as she backed away. Could it be the others—or something else?

Voices broke through the howling wind. The figures, two of them, inched closer. Her hand arrived at something cold and hard at waist level. Stone, slick from the fog.

Blood rushed in her ears as soon as her skin met the stone wall. The air wrapped its invisible hands around her head, squeezing tight. Beneath her, the ground continued quaking. Bile rose in her throat. Magic was concentrated here, and it seemed intent on tearing her apart.

But while her insides churned and her head pounded, everything else settled. The air cleared, snow settling to the ground and the wind dying to a low whistle. All was still.

And right next to her was the well, a blackened stone edifice as large as a dinner table fit for twenty people, laced with wisps of vapour over its mouth. A wave of nausea seized her when she peered over it. Her legs gave way just as Shuang and Liqin appeared on the opposite side of the well.

The cold began to creep under her skin, and the pounding in her head made her grip her knives so hard the hilts dug into her palms. She squeezed her eyes shut, trying to block out the pain. The sooner she retrieved the manual, the sooner she could leave this place. But *how*? She was near paralyzed.

Shuang's breezy voice rang out next to her. 'Looks like we're not the ones who got here first, Liqin.' She laid a hand on Desert Rose's shoulder and leaned close to hiss in her ear, 'Tell us, desert girl. What sort of magic did you use to get here?'

Desert Rose's knives clattered to the ground as she propped herself against the well. She didn't trust herself to speak in case she threw up.

'You see, this magic here only affects magical beings,' Shuang went on, gesturing at the well. 'Mortals like me and Liqin don't feel a thing. Sure, there are defensive barriers we can't break down, and we'd bleed like any human. But the magic from this well won't debilitate us.

Which means you somehow evaded Cleansing and have been disguising as mortal among us.'

She grabbed Desert Rose's hair and yanked her head back. 'You and Windshadow think you can come here and steal what belongs to us?' she hissed. 'We've worked our whole lives to enter the palace. Our parents dreamed this honourable life for us, and you two desert girls come in riding on the coattails of the Fourth Prince and try to take what rightfully belongs to us?'

Desert Rose grappled for footing. Next to her, the mouth of the well gaped like a creature ready to devour her. She couldn't tell how deep it was, but when she pushed in a couple of stones from the crumbling mouth of the well, there was no feedback.

She tried to reach for her knives, but Shuang kicked them away. 'You're no match for us, desert girl. The prince even had to teach you how to read.' She grabbed Desert Rose by the shoulder and wrenched her arm behind her back. 'You think the emperor is going to let a traitor like you into the Imperial Guard?'

'Shuang,' Liqin said from behind her. 'Let's just grab the manual and go. We need to make it back before last light.'

'Can't you see I'm busy, Liqin?' Shuang snapped.

Desert Rose gathered all her strength and elbowed Shuang in the ribs before throwing her off. She staggered towards her knives, but Shuang dragged her back before her fingers could close around the hilts.

Desert Rose was about to kick Shuang in the face when Shuang let out a pained cry and loosened her grasp. Behind her, Windshadow had an arm wrapped around her neck and another pinning her arms behind her back.

Desert Rose dived for her knives and rolled away.

'Tell me again what desert girls are here to do,' Windshadow snarled. A manic gleam in her eyes made her seem almost inhuman. She nodded at Desert Rose. 'Finish her.'

Shuang gurgled, writhing in Windshadow's grip.

'Stop it, you're going to kill her!' Liqin cried.

Windshadow did not budge. 'Like she didn't intend to kill me and Desert Rose.'

Desert Rose tucked her knives away. 'Enough, Windshadow. Stop!' She tried to pry Windshadow off Shuang, only then noticing the sheen of perspiration on Windshadow's forehead. She was fighting the same ills of the magic.

The moment of distraction let Shuang break free of Windshadow. She grabbed one of her swords and charged towards Windshadow.

Despite battling the well magic, Windshadow didn't miss a beat, dodging easily when Shuang thrust her blade at her. Quick as a blink, she vanished on the spot and reappeared behind Shuang to kick her squarely in the back. Shuang stumbled, almost losing grip of her sword. Before she could right herself, Windshadow appeared right before her and created a gust of wind that pinned her to the ground.

Desert Rose caught Liqin's eye. A moment of understanding passed between them. As skilled as she was at combat, Shuang was no match against an enraged Windshadow with supernatural abilities.

She and Liqin sprung towards the two girls. She tried to grab Windshadow while Liqin tried to pull Shuang away. But even when Shuang had the chance to escape when Desert Rose broke Windshadow's focus, she flung Liqin aside and lunged for Windshadow again, aiming her sword straight at her heart.

Once Shuang got close enough, Windshadow tripped her and disappeared like a puff of smoke. Shuang's sword went soaring through the air as she scrambled for purchase.

She let out a scream as she pitched into the well.

'Shuang!' Liqin cried.

Desert Rose acted on pure instinct, leaping forward to catch her. Shuang's palm was slick, but her grip was firm. She gave a sharp tug, and Desert Rose found herself plummeting down the dark, mossy well together with her.

The world narrowed to a circle of ghost-white sky. Desert Rose sent a silent plea to the gods, although she knew there was no way they could save her now. She was plunging down a magical well that seemed to have a mind of its own.

The gods can't save you, Rose. Only you can. You must.

She closed her eyes and reached for the water, way down in the pit of the well, clinging to it like a lifeline. The connection felt like a frayed thread, the water too far from her grasp.

But then something flared within her, sending a rush of power coursing through her body, like a flame igniting her soul. It made her ache for something—something much bigger than her that she couldn't pinpoint. Her yearning was as unquenchable as the vast desert she had left behind. She had felt it when she initiated rain at the Crown Prince's funeral, but this time it was much keener, like a fire that seared too close for comfort, a creature that sidled up to her with its fangs bared.

There was no time to consider. As darkness closed in around her and the skylight receded to a size of a coin above, she pushed past every misgiving, ignored every word of her father's warning ringing in her head.

She gave in to the fire, let it consume her.

The well gave a low rumble, sending a shudder down her spine. She felt it in her core, as though what was awakening the well was stirring up something dormant in her too.

And then she wasn't falling any more. Something caught her, mid-fall, cushioning her back. As she jerked to a stop, Shuang's hand slipped out of her grasp.

Shuang's scream echoed through the well as she plunged into the deep, dark nothingness below.

Everything fell still.

Desert Rose ventured a glance around her and found herself lying in a flat, shallow pool of water hovering in mid-air. Her pulse thrummed as she picked herself up slowly. The water platform shifted around her, shrinking to the size of a dais when she stood. She stared at the water at her feet, as solid as a rug yet undulating like a stream. The water hadn't just saved her; it was now *responding* to her.

She was alone. Now that Shuang's screams had died, there was only the faint sound of gently flowing water. Her nausea and headache had faded, replaced by an eerie calm that settled around her.

'Shuang?' she called.

No reply. Was she already dead? The thought sickened her. Had she let Shuang die? Could she risk going all the way down to the bottom of the well to find her? What if she couldn't control the water and ended up in the pit too?

'Rose!'

She looked up to find Windshadow leaning over the well, a darkened speck against the sun. 'I'm okay,' she said.

'Thank the gods you're alive. Did you find the manual?'

'No, but Shuang—I think she fell all the way down.'

A beat lapsed. 'Well,' said Windshadow. 'That's unfortunate. Wait, what do you mean *all* the way down?' She peered closer, and the silence drew out longer this time.

'I don't know how I did it,' Desert Rose said.

In all her life, she had never heard of anyone who could manipulate water this way. The tribe shamans could conduct rituals for rain, sure, but even they couldn't do what she had just done—or what Windshadow could with wind. Supernatural abilities like that were the stuff of bonfire stories, legends embellished into myths, tall tales of gods and the children of gods who had lost their way and were stuck on earth.

'We can figure out the how and why later,' Windshadow said. 'Can you try and go lower? See if the manual is there?'

Desert Rose took a deep breath and reached out to the water again. A warm energy flowed through her, all the way down to her feet, making the pool of water tremble.

And then, slowly but surely, she was sliding down.

She held on to the wall for support, her palms brushing the cold, clammy stone as she descended. Light was scant here, but by the time her eyes had adjusted to the darkness, she was already a foot from the ground.

Despite the dampness of its walls, the pit of the well was dry. Desert Rose groped her way around until her hand hit something other than loose stone and rocks.

Tucked in a corner like a forgotten thing was a bundled wooden scroll.

'Windshadow!' she called. 'I found it!' She reached for the scroll and tucked it into her tunic, half-expecting something untoward to happen. But it only glowed with a subdued golden light . . . illuminating the pile of numerous mangled, rotten corpses, and the fresh one next to her.

Alive, Shuang had been sharp-toothed and flint-eyed, all ambition and resolve, as unyielding as her double swords. Now broken and defeated at the bottom of a well, she seemed like a mere human felled by her desire for greatness.

Desert Rose held out a shaking hand to Shuang's neck, bent at an awkward angle. Her pulse was still.

Another rumble, almost a growl, came from the well. It gave a huge shudder, rattling the walls like waking beast shaking free from sleep. There was a deafening crack before stones started raining down on her.

'Rose!' Windshadow called. 'Do you have it?'

She choked on a sob she hadn't realized was in her throat. 'I—yes, I have it.'

'Well, hurry up. The well is . . .'

Another tremor set loose a cascade of stones, cutting Windshadow off mid-sentence.

Windshadow's face appeared over the edge again. 'Okay, here's what we do. I'll dredge you up, and you try using the water to lift yourself up too.'

'But Shuang—'

'Is dead,' Windshadow said. 'There's nothing you can do.'

Isn't there? She couldn't leave Shuang here among the others who had met the same fate.

'For gods' sake, Rose. Don't be a bleeding heart. She would have killed you anyway. Hurry, before the well—'

As if on cue, the well roared, sending more stones down on her. On reflex, she threw out her hands, creating a shield of water around her, sturdy enough to deflect the onslaught.

A gust of wind swept into the well—Windshadow's doing. It curled beneath Desert Rose and raised the water platform. She shot up in a spurt of wind and water, catapulting into the silvery sky.

Cold, fresh air hit her lungs as she soared through the air. The frosty, hard ground met her soon enough, and she rolled off it to break her fall, coming to a stop a few feet away from the well, soaked and spluttering.

Windshadow rushed over to her. 'All right there, *azzi*?'

Desert Rose accepted Windshadow's outstretched hand as she got up on shaky feet. 'Thank you.' Windshadow handed over her double knives, which she secured to her waist. She patted her tunic to check that the scroll was still securely tucked.

The landscape had changed during her brief time in the well. They now stood in the middle of a large circle, where five paths fanned out in different directions. Next to the well stood an imposing bronze statue, behind which was the opening to the hedge maze she and Windshadow had emerged from.

Desert Rose stared up at the statue. It was at least five times taller than her, a heavy-browed man with a long beard and an all-seeing gaze. He held a scroll in one hand and an orb in his other.

'I'm guessing that's High Priest Du,' said Desert Rose, recalling what she had read from her textbooks.

Windshadow nodded. 'Exalted and worshipped by his devotees until the first Oasis Emperor denounced magic. Also the one who erected the Wall, and the last sorcerer to be killed in this gods-forsaken kingdom.'

'So this place is the last bastion of magic?'

Windshadow shrugged. 'I suppose.' Her eyes gleamed. 'Rose. Do you realize what you just did?'

Despite her sodden clothes and boots, her body remained warm in the aftermath of using her magic.

Her magic. It sounded preposterous, even obnoxious, to think that she could possess magical abilities, much less wield it. She, who hadn't even been able to conjure a ripple during Dil Mura's lessons. If someone had told her she could one day dive into a magic well and rescue a sorcerer's manual, she would have laughed.

Behind her, voice trembling, Liqin asked, 'Where's Shuang?'

Desert Rose exchanged a look with Windshadow. Liqin threw a hand over her mouth and began to sob.

'I'm sorry.' Desert Rose took a step towards her. 'I didn't—she just—'

Windshadow tugged on her hand and shook her head. Desert Rose fell silent. What more could she possibly say?

The well gave another bellow, and the earth responded with a thunderous crack, splitting under their feet.

'Time to go,' Windshadow said.

Desert Rose glanced around. 'Where's Xiyue?'

Liqin's gaze fell to the ground. 'I don't know. We—we lost her.'

'Lost her or left her behind?' Windshadow muttered. Liqin bit her lip. 'Move.'

Liqin threw out a hand to stop Windshadow from leaving. 'Wait.' She turned to Desert Rose. 'Are you just going to leave Shuang here?'

Windshadow shot her an impatient stare. 'She's dead, Liqin.'

Liqin glowered at her. 'I won't leave her here.'

'Suit yourself. Maybe you two can spend eternity together in that well.' Windshadow took Desert Rose's hand, giving it a sharp tug when Desert Rose hesitated.

Behind them, the well let out a monstrous roar. The girls threw their hands up to cover their ears as the ground began to quake.

In a spray of sleet and stone, an anvil-shaped cloud burst out of the well and shifted into a dragon, large enough to swallow them all in a maelstrom. The dragon roared, loud enough to shake the heavens, a creature made of thunderstorm and fury.

Desert Rose seized Liqin's hand, and the three of them dashed straight for the opening in the maze. The dragon rose to its full height, rearing its long snout before diving for them. Around them, branches rustled and crackled, some snapping under the force of the gale, some snagging at their clothes.

Liqin stumbled along behind, calling out for Shuang and sobbing. The dragon went for her first, edging between her and Desert Rose and knocking her over with a blast of icy wind.

'Rose, help me hold it off!' Windshadow yelled as Desert Rose helped Liqin up. She threw up her hands, trying to tear the storm dragon apart, but all it did was disperse a few wisps of clouds from its body before it lunged and snapped at them again.

The girls dodged its swiping talons, leaving it to claw the icy ground and rip apart the hedges behind them. It opened its mouth and shot a stream of hail at them, narrowly missing Desert Rose.

There was no way they could outrun it.

Desert Rose gathered all the moisture she could find—vapour in the thin air, the sleet that the creature shook off its back, the water flowing underground, far from winter's reach, even the sweat forming on her upper lip—and built a wall of water between them and the dragon, buying them time to escape.

The dragon continued shooting hail and ice shards at them, until Desert Rose squeezed her eyes closed and threw out her hands, imagining the dragon shattering into a million raindrops.

A roar split the skies up. Wind swept across the land, almost lifting them off their feet. Desert Rose opened her eyes, squinting against the force to see the dragon burst into a shower of sleet and rain.

Sunlight filtered through the shreds of clouds, chasing away the dragon's receding shadow. A gentle breeze trailed in the wake of the storm. Their ragged breaths were the only sounds in the silence that followed.

Windshadow turned and shot her a grin. 'We make a good team, *azzi*.' Liqin plodded ahead, silent.

They returned to the gate past last light. Desert Rose shut it behind them and leaned against it, gathering her breath. The scroll remained pressed against her heart, secure despite everything she had been through.

She had done it. She had won the first trial.

What would Papa think of all this?

The thought came unbidden, and she felt a pang of guilt, as though he had been there watching her use magic. She could hear his disapproving voice, imagine his anger. He had always forbidden her to dabble in magic, told her it was too dangerous.

Maybe he was right. She *had* felt a thrill of danger when she succumbed to that force within her. But it had also felt *right*, as though she had, at last, filled a hollowness in her soul.

Xiyue was already waiting outside under a withered tree, her arms wrapped around herself as she stomped her feet to beat the cold.

'Oh, thank the Great Oasis Emperor! I thought all of you didn't make it,' she cried when she noticed them. She threw her arms around each of them. Desert Rose staggered backwards in surprise, but patted Xiyue on the back in return.

'The Great Oasis Emperor wasn't the one who got us out alive,' Windshadow said tetchily.

'Where were you?' Desert Rose asked. 'We thought you went off with Liqin.'

'The fog descended and I lost sight of them,' she said. 'Wandered around for a bit before I decided this was useless—what mortal can possibly go up against magic and hope to win?'

Desert Rose saw a tear slip down Liqin's cheek before she turned away.

Xiyue glanced around. 'Where is Shuang? Wasn't she with you, Liqin?'

'She's dead, okay, Xiyue?' Liqin snapped. 'Any more stupid questions before we head back?'

Xiyue froze, her eyes filling up with tears immediately. Liqin shoved past Desert Rose and made for the palace.

The journey back to the Hall of Valour seemed much longer than the one to the maze. A bone-deep weariness nestled within her, but Desert Rose dragged herself across the courtyard with the other girls. Ahead of them, neither Liqin nor Xiyue said a word, although Xiyue sobbed the entire way.

Windshadow linked arms with Desert Rose. As they neared the steps leading up to the Hall, she leaned over and murmured, 'Look alive, *azzi*. You just won the first trial.'

But Desert Rose was too tired to even crack a smile.

'You know what this means, don't you?' Windshadow said.

Desert Rose sighed. 'What?'

'What we did back there is much more than what the shamans can do.' Her eyes gleamed brighter than the sickle moon above. 'It means that you and I, Rose—we're gifted.'

Twenty

Meng

It was nightfall by the time the girls returned. Meng had been unable to focus on anything for the entire day until the messenger arrived at his chamber announcing that the candidates had made it back.

When he gathered back at the Hall of Valour with the housemistress, his parents, and Mian, the girls were trudging through the expanse of snow across the courtyard, thrown into relief only by the frail moonlight.

Meng released a breath he hadn't realized he had been holding. But something was amiss. There were only four of them.

'I hope the one left behind is not dead,' the emperor remarked. 'Very bad business to have apprentices die in the palace.'

'That would be unfortunate indeed, Your Majesty, but not unheard of,' said Mian.

The emperor squinted into the distance. 'I don't see them bringing anything back.'

'Patience, Your Majesty,' the empress murmured.

The girls approached the Hall, stepping into the lantern light. Their tunics were ripped, their hair windswept, and they looked like they might collapse any moment. Desert Rose looked the most bedraggled of all, with a fresh cut on her face, her tunic in shreds, boots soiled, and a blank stare.

But she was alive. She was alive. Meng felt his fists unclench.

Next to Desert Rose, the girl called Fengying—although almost everyone called her Windshadow—locked eyes with him. She almost broke into a triumphant smile until she remembered her place and lowered her gaze.

The one who died was the first girl they had brought in, the one who simply introduced herself as Shuang. Meng recalled admiring the clean precision of her double sword technique and her inexorable energy during combat. Out of all the girls, she was probably the one he least expected to have been eliminated this early in the trials.

The girls bowed and greeted the emperor in unison.

'Rise,' the emperor ordered. The girls thanked him, and he nodded at the housemistress, granting her permission to speak.

'Where is Shuang?' the housemistress asked.

One of the Capital girls, whose name eluded Meng, bit her trembling lip and lowered her gaze. Liqin let out a sob and proceeded to describe how Shuang had, in a heroic effort to save Desert Rose from falling into the well, met her own demise instead. Meng glanced at Desert Rose, but her stare was hollow, fixed on the pillar next to him.

'So do you have it? The manual?' the emperor demanded. His eyes shifted to Desert Rose, who, upon a nudge from Windshadow, pulled out a wooden scroll from her tunic.

Meng knew his father planned to study the manual for clues on finding the spring, but it seemed to him a huge waste of its potential. The scholar in him longed to pore over the manual and uncover its secrets on ancient sorcery, but—

'Hand it over,' the emperor ordered, his eyes gleaming as he eyed the scroll.

Desert Rose hesitated for the briefest moment, but surrendered it before the emperor could notice.

Up close, it looked like any other scroll: wooden and weathered, rolled up and bound by a frayed hemp string. Characters foreign to Meng were inscribed on the first column slate, the ink still dark and gleaming as though the manual had been written just yesterday. What information did it contain? Could it possibly be the secret to restoring magic to the kingdom?

The emperor tried to untie the string, but the dead knot would not budge, even under Desert Rose's knife. He gave the scroll a shake, but it remained stubbornly fastened. The emperor cleared his throat and let out a laugh. 'I'm sure we'll find a way to crack open this old thing. You have done well . . .' He raised his brows, expectant.

'Mingxi,' Desert Rose supplied. There was neither pride nor triumph in her voice. She kept her gaze on the marble ground, but Meng noticed her tightened jaw and clenched fists by her side. She remained where she was, still as stone, as the emperor leaned forward to assess her.

'Very well,' the emperor said at length. 'I pronounce contender Mingxi the winner of the first trial.'

Only then did she raise her clasped fists and meet his gaze. 'Thank you, Your Majesty,' she said. But when she turned away, her eyes spoke vengeance.

*

'You worry about her. The second desert girl.'

Meng snapped out of his thoughts to find his father observing him. The House of Night girls had left with their housemistress, leaving him alone with his parents and Mian, leaving him exposed.

'I . . . I don't,' he said.

Had he been worried about Desert Rose? He had never cared about a girl in his life. They didn't pique his interest the way his books did.

But it had been curiosity that first made him approach her at the Capital gates that night, a fascination akin to that he had for an ancient magic scroll, and perhaps a twinge of pity. Somewhere along the way, something had changed. And today, he *had* been worried about her. He had feared that she would perish in the White Crypt.

'Do you care for her?' his father pressed.

Next to him, his mother's stare sharpened.

Meng hurried to shift his expression into one of indifference, but he knew it was too late. The emperor had an exceptional ability to read people. No matter how he tried to disguise his feelings before his father, he always seemed to let something through the cracks.

'I just feel responsible for the candidate I brought in,' he replied, chasing every emotion out of his voice.

The desert girl who could retrieve water from a dry well was a potential asset to not just the Imperial Guard, but the Nightwalkers, the emperor's secret league of spies. That was the reason he had given his father at the beginning. It was the reason he had given Desert Rose the plaque that led her straight to the housemistress, with no Cleansing or Drafting.

He had brought her into all this.

Some part of him regretted it, even though he knew it was for a greater cause.

'What about the first desert girl you brought in?' the emperor asked. 'Do you care as much for her?'

When he first met Windshadow a couple of years ago, she had been part of an underground rebel faction plotting to kill the emperor, a fact his father was unaware of to this day. Windshadow was the only one caught during the raid; the rest had scattered and gone into hiding, although it might have been her intention to sacrifice herself for her comrades.

If Meng hadn't seen the trick she tried to pull in jail—using *wind* to steal the keys from the prison guard while he was asleep—he might have missed out on a valuable asset by letting her be sentenced to death. There was so much they could do, having a girl with her abilities on their side. And a rebel could always be persuaded to fight for the right cause . . .

'Whatever it is,' the emperor continued, 'they are indeed special if they managed to retrieve something protected by advanced magic.' He laid a hand on Meng's shoulder. 'You did well by bringing them in, son.' He paused. 'But I am concerned about their loyalty. We can't be sure of their allegiance.'

'The second trial can test that, Your Majesty,' said Mian.

According to the High Adviser, who had suggested the idea for the second trial, making the apprentices assassinate their assigned mark would kill two birds with one stone. For one, it would prove their skill and loyalty. For another, Geshao would no longer be a 'loose end' that the empress had wanted taken care of—another fact that the emperor was not aware of.

'We shall see,' the emperor said. 'Meng, have that manual unlocked and deciphered. I want every single secret revealed.'

Meng accepted the order, glad to finally take his leave. He tucked the scroll in his robe and made sure to avoid his mother's eyes as he stepped out of the Hall.

*

He found her in the library that night, sitting among the shelves with her knees folded and staring into space. She had changed out of her tunic and cleaned up, but there was a desolation that remained, like a new skin she couldn't shake off after the first trial.

Winter was starting to thaw—they had made it through the worst of the cold—but it was still draughty in this part of the library. He took over the tea tray from his maid and gestured for her to leave.

Desert Rose was so lost in thought that she didn't notice him approach until he handed her a cup of tea.

'You look like you need some,' he said.

She scrambled to get up, but he stopped her before she could bow to him. They had spent enough evenings here to dispense with formalities now.

'I'm fine,' she said, but accepted the tea anyway.

He pulled out two reading chairs next to the shelves and sat her in one of them before settling into the other. They sipped in silence for a while. Meng watched her as she nursed her cup, her face unreadable.

'What happened in there?' he asked.

She shook her head. Whatever it was that troubled her, she wasn't ready to share.

'Would you like to take a look at the manual?' he asked, setting down his cup of tea and pulling the scroll out of his robe. 'Apparently, it's locked. None of us knows what to do with this old thing.'

She ran her finger down the column of words on the first tab, which Meng presumed was the title. It was written in a serpentine script unlike anything he had ever encountered, although it looked like a combination of the northern Myrrhic scribble and ancient characters from the past, when Oasis Kingdom was still known as Hesui.

Meng leaned close to listen when Desert Rose muttered the title under her breath. It sounded like an ancient tongue, but the words slipped out easily. *Duru-shel Minta*. The War of the Realms.

At her words, the hemp string snapped. The manual rolled open, past her knees and onto the floor. Inside, vertical lines of script, just as unintelligible to Meng, were packed close to one another.

His excitement bloomed. 'Can you understand what it says?'

She bit her lip, frowning as her eyes ran down each tab. 'It goes back to the legend of the Sky Princess and Earth Prince, the two immortals who prompted the First War between heaven and earth.'

'Isn't that an old folk tale?'

'The Celestial King sealed the pool where magic once flowed through to keep the world in balance,' she read, tracing her finger down each line. 'And the age of darkness descended upon earth. Magic that remained on earth fell into the hands of men, and kingdoms now wield it against one another.' She glanced at him.

'Go on,' he urged.

'Oasis Kingdom might have sealed itself off to protect itself, but no amount of purging will destroy magic in this land. Magic cannot be destroyed, nor buried for long.'

He leaned closer. 'What else? Does it say how to unseal it?'

Her frown deepened as she continued reading. 'It says only the essence of the gods can free that which has been contained.'

The essence of the gods. What could that mean?

Desert Rose seemed equally mystified. She squeezed her eyes shut and let out a sigh.

Meng wrapped a hand around hers, offering a smile when her gaze found his again. 'It's okay. We'll figure it out in due time. You've had a long day, get some rest. I'll come and see you again tomorrow.'

She returned a watery smile and took another sip of tea upon his urging. He waited until she had finished her tea before leaving her to her solitude again.

He wanted to linger, to hear her talk about her home and her people again. In that moment, he wanted nothing more than to cut off his title and be free of his destiny. But that was not an option he could afford.

As he left the library, he could almost hear his mother chiding him. 'Foolish boy. Of what use is a bleeding heart to the future ruler of Oasis Kingdom?'

But for now, he would hold on to his bleeding heart, just for a while longer.

There was a time when heaven met earth
through the sacred Celestial Pool.
Gods and monsters worked together,
each with a task to do.
They guarded their realms and upheld the peace,
kept the magic flowing through.
But when two immortals broke the rules,
gods and demons took to war.
The Pool dried up and magic fell
into the inept hands of men.
And so lies the world, sickened by greed
until the Pool flows free again.
Only the essence of the gods can free
that which has been contained.

—Duru-shel Minta, folk song

Twenty-One

Desert Rose

Duru-shel Minta. Of all things, the manual that the old sorcerers had chosen to guard and hide at the bottom of a magic well contained an old folk song Desert Rose had heard countless times growing up.

After Prince Meng left with the scroll, she made her way back to the House of Night, her thoughts in a whirl. There was nothing in there that provided a concrete clue to finding the spring. Why was the emperor so persistent in dredging it up? Why would he unseal the magic in the kingdom after denouncing it for so long?

Dread slowed her feet as she approached the House of Night. Everyone had gathered in the common room for Shuang's wake. Shuang's double swords rested on the table in the middle of the room, illuminated by four white candles. Desert Rose knew there would be no spiritual send-off, but this seemed awfully bare compared to the funerals her tribe held.

She joined the Blue Cranes and Black Cranes standing in two rows behind Shimu, facing the table. On Shimu's cue, they bowed their heads and placed their hands over their hearts.

Shimu spoke on behalf of them, but Desert Rose barely heard what she said. She thought about Shuang's final moment in the maze. How she had fought so hard to win, but lost everything in the end. How her unwavering belief in her destiny had led her this far.

Despite everything Shuang had done to her, it wasn't resentment that Desert Rose felt, but a strange sense of indignation on Shuang's behalf. To think she had devoted her life to this cause only to be sent off as just another casualty.

After the brief ceremony, Desert Rose sent a silent prayer to Yeshil, the moon goddess, to light Shuang's way home. *I'm sorry*, she added, even though she knew Shuang wouldn't have cared for an apology anyway.

Shimu made the Blue Cranes wait in the common room while she briefed the Black Cranes in their dorm. The four of them remained where they were, each stewing in their own thoughts. Even Xiyue couldn't offer a hollow platitude to thaw the atmosphere.

Liqin stepped up to the table. She laid a hand on one of Shuang's swords and dipped her head. It wasn't until Desert Rose went closer that she realized she was crying.

'Liqin,' Desert Rose began, but she didn't know what else to say.

Liqin whirled around, her eyes fierce and shining. 'You could have brought her back. It was the least you could have done.'

Desert Rose wasn't sure if she *could* have, but she should have. Shuang did not deserve to be left behind in the White Crypt.

'We were supposed to join the Imperial Guard together,' Liqin said. 'Shuang is not the one who should have died.'

Shimu returned then, her weary eyes betraying her strong front. 'Tomorrow, you will begin your second trial. The trials, by nature, come with their dangers—this is what you must prepare for not just at the House of Night, but in our duty. I suggest all of you get enough rest tonight. Your next task might take you more than a day to accomplish—and some mental preparation.'

The girls exchanged uncertain looks.

'For your second task,' Shimu said, 'you are to eliminate the mark assigned to you. Whatever you do, leave no trace behind.'

Twenty-Two

Wei

According to Qiu, Geshao was expected at the end of the month. In the days he spent at Qiu's waiting for the merchant, Wei picked up what he could about herbs from his sister while ignoring Zhong's dubious stares and scathing offhand remarks. Heyang remained civil to him, never probing about his business, even though Wei knew that every day he spent at their abode was a day he put the *shouren* at the risk of being exposed.

Wei kept vigil each night, taking turns with Qara, whose tendency to pull out her dagger at the slightest disturbance reminded him of Desert Rose. Sometimes, he found his thoughts drifting to her, but instead of fighting them, he let them tide him through the night.

The day before Geshao's scheduled visit, Wei helped his sister prepare a concoction that involved crushing a shrivelled blood-coloured root and an entire afternoon of brewing.

'I hope this is a truth-telling potion or something that will make him talk,' he said as faint pink smoke rose from the bubbling mixture in the pot. An earthy, floral scent filled the kitchen.

Qiu rolled her eyes. 'No, but I have something that can weaken his defences.'

She continued stirring in languid circles, explaining the properties of the ointment's key ingredient: the Dugurian dreamroot, smuggled in from the black market. As rare as a snowbird's feather, it was lethal enough to plant nightmares in anyone who ingested it in any form, eventually driving him out of his mind.

'So this is what we'll be feeding him?' Wei asked.

Qiu bit her lip. 'This is what he ordered. He wanted a batch of night draught strong enough to knock out an army.'

'An army,' Wei echoed. '*The* army?' If it was indeed the Imperial Army he was targeting, Geshao had to be acting on someone's command. And Wei already had an inkling whom it was.

Geshao's arrival was hard to miss. He rode in a little after last light with his servant boy in tow, complaining about everything he could—the snow, the cold, the uneven terrain—as though he wasn't born and bred in the desert.

Wei and Qara watched from behind the kitchen wall as Qiu and Heyang invited him in.

'This place is more inaccessible than the caves of Mogavu. That forest is out to confuse travellers. Just burn it down,' Geshao said after shedding his coat and settling into a chair.

'If we burned the forest down, the emperor will find us and we will no longer be able to make medicine for you,' Qiu said coolly, offering him a cup of steaming floral tea Qara had prepared.

'Have you prepared what I ordered?' Geshao asked, taking a sip of his tea.

'The first batch is already in storage.'

'What business is this that requires such a huge amount of something so potent?' Heyang asked.

Geshao set his cup down and eyed the fox-man. 'Since when did I have to account for my orders to you?'

'Would you like to inspect the first batch now?' Qiu cut in. 'The next batch is almost ready as well. You should have them within the hour. Have some more tea.' Geshao ignored her and headed towards the storage room.

Qiu followed behind, gesturing for Heyang to stay put when he made to follow them. Wei pressed close to the wall as they passed, his hand gripping the hilt of his knife.

The storage room was a shadowy area in the deepest part of the cavern. Wei slipped through the wooden door after Geshao and Qiu. There was no other exit except for that door.

Perfect for cornering someone.

The room was filled with the heady bittersweet scent of the night draught, warm in their clay jars. Geshao surveyed the stock jar by jar, testing each one with a silver chopstick.

'I'll leave you to it, then,' Qiu said, turning to leave.

Wei wasted no time. As soon as Qiu closed the door, he stepped out from the rack, his hiding spot, and pressed the blade of his knife against the side of Geshao's neck. With the right amount of pressure applied, he could kill him in a heartbeat.

Geshao froze.

'Who sent you?' Wei demanded.

Geshao raised his hands slowly. 'How can I talk with a knife to my neck? Release me and I will tell you what you want to know.'

He was far calmer than Wei expected. Maybe his desert-bred nature hadn't been completely chased out of him yet.

The cold, keen edge of a blade rested against his neck. Wei stilled.

'The mark is mine.' Even muffled, the voice was unmistakeable.

He smirked. 'You've been working on your stealth.'

The blade eased off him. Wei turned around slowly to find Desert Rose standing behind him, dressed in a fitted black tunic and mask. Half her face was covered, but something was different about her. There was a keenness in her eyes that made her look feral, almost unworldly.

What had happened in the time he was out of the palace?

'When did you get in? Did you tail him all the way up here?' He nudged a finger in Geshao's direction.

'Step away from him please.' Her voice was cold. 'I have questions for him.'

'What a coincidence. I was also just about to have a chat with him before killing him.'

In a movement swifter than expected, Geshao shoved past Wei and reached out to yank off Desert Rose's mask. He let out a bark of laughter upon seeing her face.

'My, my. Little Desert Rose. All grown up and attempting to kill me,' said Geshao. 'If I had known this was how you'd end up, I would have killed you myself after Scarbrow brought you back to the tribe. His little desert mongrel.'

Wei brought the tip of his knife back to Geshao's neck, drawing a pinprick of blood as a warning this time. Geshao flinched.

'You stole something from my father,' said Desert Rose. 'I want it back.'

He ignored her. 'Scarbrow should never have brought you into the tribe, much less try so hard to find a cure for you.'

'What cure?' she demanded.

He only laughed. 'So, which one of you is going to kill me?'

'Makes no difference. You betrayed the tribe. Death is mercy for you,' Desert Rose said.

'Says the girl who wields her weapon in the name of the Oasis Emperor.' His eyes dashed to the emblem engraved on the blade of her knife.

'Cut the drivel,' Wei snarled. 'Who ordered the night draught?'

Geshao raised his brows at Desert Rose. 'Not very polite, your friend.'

'Just answer the question,' Desert Rose snapped.

Geshao's lips curled into a sneer. 'Why should I listen to an abomination like you—'

'I'll give you three counts to answer my question before I slice your throat open,' Wei said. 'One.'

Geshao laughed. 'My blood won't spill any answers.'

'*Two.*'

'The Dugur tribe made a grave mistake electing Blackstone as a clan leader instead of me. It's the start of a new era that I would have helped create. The end of the Dugur tribe is coming.'

'Three,' Desert Rose said, stepping forward with her knife—

'Wei!' Qiu burst through the door, panting. 'We need to go. *Now.*'

*

Wei smelled smoke before he saw the fire blazing outside the home. Flames leapt against the night sky, and the very air singed, pungent with thick, acrid smoke laced with something sweet and tart.

The herbs in the other storage room were burning.

Next to him, Desert Rose surveyed their surroundings. 'We're trapped.'

'Rose!' Qara cried. The younger desert girl appeared next to them and threw her arms around Desert Rose.

Desert Rose staggered back in surprise but returned the embrace. 'Qara?'

'Rose, why are you here? Where have you been? I've been so worried.'

Desert Rose pulled away. 'I could ask the same of you.'

'No time for reunions now,' Wei said, his grip tightening on Geshao as the merchant tried to break free.

Zhong and Heyang crashed in through the door, introducing a fresh wave of heat into the house before Heyang slammed the door close behind him.

'Heyang,' Qiu cried, dashing towards him and reaching for his hand. 'Where are the rest? Are they okay?'

'We don't know. We're trapped in here.'

'Someone must have planted this fire,' Zhong snarled.

Qiu's brows pulled together. 'It must not reach the scarlet clouds. Those herbs are combustible.'

'They were led here,' Zhong went on. 'Someone must have tipped them off.' He whirled around and glared at Wei. '*You.*'

'Zhong, now is really not the time,' Qiu said.

An audible sizzle came from the back, followed by a deafening roar. The ground trembled under their feet as flames leapt higher and pressed closer to the house. Fresh clouds of crimson smoke bloomed from outside and crept in from under the door, filling the air with a bitter tang.

'That would be the scarlet clouds,' Qiu said, looking rather faint. 'They can keep a fire going for days.'

'Is there a cellar where we can wait this out?' Wei asked.

'There is,' Heyang said. 'But no guarantees we'll last longer than the scarlet clouds.'

'Somebody do something!' Geshao screamed. 'I can't die here now! I have unfinished business—'

'We're trying to figure something out, in case you haven't noticed,' Wei snapped.

'There is something . . .' Desert Rose said. 'There's something I can try.'

The *shouren* brothers turned to her, realizing her presence. 'Who are *you*?' Zhong demanded.

'Not important for now,' Wei cut in. He peered at Desert Rose, trying to read the hesitation in her eyes. 'Go on. Do you have an idea?'

Desert Rose closed her eyes, her brows pulling together. Outside, the fire continued its rampage, creeping closer by the moment. The heat was scorching, almost dizzying.

'What is she doing?' Geshao cried. 'What are we waiting for?'

'Keep screaming, and maybe I'll slit your throat,' Wei warned, but he glanced at Desert Rose. What was she planning to do? His eyes were tearing up from the blinding heat and Qiu was starting to look a little faint.

When Desert Rose opened her eyes at last, an ethereal light shone from within, silver as the ghost moon on a clear winter's night, steady as the water in a moonlit pond.

It hadn't been a mistake then. It hadn't been a trick of the light the first time he had crossed blades with her. She *was* supernatural. Maybe she had been lying, or maybe she just hadn't known it then.

Desert Rose opened the door before anyone could protest, barely flinching in the face of the flames and the blinding clouds of scarlet smoke that wafted in.

Then he heard it. A gentle slosh and burble, like the gurgling of a stream nearby. The flames retreated like a creature cowering back, revealing a ring of charred grass around the house.

Wei left Geshao's side to join Desert Rose at the door, and found himself facing a towering veil of water as high as the flames could leap. It rippled and shimmered, dancing in the heat. Keeping the fire at bay.

She had created that; she was *controlling* that, as though it were nothing but an extension of her outstretched hand. Her eyes blazed stronger than the fire before them, but Wei noticed the sheen of perspiration on her face.

No time for questions. They had to move now.

But everyone else was rooted to the ground as they watched Desert Rose manipulate the veil. Wei motioned for them to follow him.

Qiu came over to him and laid a hand on his arm. 'Wei, are you sure . . .?'

Wei nodded. 'I trust her.'

'So do I,' said Qara after collecting herself.

Desert Rose pointed to her left. 'This way.'

Beyond the veil of water, a narrow archway no bigger than a stable door shifted into view, revealing the blackened remains of the forest beyond it. It held up strong and sturdy like a brick tunnel, but a closer look revealed that it, too, was made of water. Flames rippled above it, unable to reach them.

'Well, I'll be damned,' Zhong murmured, staring up at the arch.

'I will not set one foot near that sort of witchcraft,' Geshao declared from behind. 'And I still need my night draught—'

'By all means, stay here and burn with your night draught,' Wei said. 'One less person for us to worry about.'

'Hurry up,' Desert Rose said, her face flushed and strained. 'I can't hold it up for much longer. If another scarlet cloud burns . . .'

'Qiu, you go first with the rest,' Wei said. 'I'll bring up the rear.' He clamped a hand on Geshao's shoulder, flashing him a warning with his eyes. He needed Geshao alive, at least until he could shake the truth from his mouth.

If Qiu held any further reservations about Desert Rose's ability, she swallowed them and forged ahead. They dashed through the arch in a single file, led by Desert Rose. The fire bristled around them, indignant at their attempt to foil its destruction. Scarlet smoke trailed behind them from the house and pooled around their feet, frothing like an angry sea.

With a swift elbow to Wei's gut, Geshao wrenched free and scampered back towards the house, disappearing in a cloud of smoke.

'Don't be a fool!' Wei roared after him.

'Which way did he go?' Heyang said.

'He's a pain,' Zhong said. 'Leave him.'

Heyang shot him a look, then turned to Qiu. 'Wait here. I'll go get him.'

'Heyang, no!' Qiu reached for him, but the fox-man was already dashing into the smoke. Wei seized Qiu before she could go after her husband.

Moments slipped by. The fire crept closer towards them as the arch began to falter. Desert Rose's face was turning pale from exertion.

Qiu squirmed against Wei, trying to break free, but he did not relent. She cried out for Heyang, but there was only the muffled sizzle of trees burning. Zhong looked like he meant to go looking for his brother too, but Wei laid a hand on his shoulder.

He tugged on Qiu's arm, hating himself for saying it. 'We have to move.'

'No!' Qiu cried. 'I'm not leaving without him.'

The water arch began to thin around them. Desert Rose swayed on her feet, biting her ashen lip as she raised another hand to prop up the arch. If she lost control, they would burn faster than they could take another step.

But he couldn't leave his sister here.

Qiu craned her neck for a glimpse of Heyang until at last a fox zipped out of the flames, its auburn fur and tail partly singed. It fell before Qiu's feet, unconscious. She scooped it up gently and cradled it close to her as Zhong laid his fingers against its neck, feeling for a pulse.

'He's alive,' Zhong said, his shoulders relaxing.

'Okay, let's keep moving,' Wei said, reaching to catch Desert Rose just as her knees buckled.

'I'm okay,' she murmured, steeling herself, and continued to lead the way.

The arch stretched ahead. Wei lost track of time as they shuffled through, until they finally peeled free of the blistering heat. As their feet left the last wisp of red smoke behind, a blast of icy late-winter air hit them.

Wei's shoes crunched on snow again. The water archway ebbed, revealing the expanse of night overhead. Far behind them was the outcrop surrounded by burnt trees lit by embers.

They stopped at the foot of an old pine tree to catch their breaths. There was less snow cover here and denser vegetation, which meant they were lower down the mountain, but they were still out in the open. Exposed.

Wei checked for moving shadows, but they were alone, as far as he could tell. No stirring in the woods or lurking figures. Just them—stranded in the middle of Yeli mountain, home to fabled beasts, mountain ghouls, and broken magic that lay deep in its stone heart.

'What—what *was* that?' he asked once he had caught his breath. 'That water . . . thing.'

Desert Rose herself didn't have an explanation for it. What she had done was nothing like the sort of magic Wei had seen before during his time in the mountains and the desert.

Qara peered at Desert Rose, keeping, Wei noticed, a careful distance from her. 'But . . . you were never good at the natural arts.'

Desert Rose was staring into space, her eyes glazed and faraway. Her breaths came shallow and quick. It seemed like the mountain wind could sweep her away any moment.

Wei laid a hand on her shoulder. 'Are you okay?'

She made no answer, only collapsing into his arms as her last breath escaped her.

Twenty-Three

Desert Rose

She smelled bitter wood-smoke at first, then the faint saccharine scent of flowers. *The scarlet clouds.*

Her eyelids cracked open.

Overhead, stars peeked through the cloud-strewn sky. She was wrapped in someone's outercoat, lying against something—someone—warm and firm, but an unshakeable chill nestled deep in her bones. The smell of burnt herbs clung to their clothes. Next to her, a low fire crackled, offering meagre warmth against the brutal mountain cold.

'You're awake,' a deep male voice rumbled against her ear.

She jerked away, only to be assaulted by a wave of pain in her head. Her entire body ached like she had been riding all day in the desert.

Wei's face shifted into focus. 'Lie still,' he said, nudging her back into his arms.

She massaged her temples, where a headache seemed to have taken root. As far as she could tell, they were alone.

'Where are we?' she asked.

'In the middle of nowhere, but still on Yeli Mountain.'

She hated the mountain, with its close canopies and deceptive winding paths. While the desert was open and honest, the mountain held on to its secrets. It seemed too easy for someone to jump out from behind a tree and attack them any moment.

'But we're safe . . . for now,' Wei added. 'The rest went to look for the other *shouren* to make sure they're okay. Qara went with them.'

'Qara . . . has been here all this while?'

Wei nodded. 'Ever since she broke free of the clan leaders during the riot at my brother's funeral. My sister took her in.'

'The clan leaders,' she echoed. 'Did they—'

'Yes, they were the ones who rallied the *shouren*, instigated the riots.'

Did that mean the clan leaders—Blackstone and the rest of them—weren't actually allied with the Oasis Emperor? But why would they create unrest in the Capital? And where did Golsha fit into all this? What did he want with that night draught? More importantly, was he still alive? She had caught a glimpse of him dashing back into the house. Everything else that happened after that had faded into a blur.

'We left Geshao behind, most likely dead,' Wei said, as though he had heard her thoughts.

She closed her eyes in dismay. Now she would never know what he had stolen from her father or what he knew about her identity. Her life before she found the Dugur tribe was the biggest mystery of her life, one she had often wondered about despite her father's insistence that it was unimportant.

She recalled the look on everyone's faces, Golsha calling her an abomination. Unlike Windshadow, who had watched her like a proud sister when she used her magic, everyone else had regarded her with wariness and fear, even Qara.

'Aren't you afraid I might hurt you?' she asked.

'I'm not afraid of magic,' Wei said. 'What I fear is magic landing in the wrong hands.'

A chilly wind whipped past. He pulled the coat tighter around her and stoked the fire for a bit.

'When did you discover . . . what you could do?' he asked.

'At Yong's funeral—I called on that downpour to put out the fire. Then it happened again at the first trial, when we were trying to retrieve a manual from the White Crypt.'

The words lodged in her throat. She couldn't tell him about Shuang—what would he think of her?

'And?' he probed.

She told him about the maze, how she and Windshadow had manipulated the blizzard to forge a way through, about the altercation with

Shuang and falling into the well, about the water platform and fighting the storm dragon, about leaving Shuang behind, and finally, about *Duru-shel Minta*.

The power that had flared in her earlier now felt like a demon living inside her. What *was* she? Why did she have such an ability, and why was it surfacing now? Why did her power sap her of every shred of energy whenever she used it and how would she learn to control it?

'I should have saved her,' she said. 'I should have brought her back. I should have at least tried.'

'If you did, you'd be dead in that well too.' He shook her shoulder firmly. 'It was an accident. There was nothing you could have done.'

'When I was about ten,' she said, 'I heard about a boy from another desert tribe who accidentally set his camp on fire. The tribe renounced him. They thought it was dark magic; they thought he was an abomination, because it was unnatural what he could do.' She beat down the horror rising in her throat, still fresh, as though her father had only just relayed the news. 'He burned them all.'

Wei was silent. Did he regret saving her now?

At length, he said, 'Somehow, you don't look like the sort who would drown people alive just to make a point.'

'You think so? I was ready to kill your father for what he did to mine.'

'I don't think you're inherently evil, if that's what you're asking. And this magical ability, whatever it is, is not going to change anything unless you let it.'

She wished her father were here. He would lay his hand on her head and stroke her hair, disentangle her thoughts, and tell her to live her way towards the answers. He would make her feel human again, loved, not a castaway lost in a desert. Not an abomination.

But there was only Wei here and now—not a foe yet not quite a friend, an unlikely ally—his chest rising and falling steadily against her. Still, it was, for some reason, enough to calm her rampant thoughts. Her ragged breaths slowed to match his. It felt less lonely out here in the darkness, breathing in the same thin mountain air with someone else.

'For what it's worth, I don't think you're an abomination,' he added, so softly she almost missed it.

A rustle in the nearby trees startled them both.

Wei's sister stepped out of the shadowy trees with Qara next to her, carrying a small torch.

'How's your husband?' Wei asked Qiu.

'Heyang's with a healer now. Nothing too serious.'

Desert Rose scrambled to her feet with Wei's help.

'Oh good, you're awake,' Qiu said. 'Qara has filled me in about you.' She dipped her head in greeting. 'Pleasure to meet you, Desert Rose. Just call me Qiu.'

Desert Rose returned the greeting. So this was the forsaken princess she had heard whispers about in the palace. Even though she looked a little worse for wear, Princess Qiu carried an air that made her seem regal among these withered woods.

Qara wedged the torch into the ground and threw her arms around Desert Rose. She still smelled like the desert, like home. She had so many questions for her friend, but those could wait for now.

Qara peered at her face. 'How are you feeling?'

She felt drained, as though her power had carved out a hole in her gut and wrung her dry. But how could Qara understand? Even she didn't understand this thing living within her now.

'We found this,' Qiu said, sparing her from answering. She held out a gold-plated badge close to the flame. It was dirt-stained, but there was no mistaking the imperial emblem engraved on it. 'And we found the rest of the *shouren*'—Qiu glanced at Desert Rose—'with the desert clan leaders.'

With the help of the lone torch, the four of them made their way to a clearing that overlooked a shallow valley, where what appeared to be several hundred *shouren* gathered on the bank of a half-frozen ravine. Some were in their animal form—hares and boars and wolves and deer pacing in circles—while others remained human in their singed or torn clothes. There were children, *infants* barely alive, mothers, and the elderly. Some were tending to the wounded and dead, others looked as though the fire had burned the fight out of them.

Five men in dark ermine coats stood in a row in front of the crowd. On instinct, Desert Rose withdrew into the shadows, colliding into Wei behind her. She could have sworn Bataar spotted her from below. Part of her wanted to charge down there and demand to know what they had done to her father, but fear planted her firmly on the spot.

Blackstone stepped up to a mound to address the crowd. Behind him, Bataar and the other Dugur clan leaders—Bekir, Erden, Gan, and Huol—maintained a stony front.

'For generations,' said Blackstone, 'you have been abandoned by this kingdom. Look around you. Look at your wounded, your dead. This is the act of a tyrant who calls himself the chosen ruler of this land. He destroyed your home, your families, your lives. He almost killed your leader.' He gestured at an injured wolf laying in the arms of a grey-haired woman, who was applying salve to its charred fur. 'Will you continue to live in hiding, cowering in fear from the emperor, when he has more reason to fear you?'

A murmur rippled through the *shouren.* Those in animal form kicked their hind legs or thumped their tails in support.

Desert Rose turned to Qiu. 'Do they really think he cares about the *shouren's* lives or their homes and families? He's just using them for the rebellion.'

A twig snapped behind them. They whirled around to find Golsha several feet away, his face barely illuminated by the torch on the ground. His clothes were torn and half-burnt, and his soot-smeared face sported fresh cuts. He froze when he saw them, then turned tail and ran.

Wei wasted no time. Whipping out his knife, he took off after the merchant.

'Wei!' Qiu hissed, but Wei had already disappeared into the gloom. She sighed.

Blackstone continued speaking below, oblivious, but Bataar's gaze snapped up. Desert Rose pulled Qara further back into the shadows, but Bataar's eyes landed right on her. She ducked behind a tree, her heart racing.

Qara gripped her hand. 'Did he see you?'

'Go,' Qiu told Desert Rose. 'Find my brother and return to the palace.'

'What about Qara?' Desert Rose said. 'If Bataar finds her—'

'I'll take care of her. I don't trust Blackstone any more than you do. And I will do whatever I can to protect my family and friends from those clan leaders.'

Desert Rose yearned to stay with Qara, but she was still in the running for the trials and had an emperor to kill. 'Meet me at the eastern gates on the night of the Spring Ceremony at ten bells,' she told Qara. 'We will leave the Capital together.'

There were too many things that could go wrong, too many ways she wouldn't be able to escape home with her friend. But she had to believe they would pull it off. They had to.

She gave Qara's hand a squeeze and dashed through the trees. It was impossible to go far or fast in this darkness, not unless she fancied breaking her ankle on a root. There was no sign of Wei or Golsha, no stirring whatsoever. She paused to gain her bearings.

A rustle came from her left. Her grip tightened on her knives.

Out of the gloom came a hulking figure. She whirled around and struck without hesitation. Her blade ripped through several inches of cloth before Bataar caught her wrist. She aimed a kick at his chest, but he struck her in the gut before she could attack and shoved her against a tree.

Even without a weapon drawn, Bataar was far more skilled than her in combat and had obvious physical advantage, but maybe she could buy some time for Qara and Qiu to get away.

Bataar took a step towards her. She picked herself up and held out her knives, collecting her breath. 'Stay away from me.'

Bataar stopped and let out a sigh. 'Rose. I'm not the one you should fear.'

'Funny, coming from the person who shot me in the leg.'

'I could have shot you in the heart.'

'Well, thank you for your magnanimity,' she snapped.

'I never meant to hurt you.'

'But you did. You picked a side, and you helped destroy our tribe.'

'I'm helping to create change. Scarbrow has defended the tribe for decades, but we cannot remain passive any longer. Kingdoms are warring around us. It's only a matter of time before we are used as pawns by one of them, or worse, destroyed. We need to take matters into our hands instead of waiting to be attacked.'

He took her hand and gave it a gentle squeeze like he used to before they went off to explore a new territory or stake out passing caravanserais. But this time, his touch only made her flinch.

'Rose, come back with us,' he said, unfazed. 'Once our business here is finished, we can all go back home and rebuild a new tribe.'

His words ignited another spark of fury in her. 'I *had* a home,' she spat, 'until you chased me out of it.' She yanked her hand out of his grasp and turned to leave.

'My father and the other clan leaders let Scarbrow go,' he called.

Her footsteps faltered.

Bataar caught up with her. 'Before he fled, he said he was going to find a cure for you, whatever that meant.'

A cure. It was the same thing Golsha had mentioned. But a cure for *what*?

She shook her head. 'I won't believe another word you say.'

'The clan leaders only persecuted him to convince the Oasis Emperor of their loyalties.' He reached for her hand again. 'We would never have pushed Scarbrow over the edge.'

She shoved his hand away and glared at him. 'Blackstone has always wanted to be chieftain. The coup was not an act; they betrayed my father all the same. *You* betrayed him—and me.'

Bataar's gaze hardened. 'If that's what you choose to believe, so be it.' He unsheathed his sabre. 'But if you are not with us, then you are against us.'

'My father is dead because of you and the clan leaders. The ones who swore their allegiance to him!' she roared, dropping her knives and gathering all the strength left in her. The ice and snow responded to her call, seeping towards her through the frozen ground, the very air. She assembled it around her, sharpening them to flints. 'I'd rather die than join you lot of traitors.'

Bataar stared at the row of ice arrows hovering in the air around her and took a step back. 'Rose . . . what is this?'

She raised her hands. 'Let me go, Bataar, or I will do what I should have done that night.'

'This . . . this is not the natural arts.'

'I said, leave!'

Bataar sheathed his sabre and raised his hands in the air, backing away slowly. 'You belong to the tribe, Rose. I believe you will come back one day. And maybe you will see that what we are doing is for the good of our people.'

'Keep telling yourself that if it helps you sleep better at night.'

Bataar turned and left without another backward glance.

At her command, the arrows dissolved around her. She clenched her shaking fists and fell to her knees. Blood raced through her veins, and her old wound throbbed where Bataar had shot her all those nights ago.

Twenty-Four

Meng

The general brought news of the Yeli Mountain fire two days later. In the Hall of Valour, Meng perched on the edge of his seat, next to his parents and Mian.

'About a hundred-odd *shouren* were killed in the fire, as of last count,' he reported.

The emperor leaned forward in his seat. 'Is that all of them?'

'We don't know. But we have reason to believe there are still survivors.'

The emperor slammed his hand down on the arm of his seat. 'I distinctly recall my order was to leave no survivors. I want the mountain burned to its core and not a single *shouren* left.'

'But the Third Prince was there too—with a girl. And . . .' His gaze fell to the floor.

'Speak freely,' Meng said.

The general looked up, his jaw tightening. 'And the princess,' he said.

Silence curdled, thick as spoilt milk.

The general begged for pardon, but Meng cut him short. 'You said the Third Prince was with a girl? Did you see her face?'

The general couldn't identify her, but it became clear who she was soon enough, when he described the way she led them out of a ring of fire . . . by creating a tunnel of water.

If Desert Rose was on Yeli Mountain going after her mark, that meant Geshao was there too. The merchant had told him he was able to round up 'a sizeable group of rebels' who could also prepare the night draught Meng had ordered. Did he mean the *shouren*?

'I should have thrown him into prison with his mother as soon as he returned,' the emperor seethed.

'Are they alive?' Meng asked the general. His mother shot him a piercing stare, but he pretended not to notice.

The doors to the Hall swung open before the general could reply.

Wei looked the same as he did on the day he returned to the Capital—as though he had fought his way through hell. Sometimes, Meng wondered if living in the wild had made his brother more beast than human, or if it had only brought out the beast in him.

Wei scanned each of their faces. 'I have new leads from a merchant by the name of Geshao.'

*

Meng had never seen his mother quite this furious, not even when Han was banished or when Yong was officiated as Crown Prince. It was a small stroke of luck that Wei returned at this hour and the emperor decided to trial Geshao in court the next day.

Still, that didn't stop Meng's mother from pacing around her chamber now. She whirled around to glare at him. 'Do you realize what this means for us? If Geshao confesses everything, both of us would suffer Luzhen's fate too.'

'We still have some time until the court trial tomorrow, Mother. I'll settle this issue tonight.'

'You told me this would not be a problem. You told me the girl would be on our side.'

'Desert Rose would have killed him if it weren't for Wei being there as well. She has reason to side with us—Father destroyed her tribe. She just needs some time.' His mother's lips thinned. Meng sighed. 'Give me some time. I will fix everything.'

'The Spring Ceremony is in a week. The tide can turn against us in that time.'

'I am aware of that.' A hint of irritation slipped out of him.

She laid a hand on his cheek. 'Meng, we have come too far to be thwarted at this step. My only wish is to see our family reunited again. Don't you?'

And there she had him, once again, knowing this was the reason he agreed to everything she had planned. Only if he were the emperor would he have the power to piece his family back together. Only if he were the emperor would he finally have control over his own life. Only if he were the emperor would he be able to save his kingdom.

Whatever the cost, it would be worth it. He had to believe it would.

He grasped her hand in both of his. 'It's all I ever want.'

'You are all I have left, Meng. You are my only hope.' Her words felt like a rope, sometimes a lifeline, sometimes a noose.

'Everything will go as planned, Mother,' he said. 'Trust me.'

Twenty-Five

Desert Rose

Windshadow won the second trial. Not only had she killed her mark, she was also the first to return. If only Wei hadn't insisted on bringing Golsha back to the palace alive. If only her mark was not also a suspect involved in the Crown Prince's murder.

But what did it matter now, making it to the final trial? She never intended to become part of the emperor's personal guard, and the *shouren* were already planning to attack the palace. With what she was capable of now, it would be even easier than lifting a sword.

Except . . . could it really be that easy? Would the emperor not suspect a thing, having two desert girls living under his roof?

And what did it mean if she joined the *shouren* in dethroning the emperor? Was she then abetting the clan leaders, the ones who had betrayed her father?

A strange new hunger growled in her gut. There was a newly carved space where her power seemed to be growing by the day, consuming more of her.

She had never asked many questions about her past. There was no reason to: she recalled nothing about it, and Scarbrow gave her everything she could ever ask for—love, home, family, friends.

But now that she was far away from home without any of those things, and her father wasn't around to answer her questions (or shield her from the truth), she had to find the answers on her own.

Golsha knew who—or what—she was. He had been there when her father had brought her back to the tribe.

She stole down the lane leading out of the House of Night, aware of her footfalls and every breath she took. An evening this still was not favourable for sneaking out, but she couldn't wait any longer.

A rustle made her halt. Before she could duck into the shadows, Shimu appeared in front of her, her gaze piercing through the gloom.

'Where are you going at this hour, Mingxi?'

Not a single excuse came to mind that would sound believable.

'I think,' said the housemistress, 'given the circumstances so far, it's best for you to lie low. There has already been talk about your miraculous escape from the well in the White Crypt and the fire on Yeli Mountain.' She took a step closer and lowered her voice. 'Surely you know by now that to use magic in this kingdom is to court death.'

Her breath caught. 'You—you knew?'

'The Fourth Prince did not bring you and Windshadow in for no reason.'

They had known. Shimu and Matron had understood everything right from the start, ever since she showed them the plaque Prince Meng had given her. Had her entry to the Capital and her journey to this point been planned from the beginning too? How many more of them knew about her abilities? How many of them had lied to her?

She needed air. She needed to get out of this palace and back to . . . where? There was no home for her to go any more.

First things first—she needed answers.

'I just need to talk to Geshao. Please.' There was no way Shimu would allow her to visit a prisoner who used to be a tribemate. 'Prince Meng told me to,' she lied.

Shimu narrowed her eyes. 'Return by last lamp,' she said at last.

'Thank you.'

She bolted down the path before the housemistress could change her mind, speeding past the gardens, chambers, library, and astronomy tower towards the prison, keeping away from lamplight.

Flanked by two stone pillars, the entrance to the dungeons was a heavy black metal door set in a thick stone wall. Desert Rose slunk to the back to avoid the guards and slid through the crusty grills of a small window, the only one in sight.

She crept down the steep, narrow stairway leading down to the dungeon, relying on firelight from the scant torches along the stairway. A prison guard on duty was deep in slumber, his hat tipping down his ruddy face. She snuck past him and headed down the corridor.

It was slow-going, searching each cell under dim lighting. Cold drafts of wind swirled through the passage, hurrying her along.

Then came a voice, quiet and deep, not five feet away from her. She ducked behind a wall and pulled her mask higher up her face.

'I will come for you soon, Mother. Wait for me.'

'Wei, what are you planning to do?' The second voice was tight with worry.

'Don't worry, Mother. We'll be free of this wretched place at last.' Wei turned, as though sensing a presence behind him. Desert Rose held her breath.

Wei got up and headed in her direction. Before she could slip away, he reached out and grabbed her arm, leading her down the passageway. He only released her after they had rounded a bend, away from his mother's ears.

'I know why you're here,' he said, keeping his voice low. 'His cell is that way.' He pointed over her shoulder. 'I was just about to pay him a visit too.'

They wound down the passageway, where the cells became draughtier and more cramped. At last, Wei came to a stop before a cell tucked in the corner. Most of the prisoners were asleep, and this one lying near the bars was no different.

Except he lay face down next to a half-eaten bun.

Desert Rose exchanged a glance with Wei and knelt next to the body.

'Golsha?' she said, prodding him with the hilt of her knife. No response. Wei knelt before him and turned him over.

The ex-tribesman's face was ashen, lips blackened, and he was no longer breathing.

'Poisoned,' Wei murmured, checking his pulse. 'Someone didn't want him to talk.'

*

The House of Night was dark when she returned. Everyone had retired to their dormitories. Desert Rose sank into a chair in the darkened common room, her mind reeling.

Her last lead was gone, and the Spring Ceremony was looming. She needed a plan, one that did not involve picking a side, one that would allow her to escape Oasis Kingdom after she was done with the emperor.

Windshadow came in on a breeze. Desert Rose had gotten so used to the way she came and went that she never once questioned how Windshadow managed to move around so stealthily. Even now, in the common room with the door closed, she only registered Windshadow's arrival when the girl appeared on the chair next to her.

'Where have you been, *azzi*?' Windshadow leaned over and peered at her face. 'Why the dour face? Was that your first kill? Remember, we're assassins. No room for bleeding hearts here.'

Desert Rose continued staring at the ground. 'Windshadow, what do you remember of the desert?'

'Plenty. Mostly stuff I don't want to remember.' She paused. 'Why?'

'What about the time you discovered your abilities?'

She had never wondered this before, who Windshadow really was, where she came from, and what brought her to the Capital to support a prince she had no affiliation to. But it seemed crucial now to understand.

'After I fought a skin-hawk when I was ten,' said Windshadow. 'You know those things—they're relentless and won't stop until they've ripped you apart.' Desert Rose nodded. 'I finally shredded it with the biggest gust of wind I had ever summoned. The other kids in my tribe stopped picking on me after that.'

'You don't think it's strange that we are the only ones who can do this?'

'Because we're special? Who knows? Why look a gift horse in the mouth? What matters is how we use this magic, and right now we have a common enemy to fight. Everything is in place.'

'Everything?'

Windshadow looked over Desert Rose's shoulder, a smile sliding up her face. Desert Rose turned around to find Prince Meng standing at the back entrance of the common room. He approached them, serene and composed as always, as though nothing about their conversation was out of the ordinary. As though he had known all along.

He sat down next to her. 'You have witnessed what it's like under my father's reign.' His gaze was as gentle as his voice, but now when he placed his hand on hers, she flinched. 'I need your help, Rose. Your abilities can help end my father's tyranny and fix all that is wrong with this kingdom.'

'Did you know all along what I was?' she said quietly.

He sighed. 'I had a guess.'

She pulled her hand out of his. 'Was that why you brought me into the palace, the House of Night, and made me train as an assassin? So that I could be a weapon you used against your father when the time came?'

'No.' He shifted closer and looked her in the eye. 'That was not my intention. Yes, I *had* hoped you could help my cause, but your agenda turned out to match mine.' He turned away, his gaze hardening. 'My father's position was precarious to begin with, and the people are demanding for change. They deserve to be free of his rule, to see magic restored to the kingdom. And while I cannot say that I will make a good emperor, at least I can be a rational one.'

Why should she even help him? What did she care about the fate of Oasis Kingdom? All she ever wanted was to find her father, and to make the one responsible for her father's death pay.

Yet, what if Meng's rule could bring peace between the kingdom and desert tribes? What if Oasis Kingdom could become strong enough to bring the warring nations to a ceasefire?

Her thoughts drifted to what Wei had told her—that his mother would not have a chance to live if Prince Meng took over the throne, because standing behind him were the empress and the High Adviser. How freely could Meng really rule the kingdom?

'Desert Rose,' Meng said, pulling her out of her thoughts. 'Will you help me?'

Windshadow nudged her. 'We wanted our revenge, didn't we, *azzi*?' Her eyes shone in the low lamp light, bright as twin blades. 'Now's our chance.'

Twenty-Six

Desert Rose

Spring crept up on them after what seemed like an endless winter. The bitter cold tried its best to linger on, but occasionally a warm breeze that swept through the palace grounds succeeded in chasing it away.

Now mere days away from the Spring Ceremony, preparations began in earnest. Maids scurried about with rolls of silk and baskets of flowers under Matron's direction, and rehearsal ceremonies took place at the Spring Court outside the Hall of Blessings.

The House of Night, however, was filled with the sound of swords ringing.

The sword dance had a complicated choreography that involved a mixture of dancing and sparring, intricate and precise body movements while wielding double swords. Desert Rose, paired with Liqin, easily fared the worst. It didn't help that Liqin went at her with more vengeance than necessary, until Shimu threatened to take her out of the performance altogether.

On the first evening of spring, every court official, noble, and member of the imperial family gathered at the Spring Court, draped in gold-spun silks and furs and dripping with jewels in festive hues. Sapphires, emeralds, and rubies glittered atop immaculate headpieces. Nobles and ambassadors came bearing gifts wrapped in silk cloth, greeting one another far too heartily.

The courtyard was bordered on three sides by long rows of tables and cushions laden with gilded plates overflowing with flowers and fruits for the banquet. Wine goblets perched before each attendee, periodically refilled by maids. Lanterns dangled overhead, their warm glow illuminating each face. Pockets of conversation blended with the music made by zither and flute players, punctuated by occasional bursts of laughter.

At the far end of the court was the emperor's empty seat, raised above everyone else's. Matron was already seated four seats away, keeping an eye on the maids on duty.

Desert Rose watched the proceedings from the holding room with the other performers, Windshadow and Xiyue by her side and Liqin hovering a few feet away. They were in their dark blue tunics belted with a red sash, over which they wore a ceremonial dark blue robe with flared sleeves. A red mask covered half their painted faces and a red ribbon held their hair in identical buns. Their double swords tucked by their waists effectively kept the other performers away from them.

Xiyue wrung her hands, biting her lip as she stared out the window. 'Go over that last bit with me again, Liqin,' she begged.

'For the last time, Xiyue, you'll be fine. Quit bothering me about the choreography,' Liqin said, although her shaking fingers couldn't stop fidgeting with her sash.

Desert Rose took deep breaths to calm her nerves. Xiyue reached over to give her hand an encouraging squeeze, though she was antsy not for the reason Xiyue presumed. She peered out, surveying the rooftops and shadowed nooks for a sign of Wei or a *shouren*, even though it was impossible to tell the latter apart from humans. Was the plan already in action? How many of them were already in the palace?

The imperial family arrived with much fanfare, brought in on gilded sedans and with court maids parting the way. Meng stepped out with the confidence of a future emperor, dressed in a resplendent blue robe embroidered with silver. The female performers in the holding room let out a collective dreamy sigh at the sight of him. Windshadow sent her a conspiratorial nod, but Desert Rose only continued scanning the courtyard for tell-tale signs of a brewing mutiny.

The emperor launched into his speech once everyone was seated. Desert Rose let her attention drift away, her thoughts buzzing in her head.

Wei, where are you? Was he with the *shouren* now, or had he gone to break his mother out of prison? Did Meng have an inkling of what was to come?

She shook her head. *Focus, Rose.* This was her chance, at last, to get the answers she wanted from the emperor and then finish him off. There was no time to dwell on anything else. She had a promise to keep with Qara. She had to make it out of here alive.

Out in the courtyard, everyone raised their goblets when the emperor toasted to peace and prosperity in the kingdom.

'Long live Oasis Kingdom! Long live the emperor!' the crowd chorused before tipping back their drinks.

The first troupe of dancers filed out of the holding room and leaped to the centre of the courtyard as the first dish was served. Everyone plunged either into conversation or their food. It wouldn't take much to throw them all into mayhem.

The Blue Cranes were the second last act of the evening. Liqin led them out to the stage as the music shifted into a darker, urgent number. Desert Rose fell into position, seeking strength in her cold steel blades.

Meng watched her the entire time; she could feel his eyes on her as soon as she stepped out. She took a deep breath and cleared her mind, focusing only on the routine they had practised countless times. Her heart pounded along to the drumbeats from the orchestra. She kept steady while flourishing her blades and dancing in sync with Liqin, but kept her eyes peeled for moving shadows or birds circling in the night sky.

While the audience's attention had been scattered before, it was now fixed on the Blue Cranes. Their eyes trailed their movements and they gasped whenever the Cranes thrust their swords just shy of each other's skin. Set against the steady rumble of drums, the hypnotic lilt of the reed flute and accompanying twang of the lute filled the air.

No one noticed when the beasts snuck in, prowling along the rooftops as shadows against the night.

It was not until they descended upon the courtyard that the first scream erupted. The music died. The Blue Cranes stopped. Murmurs rippled through the attendees as the emperor rose from his seat.

There were no more than fifty of them, as far as Desert Rose could tell, but they came in various forms—furred, fanged, hoofed, winged and clawed. Hawks and ravens swooped down from the sky, and serpents slithered down the pillars. Wolves, tigers, bears, and foxes tore through the crowd, aiming for court officials and military generals.

'Guards!' the emperor roared, staggering back. But no one came. Even without Golsha's night draught, the palace's defence had been immobilized.

Guests, performers, palace maids, and servants scrambled to escape, knocking over tables and wine goblets and platters of food, colliding into each other, tripping on their robes. By the far end of the banquet table, a group of drunk male officials attempted to fight off a tiger.

With the ceremony effectively interrupted, the Blue Cranes disbanded, Liqin fending off the animals while Xiyue guided a few court officials to safety. Desert Rose found Meng amongst the crowd, helping his mother up next to an upended table. He caught her gaze and nodded at her, urging her along, before leading the empress and the High Adviser through a narrow corridor that led to the Lotus Garden.

Windshadow grabbed her hand. 'Time to move!' she crowed, tugging her towards the emperor, who was still expecting the imperial guards to come to his aid. Windshadow took the emperor by one arm. 'Don't worry, Your Highness. We'll take you to safety.'

Desert Rose grabbed his other arm, and they dragged him towards the astronomy tower. Her sword swung heavy by her side, a reminder of what she was about to do. They wove through the chaos, sidestepping snakes and darting around people, keeping their grip on the emperor as they ducked into the alcove and hurried down a series of hallways.

Far away from the courtyard, the astronomy tower was cloaked in silence. Their shuffling footsteps and the emperor's laboured breathing echoed in the unearthly calm here.

'Where are all the guards?' the emperor demanded. 'What is going on?'

Windshadow shoved him through the double doors. 'Let's get you to safety before we explain, Your Highness.'

Desert Rose peered around to confirm that they weren't being tailed before sealing the doors. Swift as a breeze, Windshadow whipped behind the emperor and pinned him to the ground, jamming her knee into his back.

'Sorry we have to do this, Your Highness,' she said as he struggled. 'Actually, no. I'm not sorry at all.' Windshadow glanced up at her. 'Are you, Rose?'

The emperor strained to look up at her. The same coldness lay in his eyes when he had used his son's funeral to rally the people's support for him, when he had ordered for the rioters to be put down. She saw in his eyes everything that had unfolded that fateful night, when she was forced to flee her home and watch her father persecuted by the clan leaders, when she was shot by the boy she had once called a friend.

A flame kindled in her gut. She took a step closer to him and pulled down her mask. 'Not one bit.'

'You should have known better than to let outsiders into your kingdom, Your Highness,' Windshadow said.

He laughed. 'You think you can get away with killing the *emperor*?'

'Right now, we are alone here while your army is disabled and the *shouren* are invading your palace. I'd say our odds are pretty good.'

'There are witnesses,' he hissed. 'Even if you manage to kill me, you will be hunted down like the animals you are, with your wild, dirty magic. Your tribe, your family—they will pay for your crimes.'

Desert Rose leaned down to look him in the eye. 'They already have.' Her vengeance burned in her, now leaping and roaring like a bonfire. 'That's what happens when you destroy our families and our homes. We have nothing left to lose.' She pressed the tip of the blade against his neck, watched the colour drain from his face as her blade drew blood.

A bit more pressure and she could stab his throat . . .

'I know where your father is!' he cried.

He's just trying to save his hide, Rose. But she faltered nonetheless.

The emperor seized his chance. 'I know you're the Dugur chieftain's daughter. I know where your father is. He's not dead. Spare me and I will tell you where you can find him.'

She leaned close to him and hissed in his face, 'Don't lie to me. He's dead. Prince Meng told me you killed him.'

His brows twitched in confusion before realization dawned in his eyes. 'Meng told you that I had your father killed? Do you really think I would concern myself with the fate of an ousted chieftain? Dead or alive, his tribe has turned his back on him. He is no threat to me.'

If the emperor were telling the truth, it would support what Bataar had told her.

But that would mean that Meng had lied to her.

The emperor's laughter interrupted her thoughts. 'Meng, of all people. He sent two desert girls to kill me?' He laughed again, as though he had forgotten there was a sword against his throat. 'My fourth son. Oh, how we've read the stars wrong!'

'Hilarious,' Windshadow said dryly.

The doors swung open to reveal Wei and his mother still in her soiled prison tunic and a man's coat that drowned her petite frame. How did he know to find them here? Had he followed her?

He registered no surprise when he saw her holding the emperor at sword-point. 'Rose, don't.'

'You said you wouldn't stop me.'

'This is a trap.'

'Wei,' the emperor snarled. 'I should have known you both would be part of this. Ganging up with the *shouren* against me.'

Wei ignored him and said to Desert Rose. 'We need to leave—now. The empress is on her way—with guards.'

But she was so close now. All she had to do was let her blade finish the job.

'Rose, come on,' Windshadow urged. 'Do it and we can all go.'

Wei's attention flicked to Windshadow. 'Windshadow, am I right? I hear you have quite the way with wind. Was that how you entered my brother's chamber the night he was murdered?'

The emperor turned to Windshadow, his face flushed with rage. Luzhen's hand flew up to cover her mouth. Desert Rose stared at the other desert girl, almost releasing her grasp on her sword as she understood at last.

Of course, it would have been easy for Windshadow to sneak past the guards. To slip into a private chamber without a sound. To spike the Crown Prince's food and then disappear on a breeze.

'Not sure if you know this,' Wei went on, 'but you left some sand behind that you forgot to clean up.'

But why would Windshadow kill the Crown Prince? What was he to her?

The answer hit her like a blow to the gut. 'Prince Meng,' she murmured. 'You were working under his orders.'

All those times Windshadow had urged her to trust in the Fourth Prince. And what he had said about not being able to create any change unless he was emperor. This was all his doing; he had planned every step of the way. Arranged the Crown Prince's murder. Brought in two desert girls who bore a grudge towards the emperor. Made them kill the emperor so that he could finally ascend the throne. Maybe he was the one who had killed Golsha too.

She stared at her desert friend, hoping she would refute Wei's claims, but Windshadow had disappeared. Instead, a rough gale swept through the chamber, shoving her towards the emperor.

Her sword plunged straight into the emperor's throat, right down to the hilt. The emperor let out a choked gurgle, his eyes bugged as he stared at her.

Cold horror washed over her, turning her arm numb. She had killed him. Windshadow was gone, and all that remained was her sword lodged in the emperor's throat. Whatever answers he had about her father, she would now never know.

'Murder,' a voice declared, sharp and imperious.

The empress stood in the doorway, flanked by two guards. Behind her, Meng stared at Desert Rose with an unreadable look on his face.

Had he planned all this too—with Windshadow setting her up, and the empress and guards catching her in this moment? Had this all been his ploy to bring her to this very moment, make her the scapegoat of all their crimes? Had there ever been one moment where he was truthful to her? She tried to find an answer in his eyes, but they gave nothing away.

Now that the emperor's blood was on her hands, she saw everything with perfect clarity.

Azzi. Her desert sister had betrayed her. And so had Meng.

Meng took a step towards her, but the empress pointed an accusing finger at her.

'Seize the murderer!' she ordered. 'And the fugitive!'

Wei seemed well prepared for this. He knocked out the guard nearest to him before they could react to the empress's order. Desert Rose shook herself out of shock and took Luzhen aside as Wei felled the guards one after another, leaving no room for them to counter.

With no guards left to protect her, Empress Wangyi ducked behind Meng, who stood between her and Wei, daring Wei to take another step closer. They faced each other head-on, neither willing to budge, until Meng pulled out a knife tucked in his waist and went for Wei's neck.

Wei swerved and gave Meng a hard shove, sending him and the empress colliding into a pillar. He grabbed Desert Rose and his mother, and they bolted out of the astronomy tower.

Desert Rose ignored the blood pounding in her ears, the magic rushing through her veins ready to spill out, the nagging wrongness at the back of her mind. She had killed the emperor like she had set out to. But she felt no satisfaction or triumph, only the same hollowness that her father's absence had carved in her.

But there was no time to dwell on that now. Qara was waiting for her. Together with Wei and his mother, she sprinted blindly down the hallways, stepping over fallen soldiers and guards, eager to put as much distance behind her as possible. Eager to leave this Capital life behind at last.

Twenty-Seven

Wei

Within the Red Circle lay a secret passageway that would take them out of the palace. It was meant only for the imperial family in times of emergency. When Wei was little, Matron had showed him that exit once. Back then, he hadn't yet seen the need for it.

Now, though, he was relieved to find the nondescript wooden door set in the grey stone wall in the corner of the library. He let his mother duck through it first, then gestured for Desert Rose to follow suit. Her eyes met his as she hesitated for the briefest moment before stepping through.

Behind the door was a narrow stone alcove that could fit no more than four people. Beyond that, a flight of stairs led down to a well of darkness.

Every shred of light was extinguished once Wei shut the door behind him. He ventured forward and offered his hand to his mother, who in turn took Desert Rose's. They inched down the stairs until their feet hit cold, damp stone. Every rustle here they made echoed in the silence.

They forged ahead.

At one point, after what felt like an endless walk, Desert Rose said, 'I hope you know where you're going.'

'Feel free to turn back any time,' Wei replied.

The tunnel seemed interminable. He had no way of telling where they were or where they would end up. And the going was slow—they had to pause for rest several times when his mother grew dizzy from the scant underground air.

At last, they came before a wooden door. It didn't budge when he pushed it, but surrendered after he gave it a hard shove. It groaned on its hinges as it swung open, revealing a storage room of sorts. As big as a travelling tent, it had walls lined with racks, cupboards, and sealed sacks of dry goods stacked in neat rows.

Beyond those stacks was the front door. Wei pushed it open gingerly and they stepped out into a sundry shop, closed for the day. The darkness gave them some cover, but the uncooperative tunnel door had already alerted two pairs of patrol soldiers to their arrival. They stormed into the shop, weapons drawn.

'Surrender your weapons!' one of the soldiers commanded. Wei drew out his sword as two of them dove straight at him.

Wei dodged by a hair's breadth while Desert Rose pulled his mother aside and knocked another soldier out with a swift blow to the neck. Another charged forward, swinging his sword at Desert Rose. Wei slammed his blade against the soldier's sword before it could reach her.

'We have orders from Prince Meng to bring the girl back alive, or she will be charged with treason,' said the soldier. 'Empress Wangyi will testify as a witness.'

Wangyi. Meng. His father. They were supposed to be his family, yet it seemed like no matter how hard he fought, he somehow always ended up running from them like a hunted animal.

A wave of fury rose in him. Out of spite, he slashed a soldier next to him across the gut. The soldier dropped his sword with a groan and collapsed to the ground. His wound was not fatal, but the blood loss could be.

The remaining two soldiers threw out their shields. 'Prince Wei,' one of them said. 'All Prince Meng wants is the girl. He says he is willing to let you and the prisoner go.'

'How magnanimous of him.' Wei turned to Desert Rose. 'Do you want to go back to the palace?'

Desert Rose shook her head. 'He lied to me and used me. The palace is the last place I will go.'

Wei shrugged at the soldiers, pushing aside the strange pang of relief in him. 'You heard her. Now, I suggest you step aside and let us through, or I will cleave my way through like I have before.'

The soldiers exchanged a look.

'We could go for another round, or you can save him.' He glanced at the soldier, who now lay gasping in a pool of his blood. 'Your choice.'

'I'm sorry, but orders are orders,' said the soldier. He grabbed Wei's mother and dragged her away from Wei, holding out his sword. 'Surrender the girl and we will let you and the prisoner go.'

The prisoner. Once the empress, his mother was nothing but a fugitive to them now. The imperial army was now a headless beast, its loyalties shaken now that the throne was vacant, but it seemed that Meng and Wangyi were already in command.

'Release her,' Wei said quietly. 'I will not repeat myself.'

The soldiers shared another look, but did not budge. Wei lashed at them with his blade. Appearing behind them, Desert Rose delivered a well-aimed blow to their necks, knocking them out before either of them could detect her presence.

'You're welcome,' said Desert Rose. Wei felt his lips creep up in a smile.

They bolted towards the doors, but what greeted them outside made them stop short. A platoon of soldiers, at least fifty of them, stood before them like an impenetrable wall, weapons at the ready. Even if they made a good team, there was no way he and Desert Rose could take on all of them.

'I hate to state the obvious,' Wei muttered, 'but it looks like we're outnumbered.'

Desert Rose did not respond, not even when the general stepped forward and ordered them to surrender. She only closed her eyes and raised her hands as though she was gathering all the energy she could find.

Wei recognized that look. He had witnessed it on Yeli Mountain. Whatever she was attempting now would likely get her stoned here in the Capital. Even if there were no civilians around at this hour to launch a witch hunt, practising magic in the Capital was punishable by death.

'I'm not sure revealing your powers in public is the best move,' he said.

'You have a better idea?' she retorted without opening her eyes.

Upon the general's lead, the soldiers advanced.

'Stay inside, Mother,' Wei said, nudging his mother back into the shop. To Desert Rose, he muttered, 'Whatever it is you intend to do, make it quick.'

Gripping his sword, he charged straight at the incoming soldiers. But he had only managed to defeat ten of them before they had him on his back, pinned under the tip of their swords.

A low rumble, followed by the sound of rushing water, made everyone pause. Seizing his chance, Wei leapt to his feet and knocked out a few more soldiers as Desert Rose worked her magic. All he needed to do was buy as much time as he could for her.

Desert Rose opened her eyes at last. A pool of water appeared under the soldiers' feet, spreading across the ground and rising as high as their boots. Wei bounded up the steps to the shop and back to Desert Rose's side as the water level climbed to the soldiers' knees. They scrambled and collided into one another, but the general only stared at the rising water, then up at Desert Rose with her hands raised.

'Seize the witch!' he roared.

Desert Rose was ready for them. She flicked her hand and washed them off their feet. Several soldiers picked themselves up quickly and continued to wade towards her, but she was already creating another platform of water. It scooped her up, along with Wei and his mother, and lifted them into the air. Despite its undulating surface, it was as sturdy as a horse's back.

Wei's mother clutched on to him as she watched Desert Rose control the platform. He gave her hand a reassuring squeeze. 'Trust her,' he said.

Desert Rose held out her hand. 'Take my hand!' Wei grabbed it, keeping his arm around his mother. 'Hold on tight.'

They careened past the general's head and over the troop of soaking soldiers. She flicked her hand once more, harder this time, sending all of them soaring into the sky with a powerful jet of water. Another flick of her wrist and they went crashing down on roofs, balconies, pushcarts, and the ground.

Wei stared at Desert Rose as they took off. 'Remind me never to make you mad.'

They lunged towards the Capital gates. As the scene receded behind them, the pool of water subsided as quickly as it had appeared.

More troops of soldiers swarmed in on almost every street they passed, launching their spears and arrows at them. Desert Rose dodged each one of them, raising the platform, dipping it, and swerving sideways. Wei tightened his grip around his mother and used his body to shield her and Desert Rose from the incoming attacks. Twice, his mother almost lost her footing and would have slipped off had Desert Rose not picked her back up.

The platform sailed high out of range, skirting past windows and balconies, where some occupants had rushed out to watch. There was no need for discretion now that almost the entire Capital had been alerted.

When the Capital gates came into sight at last, Desert Rose lowered the platform as she scanned the vicinity. 'Qara, where are you?' she muttered. It would be impossible for Qara to roam the streets with the Capital now on high alert, but Desert Rose seemed adamant to find her friend.

By then, the Black Guards, the elite forces led by General Yue, had caught up with them.

'Cease your magic at once!' General Yue ordered.

Desert Rose sped up.

Arrows arced through the air, aimed right at them. A couple grazed past Wei, one snagging at his coat, as Desert Rose wove through the streets, her eyes peeled for Qara.

Wei found her crouched among woven baskets in a street stall, staring up at the sky. He pointed. 'There she is.'

Qara ventured out as they dived towards her. She took Desert Rose's hand without question and hopped onto the water platform, which grew to accommodate her.

Just ahead of them was the stone wall that bordered the Capital. The red gates loomed closer and closer, until they finally soared over the wall, dodging more arrows launched from the guards stationed there.

Desert Rose keeled over at last, shaking, her face gleaming with perspiration. Beneath them, the platform gave a worrying lurch. With a sweep of her hand, she drove the platform eastward, heading straight for the desert.

The night breeze hit them in the face, fresh as spring water. Wei drew in a deep breath. They had made it out of Oasis Kingdom at last.

They cruised over taverns and inns and a bazaar closed for the night. Behind them, the torches on the Capital wall faded into pinpricks while the indigo sky stretched overhead. Wei directed the way to Red Moon Tavern, where Zeyan and Beihe were waiting.

Her knees buckled as soon as she set them all on the ground. Wei caught her and propped her up. 'I've got you.'

They crept into the inn through the creaky back door, Qara bringing up the rear. All the lights were out, save for the lanterns hanging by the four corners of each level. As far as Wei could tell, they were alone.

'We're almost there,' he murmured to Desert Rose as they tiptoed up the stairs with Qara supporting her on the other side.

Zeyan and Beihe were holed up in the room at the end of the hallway. They threw their arms around Wei as soon as he entered the door and set Desert Rose in a chair. Neither of them mentioned the absence of the others, but an unspoken moment of sorrow passed between them. This was all that remained of their crew, and it was all because of him.

Zeyan smiled at Desert Rose. 'Hello again.' She nodded back with a wan smile.

'She needs rest,' Wei said.

Behind him, his mother lingered at the door, watching them as though she wasn't sure if she should join them. There was so much of his life he had not shared with her, so much that was unlike everything she had known. Would she accept it, or condemn him like his father had?

He held out a hand towards her. 'Mother, I would like you to meet my friends.' She inched into the room and went to his side. 'You already know Zeyan, son of ex-General Luo. This is Beihe, we met in the Palamir Mountains. This is Qara, she's from the desert. And this is Desert Rose—she's . . .' He glanced at her. How could he begin to describe their strangely intertwined fates after everything they had been through together?

'A friend,' Desert Rose said. Wei felt his lips slide up into a smile.

'You saved our lives,' his mother said, grasping Desert Rose's hand. 'Thank you.'

Zeyan nudged him. 'Less than one season back in the palace and you're already back out.'

Wei shrugged. 'Rogue princes are better off staying rogue.'

Twenty-Eight

Meng

They had done it. *He* had done it, just like his mother and Mian had expected him to.

From the secret alliance with the desert clan leaders to Yong's death to the final act at the Spring Ceremony, he had accomplished every carefully planned step that took him to this point. And even with someone as unplanned as Desert Rose entering the picture, he had pulled it all off.

Desert Rose. Every time he closed his eyes now, the image of her standing before his father—her sword dripping with his father's blood—would flash by. What had he done? And why could he not stop worrying about her?

An inexplicable hole inside him grew bigger with each passing moment. None of this made sense to him. He had risen to meet his destiny at last. He should be proud, joyous, *over the moon.* Yet, for some reason, he felt like he had lost.

He stood with his mother on the platform at Five Wall Court now, overlooking the Imperial Army, scanning each of their uncertain faces. Their loyalties, he knew, were now divided. The old guards standing at attention at the front regarded him with scepticism, and the younger ones at the back shifted with unease. How many of them would fall behind him, and how many more would revolt?

In front of him, Mian cleared his throat before addressing the crowd.

'In light of recent events, which resulted in the untimely deaths of our great ruler, the Fifteenth Oasis Emperor Zhaode, and his second son, Crown Prince Zhaoyong, it is hereby declared that Fourth Prince Zhaomeng will be ordained as the interim emperor.'

He didn't say what everyone knew—that it was a matter of time before Meng was officiated as the emperor.

The soldiers traded glances among themselves. Meng knew what they were thinking—that his new position was unearned, that he would prove to be an inept emperor, that he had to be involved in those deaths in some way or another, perhaps orchestrated them himself. Soon after last night's tumult, he had already caught wind of the rumours. It would take a lot more than a declaration to convince everyone that he was worthy of the throne.

There was so much to repair, not just the physical damage that the *shouren* had wreaked before they fled or were put down, but also the relations with nobles and foreign ambassadors, the crippled army with its leaderless troops, and the court officials' trust in him.

And then there was Desert Rose, now a fugitive along with Wei and his mother.

Weariness washed over Meng. It seemed like no matter what he did, he always ended up putting out fires everywhere, trying to stay in everyone's good books.

Still, he kept his calm as he stepped up to address the troops.

'The events that have transpired over the past few months are proof that the kingdom is on the precipice of a revolution. The world beyond our borders is changing and so must we, in order to survive and honour the legacy of my father and forefathers. A loyal military provides the strength an emperor needs to lead his kingdom. From now on, with all your support, I promise to bring Oasis Kingdom into a secure and prosperous future.'

Silence took hold. Then, like a clarion call, General Yue bellowed as he sank to one knee and raised his clasped fists, 'Long live the Sixteenth Oasis Emperor Zhaomeng!'

Every soldier in the parade square followed suit. 'Long live the Sixteenth Oasis Emperor Zhaomeng!' they chorused.

Meng felt his mother squeeze his hand as she sent him a beatific smile. It had been a long time since she looked so proud of him.

*

The housemistress seemed uncharacteristically subdued. She sat facing him in the middle of the common room, where she had, many nights ago, warned him to stay away from her charges.

Her eyes fell to the tea tray between them. 'I don't know her whereabouts, if that's what you are here to find out.'

'That's not why I'm here,' he said, although that *was* what he had hoped.

While Desert Rose might be at large, Windshadow had showed up soon after his father's funeral ceremony to remind him of his end of their agreement—to free her tribe from Oasis occupation once he became emperor.

'I accept whatever punishment you may issue, Your Majesty. I bear full responsibility for the fact that my apprentice has committed a crime as heinous as such under my tutelage and supervision. This is an immense shame for the House of Night.'

'I'm not here to punish you either, Housemistress. I'm partly responsible for bringing her into the House too.'

Other than the ones in the chamber last night, no one knew about his connection to Yong and his father's death. The only one who might speculate was the housemistress.

She understood his intention right away. 'You could not have pre-empted what was to come. The girl has betrayed your trust, as she has mine. I do not doubt your motives in the least.' He nodded. 'May I ask, then, what Your Majesty's purpose is for visiting at this hour?'

'I would like to have something of Desert Rose's.' He offered no further explanation, not even when the housemistress left briefly and returned with Desert Rose's textbooks and notebooks, curiosity plain on her face.

In the library, Meng sat at the last spot he had shared with Desert Rose and laid out the books before him. He flipped through every page, tracing the characters she had written in uncertain strokes when she was still learning to write in the Oasis language. The memory of her hand in his drifted back.

Had she managed to return to the desert, to what was left of her tribe? Was she still with Wei and Luzhen? Would she ever forgive him?

Another memory sprung to mind, unbidden. Way back when Meng was a boy and had just learned how to read, he would spend occasional evenings with his father here. 'With an intellect like yours, Meng, you will do great things one day,' his father had told him. Meng guessed this was not what he had in mind then.

Hot tears gathered in his eyes—whether from the thought of Desert Rose or his father, he wasn't quite sure. He dived back into the papers and came to a stop at one filled with her name, the one she used in the palace: Mingxi. At the bottom right corner, she had written her real name in the Dugurian script, as though she had feared she would forget it.

'Meng,' a familiar voice said as a shadow loomed over him.

Meng set aside the papers and got to his feet. 'Mother—I mean, Empress Dowager.'

His mother took in his tear-filled eyes and the papers filled with Desert Rose's name, and narrowed her gaze at him. 'Those tears had better not be for that desert girl. She has caused enough damage in the kingdom, and to your reputation. You need to focus on the next steps.'

Of course, she didn't care that the wrong desert girl had been framed for the murder. Or that they had just sent off the late emperor on his final journey. None of that mattered as long as they were now in power.

She grasped his hand. 'It's hard to seize the throne, and even harder to retain it. There is so much to do now, Meng. There's no time for grieving.'

'I understand, Mother,' he said, like always.

She smiled, placated. 'Now, I think it's time we bring your brother back. Don't you?'

Twenty-Nine

Desert Rose

They had some time to go before day broke, enough to steal some sleep but not quite enough to enter a restful slumber.

Desert Rose lay in bed, staring up at the ceiling and wondering if sleep would ever be restful again. Every time she closed her eyes, she saw her hand on the sword that drove through emperor's throat, the blood on her hands. Vengeance sounded noble, but there was nothing quite as brutal and horrific as the hatred and anger that rose in her moments before she killed the emperor.

Thoughts of Meng and Windshadow continued to taunt her. Windshadow calling her *azzi* and Meng's hand on hers. Had anything they said to her ever been true, any gesture of goodwill been genuine, any shred of kindness from the heart?

In the end, she threw off her covers and headed down the hallway towards the balcony. Perhaps some fresh air could calm her mind.

The inn was quiet at this hour. Floorboards creaked under her feet, even though she trod as lightly as she could.

The balcony was not empty like she had expected. Wei stood before the banister, his shoulders tensed as he stared out into the pitch-black night. She joined him without a word, grateful for some company.

'You should get some rest,' he said, still looking ahead. 'We need to keep moving.'

'I can't sleep.'

He didn't ask why. Maybe he already knew. Maybe he saw the same things too when he closed his eyes.

'When I was twelve,' he said, 'my father sent me out to the desert on my own. He knew how much I longed to venture beyond the kingdom.

That's what I want to believe—that he sent me there out of love, not hate, even though I almost died . . . had you and your father not saved me.'

It was him, Desert Rose realized at last. He was that young boy from the Capital who had almost frozen to death when she found him. She had recognized him right from the start, subconsciously, when she dreamed about that boy the night she broke into Wei's tent. What were the odds that they would cross paths again this way?

Wei let out a small laugh. 'I envied you for having a father like yours. I thought maybe if I had died out there, my father would care at last. But then I realized that the best revenge against him was to stay alive. To become the stone in his shoe, just like he had always regarded me.' A tear slipped down his face as he turned to her. 'How can I hate him and still want his love?'

Desert Rose stared at him, unable to find the right words. If she looked closely, she could still find traces of hate in his eyes, but it was sorrow that racked his body now.

'I'm sorry.' She hated how trite, almost patronizing, her words sounded.

'I don't blame you. I was ready to kill him myself, for what he had done to my mother. And with all the enemies my father had, someone else would have done the deed, even if it weren't you.'

She reached out, hesitating for a heartbeat before laying a hand on his shoulder. He shifted closer to her, and she found herself pulling him closer until they were leaning into each other, as though they were trying to fill up the space left behind by the people they had lost.

They remained that way, folding into each other for warmth, until first light started to creep across the sky, turning it a bruised shade of purple.

Wei broke the silence, his voice quiet and subdued. 'What are your plans now? You came all this way to find your father.'

She had. And not only had it been a wasted trip, she also had more questions than ever before. About who—or what—she was. What else she could do? Were there others like her and Windshadow out there? Did her father know about this all along? Was Bataar telling the truth about the fake alliance with the emperor, and about her father's last words to him?

'Do you believe he's still alive?' Wei asked.

Even in the deepest winter and the driest desert, hope springs eternal. It was her favourite Dugurian saying, one that her father had imparted to her.

Her father was chieftain. He was Scarbrow. He was the bravest, most resilient man she knew.

'I do,' she said.

He nodded. 'Then keep that hope close to you. Let it keep you going. You'll be reunited with him someday.'

Just like he had reunited with his mother.

'*Laisha.*' The word escaped her like a breath. It sounded almost foreign on her tongue now. 'Home. I would like to go home.' *If you ever get lost, Rose, just go home. I will always be there.* That was what her father used to tell her.

Wei sent her a wan smile when she told him that. Unlike her, he didn't have the promise of a home waiting for him, only a vast, wild world in these chaotic times.

'You can come too, if you'd like,' she said. 'For refuge, until you find a place to settle down.'

His smile grew wider, this time chasing the sadness from his eyes. 'I'd like that.'

There would be time to chase answers, to mourn the people they had lost, and to forget the ones who had let them down. For now, as a fresh dawn spilled its light across the horizon, they would keep moving forward, into the desert that spread itself far and wide before them, beckoning them home.

It is said that the Sky Princess and the Earth Prince had conceived one illegitimate child, whom they named Jin. But despite being the direct descendent of immortals, Jin received no blessings from the gods. Instead, he triggered the largest war between the celestial and earthly kingdoms.

The war raged on for centuries (although mere months in celestial time), almost tearing the two realms apart until a precarious truce was called. Meanwhile, the Sky Princess and Earth Prince were sentenced to spend eternity apart in solitude, and the child was left to fend for himself in the great, wild Khuzar Desert on Earth.

After the war, the five Elemental deities—who each personified earth, water, fire, wind, and metal—took pity on the child and blessed him with their essence so he could better survive on his own. But it was that mix of essences that eventually destroyed Jin from within.

Before he died, Jin vowed to set right the havoc he had wreaked. After marrying a mortal woman, he made his descendants, what we now call the Damohai, guardians of the desert. It is said that out of this elusive tribe of nomads, five will one day gather to reunite the heavenly and earthly realms again, each embodying the elements that had both protected and killed Jin.

The Damohai waited centuries for the five Elementals to appear in their midst, not knowing when or where they would appear. But even in their time of need, when their empire was wrested from them and they were forced to retreat into the Flaming Mountains, no one showed up to lead or protect them.

Could it be that the Elementals' essence had killed them before they could reunite with the Damohai, that they were indeed cursed to die from their powers unless they made their way to the Immortal Spring? No one knows for sure.

Perhaps these are myths that became stories over time. Perhaps the great Khuzar Desert, once a battleground of the gods and meeting place of two eternally doomed lovers, holds far more mysteries than we can ever know.

Perhaps one day, the Elementals would show up to reunite heaven and earth, and rebuild what was once the largest empire in the world.

Until then, men continue to wield magic as their rightly weapon and tear the world asunder.

—Excerpt from *Land of Sand and Song: Tales from the Khuzar Desert*, by Lu Ji Fang

END OF BOOK 1

Acknowledgements

This book has been years in the making and took a village to see it to fruition.

First, the journey began with Mr Martin Chan, without whom I would never have thought it possible for me to write my first novel at the age of twelve. (The 'novel' was terrible, but I fell in love with the process since then.) Fast forward to today, and the list of people I'm grateful to has only grown longer.

Thank you to writer friends and critique partners who made this road a lot less solitary: Meredith Crosbie, Nicole Evans and Rebecca Donahue for the long emails, text messages and Zoom calls about writing, dreams, books, life and everything in between. Special shoutout to Meredith for being my biggest cheerleader, for sitting through draft after draft with the same amount of enthusiasm (and for using Ben Barnes gifs as motivation whenever my optimism flagged).

To Marie Lu, Alwyn Hamilton, David Yoon, and Ning Cai for your kind words of encouragement about this novel back when it was still a scrappy first draft. Marie, you made me believe in it enough to keep going at it.

To Leslie W for being such a pillar of support with whom I can talk all things books, writing and publishing without reservations, for catching last-minute typos (!!!) and for keeping me consistently motivated and excited with new projects. To Joelyn Alexandra for consistently feeding me and Leslie with writing resources.

To Valerie Wong, who literally beta-read the final draft in two days before offering lengthy feedback that had me in stitches.

To Vivien He, Jarrod Jonah Chee, Fong Sook Han, Grace Lee, Sheila Chiang and so many more for spreading the word about this book and for every word of encouragement along the way.

To my dad, for keeping me fed and (mostly) sane while I was on deadline, and for supporting my dreams after all these years. Thank you for always being in my corner.

To Penguin Random House SEA for taking a chance on this ambitious little book and giving it a home at last. Thank you to the tireless team—especially my editor Nora Nazerene Abu Bakar—that made this book come to fruition.

To the book community I've met along the way—reviewers, bookstagrammers, booksellers, and more—who make the community such a vibrant, inspiring, and rewarding one that feels like a second home.

And lastly, to my dear readers who picked up this book and made it all the way to the end. This story begins with me and ends with you. I hope you enjoyed the journey!